Private Property

Private Property

La Jill Hunt

www.urbanbooks.net

Urban Books, LLC
300 Farmingdale Road, NY-Route 109
Farmingdale, NY 11735

ISBN 13: 978-1-62286-271-9
ISBN 10: 1-62286-271-6

First Trade Paperback Printing August 2019
Printed in the United States of America

10 9 8 7 6 5 4 3 2 1

*This is a work of fiction. Any references or similarities
to actual events, real people, living or dead, or to real
locales are intended to give the novel a sense of reality.
Any similarity in other names, characters, places, and
incidents is entirely coincidental.*

Distributed by Kensington Publishing Corp.
Submit Orders to:
Customer Service
400 Hahn Road
Westminster, MD 21157-4627
Phone: 1-800-733-3000
Fax: 1-800-659-2436

Prologue

Qualified Buyer

Darby Davidson was tired. She had been showing houses to her latest clients all day long: an NBA player and his fiancée, whom he introduced as Squirt. She couldn't have been a day over 22. Darby figured the marriage, if they made it to the altar, would last all of forty-five days based on their interaction. His money would be better spent on a two-bedroom luxury condo and an investment fund, but he was hell-bent on buying a "dream crib with all of the fixin's so all the haters and the chicks who dissed me see what they now missin'." Darby suggested otherwise, but he wasn't trying to hear it. He told her he wanted the biggest house his money could pay for, and right now, he had quite a bit. The bill for her two preteen sons' braces and their upcoming vacation trip to Hawaii told her she needed all the commission she could get.

But so far, none of the houses they had seen were what he wanted. She decided to take a chance and bring him to a new development, hoping she would have some luck there.

"This place is far," Squirt whined from the back seat of Darby's Range Rover.

"It is located in a secluded area, but that's a good thing," Darby told her, trying not to sound frustrated. She seemed to have a problem with every house they had seen, yet she wasn't putting up a dime.

"That means no one will be popping up on us out here. I like that!" Her client smiled and nodded, his face hidden behind the huge sunglasses he wore. "All of this is new construction?"

"Yes," Darby told him. "Right now, there are only about a dozen homes completed, including the one I'm about to show you. The neighborhood sits on approximately one hundred and twenty-three acres, and once it's finished, there will be approximately sixty homes, give or take. There are also several amenities, including a kid's play park, beautiful gardens, and some of the homes sit on the waterfront, which is a man-made lake."

"The Manors of Harrington Point." He read the sign as Darby turned into the community. There was a centurion-style gatehouse and sculptured brick walls that lined the lushly landscaped entrance. Flowering trellises, winding brick walkways, and iron branches graced the edges of the main roadway and the park area. As she continued driving, they were greeted by a sweeping bridge, which led to a fifty-foot glass dome pavilion and a cascading waterfall. "This place is amazing."

"This place is far!" Squirt sighed.

"It is beautiful," Darby said, ignoring her comment.

"I don't wanna stay way out here. This ain't even a gated community. What type of stuff is that?"

"Like I explained, it's a new development, and there aren't a lot of residents. Right now, it's very private and very secure, so a gate isn't necessary. And there are plans to have continual rolling security as more homes are built."

"It must not be no important people who stay out here," Squirt said.

"That's not true. There are some very prominent residents: famous actors, singers, producers, athletes . . ."

"How much do these houses run?" he asked as they made their way through the neighborhood.

"The average right now is about three to four," Darby told him.

"Three to four hundred thousand?" Squirt questioned.

"Three to four million," Darby corrected her.

"I know that house ain't cost no three million dollars." Squirt pointed at one of the smaller houses they were passing.

"Actually, that's the home of the man who owns all of the property in Harrington Point," Darby told them. "He lives there."

"He owns all this land and lives in that small house?" He laughed.

Darby looked over at the house they were referring to. It did seem small compared to the other houses in the Point, but Darby didn't consider 5,300 square feet small. The house also sat on the largest lot. Rumor had it that the land belonged to the Harrington family for several hundred years and was passed down from generation to generation. It sat vacant for years, until finally the owner's great-great-grandson came forward and decided to have a vacation home built on the lake as a surprise wedding gift for his bride-to-be. The construction had just been complete when, sadly, his fiancée died unexpectedly in her sleep. For a while, they even suspected him of killing her, until they found that she died from natural causes. Shortly after her death, he decided to move into the home and develop the neighborhood. From what Darby understood, he was a multimillionaire ten times over, but you would never be able to tell it.

She continued down the streets until they arrived at the house for sale. She pulled into the circular driveway to the covered front entrance and parked. The house was Darby's favorite listing. It was one of the largest homes in the neighborhood and was her dream home. Every potential buyer to whom she had shown the house had also fallen in love with it, but so far they all opted to have theirs custom built on the available lots.

"This place is huge!" he gushed, hopping out of the truck.

Darby didn't know which of their outfits fit the tightest: his skinny jeans and T-shirt or Squirt's sequined halter mini-dress. She had to admit, despite his fashion choices, he was an extremely handsome young man, and he seemed to have a genuine heart, which was why she tried to give him sound real estate advice and direction. She also wanted to tell him that he may want to hold off on giving Squirt his last name, but she felt that would be overstepping.

"It's ten thousand square feet," Darby told him. "Six bedrooms, six bathrooms, and ten fireplaces."

"Damn," he said, taking off his sunglasses.

Darby opened the door, and he followed her inside. "Marble flooring, state-of-the-art kitchen, all the amenities you want, and more."

"Wow," he said, walking around. "Squirt, do you see this?"

They turned and noticed she wasn't even in the house. Darby found her outside standing on the manicured lawn, talking on her phone. "I told him that, Ma!"

"Squirt, what are you doing? Come inside. You gotta see this place!" he told her as he stepped outside.

"I don't wanna go in. I don't like it." Squirt tossed her long blond hair extensions over her shoulder and put her hand on her hip.

Darby was confused. This home was the biggest and most fabulous house that she had shown them, so she thought it was a shoo-in. Based on his reaction, she knew he felt the same way.

"You haven't even seen it."

"What's wrong?" Darby asked, walking over to the couple.

"I don't like the vibe out here, and it's too far. My mama ain't even gonna be able to take the bus out here."

"My point exactly," he mumbled.

"What?" Squirt snapped.

"I mean, my point is that we can send a driver to get her when she wants to come out here," he quickly said.

Darby stared at the young couple. "Why don't we just take a quick peek inside so you can—"

"I don't wanna look inside. Look, I need to get home. Come on, I'm ready to go!"

"But we didn't even finish looking—" He paused, stared, then nodded at a car that was driving down the street. They all watched as the four-door Porsche passed by, driven by a female wearing dark shades.

"Who was that?" Squirt snapped, looking over at her fiancé.

"I don't know." He shrugged. "That car was hot!"

"I swear! This is exactly what I be telling you!" Squirt yelled.

Darby took a step away from the couple, hoping they weren't going to create a scene. Although the neighborhood was fairly empty, she didn't want to run the risk of anyone looking out their windows or driving by and seeing them arguing on the front lawn.

Looking at Squirt like she was crazy, he asked her, "What are you talking about?"

"You out here waving at bitches like you ain't put a ring on my finger a month ago." Squirt held up her finger, which held one of the biggest diamonds Darby had ever seen.

"When did I wave at anybody? Did you see me wave?" he turned and asked Darby. She just shrugged.

"Is that why you wanna move way the hell out here? To be closer to that skank?" Squirt stood directly in front of him. His six foot, nine inch body loomed well over hers, but she didn't seem to care. She squared off with him as if they were the same size and she could take him down.

"I don't even know who that was, I swear."

"If you wanna buy this house, then fine, but I ain't living here wit' you, that's for damn sure," Squirt said and headed for Darby's truck.

Clearly embarrassed, he looked over at Darby and said, "She's tripping. I do wanna see the house. Maybe we can do this some other time without her."

"That's fine. Let me lock up the house."

Another wasted damn day, she thought as she took one last glance into the gorgeous home. She glanced down at her watch. It was late, and it would be an hour-long drive back to her office, where her client's Maybach was sitting in the parking lot waiting for him and Squirt. She still had to pick up her boys from soccer, help them with homework, prepare dinner, prepare them for school, and go over paperwork for her staff meeting in the morning. If she was lucky, the one bottle of chardonnay she had chilling in the fridge would be enough to help her relax from the day and get through the full night she had ahead. In a perfect world, she would have met an amazing, handsome, funny, successful guy who was a great role model for her sons and a great lover for herself.

Better luck next time.

Chapter 1

Bishop Walter and First Lady Olivia Burke

1547 Harrington Way

Olivia Burke slipped her feet into the leather slippers lying in front of the sofa, and she stood up. She was tired, and as hard as she tried to stay awake until her husband got home, she wouldn't be able to. The church Walter was ministering at tonight was only an hour away, and she thought he would have been home by now. It was already nearly two o'clock in the morning, but knowing her husband, he had probably gotten caught up talking to some of the other ministers after the revival service and hadn't even left yet.

As the bishop and founder of one of the largest mega-churches in the state, Walter Burke was always in high demand. From local pastors just starting out who needed encouragement, to business owners looking for an opportunity to get into his ear about the next "big thing," people sought not only spiritual advice but investments in their ideas. Over the years, her husband had grown into a patient man, willing to listen when he could. He had evolved over the nearly thirty years that they had been married, and she loved him even more now than she had when they first met.

As she walked out of the den of their massive $4 million palace they called home, her eyes fell on a framed photo of the two of them. It was a bit faded, taken on one of their first dates, and they looked almost unfamiliar to her now. They had come a long way from the teenage couple who both grew up on the streets of Detroit in the late sixties. Walter was her first love, and she couldn't imagine her life without him. Then again, she never would have imagined the life they were living now.

Her eyes fell on another picture of their twin boys, Malachi and Micah. The 2-year-old boys in the photo dressed in identical blue and white sailor suits were now twenty-eight, tall, and handsome. But their similarity in looks was the only thing her sons had in common. Micah now served as the youth pastor of Greater Works Assembly of Faith, founded by his father. Malachi was serving in another capacity, as an inmate in a low-security prison for the past eighteen months. Unlike her husband, who refused to go and visit their son, Olivia made it a point to go and visit at least once a month. Olivia remembered the last visit.

"You're looking even more handsome than the last time I saw you, baby," she told Malachi when she hugged him. She wasn't lying. His six foot frame held his 200-pound athletic build well. Both of her boys had their father's strong chin, seductive brown eyes, and thick eyebrows. From her, they inherited their smooth, caramel complexion, dimpled smiles, and unbelievably straight teeth without the help of braces.

"You say that every time you see me, Mama." Malachi hugged her back. They walked around the yard of the facility.

Olivia always made it a point to keep their conversation light and casual, mostly about her duties in the church and the members Malachi was familiar with. She rarely brought up his father or brother, because she knew there was a chance it would cut her visit short. However, knowing her son's release date was approaching, she decided to test the waters.

"Well, I am biased, but it is the truth. You know your mama doesn't lie. Besides, I won't have to say it much longer, because you only have a couple more weeks until I get to see you every day." Olivia smiled.

"Yeah, I can't wait to get out of here, but I don't know about seeing you every day," Malachi laughed.

"I am already getting your room ready. The new house is amazing, and I know you're gonna love being home. We're planning a dinner—"

"Mama," Malachi interrupted her. "Please don't."

"Don't what, Malachi?" Olivia stopped walking and turned to face her son.

"Don't make any plans for me when I get out of here. I'm good." He shrugged.

"I know you're good, and it's gonna be good for you to be home."

"That won't be happening, Mama. Don't play. You already know that."

Olivia shook her head. "Why won't it be happening? We are your family. I understand the relationship between you and your brother and father is strained right now—"

"You think?" Malachi laughed. "I don't think the great Bishop Walter Burke would be too happy having his ex-convict of a son at the crib. You know that. And neither would his puppet, Micah."

"Don't be rude, Malachi. I raised you better than that," Olivia said sternly. "Your father and brother love you very much, and so do I."

"This has nothing to do with love, Mama. Come on, neither one of them has taken the time to visit or even write to me in the past year and a half."

"You know both of them have been extremely busy. And your father has made sure you have been well provided for during this entire ordeal. Do not discredit that," Olivia told him, trying not to become upset.

"Yeah, he made sure I had a good lawyer and money on the books every month. He should get the 'Father of the Year' award. Where are the nomination forms? Mama, please don't stand here and try to defend him—"

"I'm not defending him."

Malachi sucked in and quickly said, *"Fine, maybe defend isn't the right word. How about justify his actions or lack thereof while I've been in here? Or Micah's. It's okay. I am good, and I will be good once I get out of here."*

"Malachi, I want you home."

"I love you, Mama, but that's not my home. It's yours." Malachi shook his head.

"It's our home. You have just as much right to be there as anyone else. As a matter of fact, we've made provisions for you to be there. The house is everything you could ever imagine and more. It's our dream house, Malachi. Remember when you were little and you would draw pictures of mansions and hang them on the refrigerator and say, 'Mama, one day we are gonna live in a house like this!' Well, that's where we live." Olivia laughed. *"I just knew you were gonna end up being an architect."*

"Too bad I ended up being a dope dealer, huh? I guess it's true what they say." Malachi sat on top of a nearby picnic table. *"The apple don't fall—"*

"You're not a dope dealer, Malachi! You are more than that. You are a child of the highest God. You are smart and talented, and you're my son, so act like it. This situation you're in now is just temporary, and you will come out of it just fine."

"I hear ya, Mama."

Olivia walked over, smoothed down her skirt, and sat beside her son, taking his hands into hers. *"Malachi, you are so much like your father, it's unreal."*

"I am nothing like him," Malachi snapped.

"You are. Both of you are as stubborn as mules. Look at me. Promise me you will at least think about coming home, please."

She stared into her son's eyes and smiled, hoping she could will him into saying yes. She thought about telling him about his brother's upcoming nuptials but decided to save that news for later.

"I will think about it, Mama," Malachi relented.

Olivia leaned over and kissed his forehead. "Thank you. I know you're gonna love it. It sits on the water, and it even has a dock and a lift for two boats."

"I said I'd think about it. I didn't say yes."

Since that visit, Olivia had been praying every night that her son would come home. She needed for her family to heal, and in her heart, she believed Micah's wedding and Malachi's homecoming would be just the events to bring her broken family back together. It had been too long, and now it was time for them to let go of the past. Her husband and her boys were all she had, and she was going to do everything within her power to pick up the pieces left after they'd been torn apart.

The house phone rang, and Olivia put the picture that she was staring at down on the table. She walked over and answered, "Hello."

"Hey, sweetheart, I'm almost home," Walter told her. "I know you're up wondering what's taking so long."

"I'm not wondering, Walter," Olivia told him. "I know you were stuck after the service, running your mouth."

"I wasn't running my mouth, woman. I was listening to other folks run theirs." Walter laughed. "So go ahead and get upstairs and in bed. I'll be home shortly to tuck you in."

Olivia tried not to blush, but she couldn't help it. After all these years, her husband still had that effect on her. "Walter, where is Frank? I hope he can't hear you talking like that."

Frank was her husband's right-hand man and security who had been by his side since he started "Greater Works," as they'd called it over twenty years ago in a storefront.

"Frank is right here beside me driving, and I don't care if he hears what I'm saying. You're my wife, and if he knows like I know, he needs to be calling his own wife and telling her he's about to come home and handle his business too," Walter teased. "Now, go get ready for the bishop. I'll be home soon. As a matter of fact, don't get in the bed. We still got a couple of rooms in that big, new house of ours to christen, remember?"

"Walter! Stop it!" Olivia giggled. When they toured the 10,000-square-foot architectural masterpiece they now lived in, Olivia immediately fell in love. Walter, however, complained that it was too much house for just the two of them. Olivia pointed out that Micah could live in the adjacent two-bedroom apartment and be closer to his father to work on their ministry together, and then she threw in the promise that they would "christen" any of the rooms that he saw fit. That was all that needed to be said. Within days they'd decided the house would be theirs, and as soon as the sale had gone through and they'd been given the keys, her husband had smiled as she started making good on her promise before they had even brought in a piece of furniture.

"I'll see you in a few, O'la. Love you." Walter called her by the nickname he gave her when they first met.

"Love you too," Olivia said and hung up.

A little while later, she was about to head up the spiral staircase when she peeked out of the front window. A flash of light in the distance caught her eye through the window. At first she thought maybe it was a falling star, or maybe even fireworks.

She looked closer and then realized exactly what it was.

Chapter 2

Riley Rodriguez

1726 Harrington Court

"Damn." That was the only thing Riley Rodriguez could think to say as she stared at the large plasma television in her bedroom. She reached over to the nearby nightstand and picked up a lit joint, taking a long drag as she watched herself on the screen, naked and having sex with a man she barely knew. From what she had been told, he was an up-and-coming rapper named Touché.

Riley stared at herself. Her eyes were closed, and she was moaning in ecstasy as Touché pushed her back, opened her legs, and began pleasing her with his tongue. Her fingers gripped the headboard of the king-sized bed, and from the look on her face and the sounds of her moans, Riley was enjoying herself. But for the life of her, as she watched it play out on the screen, Riley couldn't remember any of it. Nothing was familiar: not the bed they were in, not where they were, nor when the entire escapade took place. One thing she was grateful for was that her face was beat to the gods. Her weave was tight as hell without a hair out of place, and her manicure and pedicure were perfect. Not to mention that whenever this had gone down, it was during a time when she had to have been hitting the gym, because her body was contoured in all the right places and there was not an ounce of fat to be seen. It was a clear picture taken at a great angle, and now the whole world was about to see it whether she liked it or not. The paperwork had been signed, the distribution deal made, and instead of being the star of the most popular family television show from the eighties, she was about to be another kind of star—a porn star.

Riley had been in the spotlight since birth. She starred in her first television commercial when she was barely 3 months old, and by the time she was the age of 6, she had one of the most recognizable faces in the U.S. and some foreign countries. Whether it was a commercial for cereal, toy stores, fast-food restaurants, or clothing stores, if they needed a cute face, then Riley was it.

At the age of 8, she starred in *Family Brides,* one of the highest-rated television sitcoms, until she was in her early teens and the show ended. Afterward, she was the lead in a teen dance movie that became an instant hit. Against the wishes of her parents and agent at the time, she played the love interest in a hard-core rap video that was so risqué it was shown on the music channels only after prime time. Riley thought it would have led to more adult roles, but instead, the offers stopped altogether. She didn't let it bother her, though. She felt that it was a sign from God that after working nonstop for years, she needed a break. That break included rest, relaxation, lots of booze, and narcotics: prescription and illegal. The past five years had been a blur, much like her memory of the pending sex tape she was watching.

Riley took another drag from the joint and turned the TV off. She had seen enough. Reaching over into her nightstand, she took out a book titled *For the Love of Thomas.* It was about a woman named Sally Hemmings, the mistress of Thomas Jefferson. Riley came across the book during her last stint in rehab. Another female resident was engrossed in it nightly, and Riley was curious about what had her attention so much that the girl wasn't even interested in sneaking out and getting high with the rest of the celebrity residents. She gave the book to Riley, and from the moment Riley began reading the woman's story, she was hooked. She had read it three times since being released from rehab. It was as if she was obsessed with Sally Hemmings's story. She even dreamed about the strong woman and all she endured. It was as if she knew her, like they met in a former life.

"Riley, are you up?"

Riley quickly put the joint out and fanned the air. Trying to be as quiet as possible, she reached into the nightstand and pulled out a small bottle of spray from Victoria's Secret, quickly trying to cover the scent. Riley held her breath and closed her eyes, hoping the person on the other side of the door would assume she was asleep and go away.

"Riley, I know you're still up. I smell the weed. I'm coming in." The bedroom door opened, and in walked Eden, Riley's younger sister, carrying a basket of folded clothes and a pile of mail. The two women looked similar, but whereas Riley's body was the epitome of a Victoria's Secret model, Eden was not so lucky. Although she was just as beautiful as her older sister, the only modeling she could do would be for Lane Bryant.

"My bad. I didn't hear you," Riley lied.

"Sure you didn't," Eden said, putting the basket on the dresser and tossing the pile of envelopes at her. "Here's your mail. I've already gone through it, and I've also talked with Chet and made sure everything is paid for the month." As usual, it seemed as if the roles had reversed and Eden was the older sister, not Riley. For the past few months, she had stepped in and taken over as Riley's personal assistant, manager, agent, chef, housekeeper, and anything else Riley needed. Riley had gone through many employees and couldn't keep anyone around other than Chet, her accountant, and Jeff, her part-time security guard.

"What about my credit cards? Did he reactivate them?" Riley asked. Chet had canceled her cards and closed her checking account, claiming that her reckless behavior was about to cost her everything she had worked for. He was so controlling, but one thing she could say was that he was brilliant when it came to her money. Even after the craziness of the last five years, Riley was able to purchase the sprawling mansion she wanted in Harrington Point, and still have a Porsche, a BMW SUV, and an Audi convertible. In addition, she had a nice chunk of change in the bank, investments, and a monthly stipend, albeit minuscule and barely enough to live on in her opinion.

"You don't need those credit cards. You have your monthly allowance if you want to shop," Eden told her.

"That's barely enough to eat," Riley complained, lying back on the huge pillows at the head of her bed.

"Maybe if you didn't spend so much on weed, it would be enough to shop." Eden shrugged, sitting on the edge of the bed.

"Don't judge me. I have a lot going on right now," Riley said. "I'm stressed about my new porn career."

"Stop it." Eden shook her head. "It won't be as bad as you think."

"I really don't think it's gonna be that bad. I mean, look." Riley picked up the remote and clicked the television back on. Immediately sounds of her and Touché moaning filled the room. "I look fucking amazing. Or should that be I look amazing fucking?"

Eden snatched the remote from her and clicked the screen off. "Riley, you don't have to play hard-core with me. I know you didn't want this to happen. It's kind of an unfair situation." Eden sighed.

"Hey, it happened, and it's my fault. I'm not blaming anyone." The last thing Riley needed was anyone feeling sorry for her. Her pride was one of the few things she had left these days.

"Have you talked to this Touché guy? What does he have to say about it?"

"I don't even know that motherfucker!" Riley reached into the drawer and took the blunt back out, along with a lighter.

"What do you mean you don't know him?" Eden said, taking the items out of her sister's hand.

"Eden, this is gonna sound crazy, but I don't remember even meeting that dude or anything that happened on that screen." Riley frowned.

"That is crazy and dangerous, Riley." Eden shook her head and gave Riley a sympathetic look.

"One of the downfalls of getting high, li'l sis. Listen to me when I tell you this: just say no . . . to drugs and sex. It leads to starring in porn movies with random strangers. Now give me my stuff back." Riley held her hand out.

Eden ignored her and reached for the book instead. "Hey, I read this. This is a great book."

"I know. I read it too, three times. This is my fourth," Riley mumbled.

"Really?" Eden looked surprised.

"Yes, heffa, I do read. Well, sometimes when I'm not busy filming pornography." Riley laughed.

"Stop joking about it, Riley. It's not funny, and I know you're pissed. I don't blame you. It's okay to admit that," Eden insisted.

"It's cool."

Turning back to the book, Eden said, "I wonder who they're gonna get to star as Sally in the movie that's coming out. I heard they were thinking about that Lauren Carmichael chick."

Riley sat up in the bed. "Movie? What movie? They're making this into a movie?"

"Yeah. I read about it in *People* the other day. Some big-time preacher bought the rights. He hired that guy who won the Oscar last year to direct it."

Riley looked down at the book in her sister's lap, and a chill went down her spine. She finally realized why the book had been so moving and why she had felt so connected to Hemmings while reading it. "I knew it!" she screamed.

"You knew what?" Eden looked confused.

"I am Sally Hemmings!" Riley announced. Eden looked at her as if she were delusional. Riley realized she may have sounded a little bizarre, but she meant what she said.

"Yeah, you definitely need to lay off the weed, Riley. Is this stuff laced?" Eden sniffed the blunt she was holding, then quickly put it down.

"I want that role. I've gotta get it," Riley told her.

"Um, you do realize Sally Hemmings was a black woman, right?"

"Whatever. I want this. Besides, even being Puerto Rican, I am way blacker than Lauren Carmichael's high-yellow ass," Riley said. "And she can't act. Did you see when she guest starred on that episode of *Law & Order?* She sucked!"

Lauren Carmichael was Riley's well-known archnemesis. For years it seemed as if whatever roles Riley didn't get went to Lauren and vice versa. When Riley turned down the sequel to the teen dance movie she'd done, the role went to Lauren, who went on to star in the Broadway version of the movie.

"Riley, you haven't acted in years," Eden told her. "You just got out of rehab last week, and considering the next movie that you're starring in is about to be released"—she paused and looked at the television—"I don't think they'll even consider you." The look on Riley's face made Eden add, "I'm just being honest."

Realistically, Riley knew that Eden was right. It didn't make sense that she wanted to play this role. But she knew that this was something she had to do, something she was born to do, and something she would do. She just had to figure out how to do it.

"That part is mine, Eden. I can feel it."

Eden didn't respond right away. She just stood, staring at Riley for a few moments. Just as Riley was about to ask what was wrong, Eden said, "Then there's only one thing to do. Make it happen. Where do we start?"

Riley jumped out of bed and smiled. "Where else? We call Peri!"

"Peri?" Eden gave her a confused look.

"Yes, Peri. Grab my phone from the dresser please?" Riley asked as she began dancing around the room.

Eden got off the bed and walked over to the dresser, grabbing Riley's cell phone and passing it to her.

Riley unlocked the screen and was about to tell Siri to call Peri when, suddenly, she heard Eden's voice. "What in the world?"

"What?" Riley frowned. "Is someone out there?"

"Give me your phone! Now!" Eden screamed.

Chapter 3

Peri Duboise

1974 Harrington Way

"Do you love me, Peri?"

"Of course I do." Peri sighed, flipping through the latest issue of *People* and sipping a glass of merlot. It had been an exhausting day. All he wanted to do was relax, but hearing the tone in Logan's voice, he knew that wasn't going to be happening.

"I'm not feeling the love at all. As a matter of fact, I haven't felt much of anything from you the past few days. What's going on?"

Peri glanced up from the magazine, put the glass of wine down, and stared at the computer screen, where he was FaceTiming with the sinfully gorgeous fitness model. Somehow he thought dating someone out of his comfort zone would bring a different result. Normally he went for the quiet, nerdy type: the business owners, computer geeks, and even a few college professors. Logan was energetic, talkative, and rambunctious, in and out of bed. It was new and refreshing when they first began dating. Peri couldn't wait to see his lover and, while they dined on gourmet meals at the hottest restaurants, listen to the entertaining tales of the daily excitement that happened in the gym or on the set of a magazine shoot. Afterward, they would hit the nightclubs, always enjoying

VIP treatment wherever they went. Logan's face was recognizable, especially since it was on billboards all over town promoting the biggest fitness chain in the city, in addition to being featured on the cover of various fitness magazines. However, to Peri, it seemed that even if the face had never been seen, it was the magnetic personality of Logan that drew people in, including him.

Peri was having the time of his life, but over time he realized he was no longer interested in enjoying the nightlife, and Logan became somewhat draining. At first, he thought it was because of the slight age difference. Peri was pushing 40 and Logan was only 28. But dating someone younger wasn't anything new for Peri. Slowly he began to realize that it wasn't the age factor but that Logan wasn't the one. As much as Peri loved Logan, he was not in love. And that seemed to be the issue he had been experiencing in all of his relationships over the past few years.

"Logan, babe, it has been a long day. You already know that. These events are stressing me, that's all." Peri wasn't lying. He was in the middle of planning weddings for two celebrity couples. The first bride was a news anchor for NBC. Actually, she wasn't the problem, but her fiancé, a decorated war veteran, needed to micromanage every detail due to his desire for everything to appear perfect.

The second bride was the daughter of an oil tycoon. Her father was sparing no expense to make her every wish come true, no matter how outrageous. Peri had spent most of the day attempting to convince her that her Venus-inspired Grecian-themed wedding may have seemed like a great idea, but requesting that her guests arrive in togas may not be in the best taste. Thankfully, he was able to persuade her. Both weddings were taking place within three weeks of one another, within the next ninety days. Peri had enough on his plate. The last thing he needed was Logan being a clingy significant other.

"I understand that, Peri, but this relationship, which seems to be going nowhere, is stressing me," Logan snapped.

The vibration of his cell phone was exactly the saving grace Peri needed at that moment. He picked it up and said, "Hold that thought," to Logan. Then, into his cell, he said, "Hey, what's going on? I'm FaceTiming with my babe, so make it quick!" He winked into the camera. Logan's facial expression let him know that the conversation was far from over.

"Peri, turn to VH1 right now! The deejay Madison wants for her reception is being featured," April Kirby, his assistant, said. "This guy is getting like two hundred eighty grand a show in Vegas. There's no way she can get him. That's almost half her budget."

Peri grabbed the remote and clicked his television on. Sure enough, on screen was DJ Avenger, the deejay his client had requested for her all-white toga soiree. Peri watched and learned that not only did DJ Avenger make over a quarter of a million dollars to play a club or event, but the deejay was also booked up for well over a year.

That's ridiculous, Peri thought. April was right. It looked as if there was no way his client would be able to have him for her wedding.

"Babe, let me call you back," Peri leaned up and said. "It's April, and we have a mini crisis on our hands."

"There's always a mini crisis on your hands, Peri!" Logan snapped.

Peri turned on his speakerphone and said, "April, please confirm for Logan that this is an emergency!"

"Hi, Lo-Lo!" April yelled through the phone as Peri held it up for Logan to see.

"Hi, April. Fine, Peri. But you'd better call me back, because we're not done," Logan said just before the screen went blank, letting Peri know the call had ended.

"Um, Peri, I wouldn't exactly call this an emergency," April said.

"This guy is hella paid. Are you watching this?" Peri asked, his face glued to the television screen.

"I know. It's crazy. He's like a millionaire, and all he does is spin records at clubs and parties," April replied.

"I'm in the wrong damn profession, that's for sure," Peri said as he watched DJ Avenger avoid the paparazzi waiting for him outside of a Las Vegas hotel. He was an average-looking guy, medium build, dark features, and dressed simply in jeans, a plain T-shirt, sneakers, and a pair of aviator shades even though it was after dark. Peri hated people who wore sunglasses at night. It seemed so extra and cliché. "He's cute."

"Yeah, he's a'ight, I guess. But he's no Logan. And why were you rushing to end your conversation with him? This is far from an emergency, which you claimed it to be. What gives?"

"Nothing," Peri said, sitting back and contemplating how he was going to tell his client that she was going to have to hire another deejay. He had better come up with other suggestions to counteract the temper tantrum she would probably have when he told her the news.

"Trouble in paradise already?"

"No, no trouble. Just the same old same old. I guess we are at the point where there seems to be a need for a title, and you know how I am about that."

"Oh, God, here comes the breakup," April groaned.

"No one said anything about breaking up. You're being as ridiculous as Logan is," Peri said, reaching for his laptop and beginning a search in Google for celebrity deejays. The first person to pop up was DJ Avenger. Peri quickly scrolled past his name and picture. "You're damn sure not an option. Anyway, April, we gotta come up with someone else and do it quickly," Peri told his assistant.

"I'm thinking we may be able to get the deejay who's on the new *Love & Hip Hop*. He seems pretty cool," April offered. "And he is fine!"

"I'm not worried about how he's gonna look on camera. I'm more concerned with his ability to entertain the guests and satisfy the need for the bride to name-drop."

"Well, you were the one who pointed out how cute DJ Avenger was, so I thought looks mattered. No need to get an attitude, sir. Maybe you need to call your boo back. Sounds like you need a little something something."

"I don't have an attitude. I'm just tired, and you don't have to be so sensitive. Maybe you need to find someone to break you off so you won't be so offended. It has been a minute, hasn't it?"

"Shut up, you jerk!" April laughed. "I can't stand you!"

Peri couldn't help but laugh at his assistant. He and April had been friends for years. They met while both were working at a coffee shop near Baxter College, where they were both enrolled. She was studying business administration in hopes of landing a job in corporate America, and he was a student hoping to land the older professor he was sleeping with.

The daughter of the coffee shop owner was diagnosed with cancer, and Peri decided to do a fundraiser to help out with her medical expenses. The event not only raised over $5,000, but it sparked something within Peri and catapulted him into his career of event planning. He had found his niche and passion.

As his clientele grew and he became busier, Peri became overwhelmed. April took pity on him and began helping him out, telling him it was only temporary until she found a real job. Peri promised that he would look for a permanent assistant, but deep down they both knew it was a lie when he said it. The two worked well together. She could handle his temperament, and she somehow knew what he was thinking without him even saying it. April Kirby was his best friend and the only family he had.

Following up on her lack of love life, Peri said, "What happened to the guy from the Jag dealership? What was his name? George? Glen?"

"Greg. And I don't talk to him anymore. He's boring. All he talks about are cars and the people who buy them."

"Maybe he's trying to impress you."

"Then he should try talking to me about the last book that he read or movie that he saw. Not some businessman who came and dropped fifty grand as a down payment for a car. I'm not impressed."

"Now if he were the man who dropped the fifty Gs down—"

"That might be a little more impressive." April laughed and then quietly said, "Speaking of fifty grand, you got another medical bill in the mail. It's a pretty big one."

Peri paused for a few moments and then said, "Pay it."

"Don't you want to know what it's for?" she asked.

"Nope, just pay it," Peri told her.

"When is the last time you talked to him?"

"Pay the bill. Keep looking for a deejay. Meet me at the venue in the morning at eight thirty."

"Peri—"

Peri hung up. He didn't want to talk about anything else. Picking up his glass of wine as he got up from the sofa, Peri walked into the kitchen. He poured the red liquid down the sink, watching as it went into the drain. It reminded him of the color of blood.

He closed his eyes and tried to think of something else, but he couldn't.

Damn April for bringing up the bills. All she had to do was pay them like I told her to. She didn't have to say anything. There's so much money in my damn bank account, I wouldn't even have missed whatever she had to pay. Just pay the damn bill. Not that his ass even cares that I am the one paying it. He probably doesn't even appreciate all that I do for him. Mortgage paid off, car paid for, and now I'm paying medical expenses for a man who despises me more than anyone else on earth. Little does he know the feeling is mutual. I hate him as much as he hates me.

Peri rinsed the glass out and turned off the light. He walked back into the living room. Just as he was about to close his laptop, a signal notified him that there was a FaceTime call. Peri declined it quickly, then paused for a second and turned his attention back to his computer screen. He scrolled back up to the top of the celebrity deejay list he'd pulled up moments before.

He couldn't help looking at the picture of DJ Avenger smiling on stage. There was something about the picture that made Peri laugh, and then he realized that it was because of the familiar look in DJ Avenger's eye. It was the same look that Peri had at the end of a successful event when he knew that everyone was satisfied: the clients, the guests, and most of all, Peri himself.

Suddenly, there was a flash of what looked like lightning in the window. He walked over to see if there was a storm approaching. To Peri's horror, it wasn't lightning at all. He ran and grabbed his phone off the sofa, dialing 911 as he opened the door and ran toward the brightness across the street, praying the entire time.

Chapter 4

Jonah Harrington

1976 Harrington Way

Sweat was pouring from Jonah's face as the sound of Eminem telling him to "Lose Yourself" blasted in his ears. Although it was after two in the morning, he had been running on the treadmill in the fitness room of his house for almost forty-five minutes. Working out was what he did when he couldn't sleep. It was much healthier than eating snacks in the pantry, which was what he really wanted to be doing.

He changed the setting on the machine to cool-down mode and inhaled deeply. The song ended, and as soon as the intro to the next song began, he stopped so suddenly that he was almost thrown off the treadmill. He quickly hit the skip button on his iPod, but it wasn't fast enough to stop the memory. He was taken back three years, to the day that he and his best friend, Zeke, walked into a local sneaker store he'd found on the internet. Zeke was looking for a particular pair of Nikes that he saw in some men's magazine.

"Man, look, I am not spending my entire day off with you going around, looking for some gym shoes," *Jonah said when they walked into the sleek store. Rap music blared through the speakers of the store where everything seemed to have a designer label. Jonah*

knew this was way different from the typical stores where he shopped, which mainly consisted of Old Navy, Aeropostale, and occasionally JCPenney when he needed fancier attire.

"They aren't 'gym shoes.' They are limited edition Yeezys, and this spot has them. I already called and checked. I told the chick I talked to that I would make it worth her time if she hooked me up."

"Yeezys?" Jonah shook his head. "What is a Yeezy? Is that a new brand?"

Zeke found that funny and slapped Jonah's back so hard that it stung a little. "Damn, Jonah. I swear, the more I try to make you hip, the more you disappoint me. Yeezy as in Kanyeezy, Kanye West, the rapper. Come on, dog."

"Ohhhh." Jonah nodded and followed his friend through the store, trying not to stare at the outrageous numbers on the price tags that caught his eye.

Suddenly, Zeke stopped. "Daaammmn! Jackpot!"

Jonah glanced to see what he was referring to, thinking it was maybe one of the T-shirts hanging on a nearby rack that had a sale price of $75. Zeke wasn't talking about anything hanging on the rack. He was staring at the girl standing behind the register.

Jonah stopped and stared himself. The girl was gorgeous—slender with a bright smile and an infectious laugh that lit up the entire store. The line of customers, which was made up mostly of men, didn't seem to mind waiting because they got the chance to enjoy what she was saying as she rang them up.

"Thanks again, and I'm glad you found what you were looking for." She smiled.

"Oh, I definitely found more than that, and I will be back. You can bet on it," the guy said, reaching for the bag she was passing him.

Jonah could see Zeke plotting as he waited in line. As soon as he got to the front, he smiled and said, "Hello, beautiful. I called a little while ago, and you're holding a pair of limited-edition Yeezys for me."

"Hmmm, are you sure? We don't normally hold items, especially anything of that caliber."

Jonah saw the smile on Zeke's face drop just a bit, and he waited to see what would happen next.

"Yes, I'm sure. I called before driving all the way over here. I told the person on the phone that I was on the way and I was coming right over." It was clear that Zeke was trying to remain calm.

"Okay, let me check right quick. What's the name?"

"Zeke, but I didn't give anyone my name. The woman on the phone double-checked to make sure you had them and then said she would hold them in the back for me as long as I got here before you all closed."

"I'm the only woman here, and I haven't talked to anyone on the phone. Are you sure this is the right store?"

"This is the only Stadium in the area, right?" Zeke asked.

"Yes, as far as I know." She nodded.

"Then this is the store I called."

"Give me one minute. I'll be right back," she said, excusing herself.

"Man, this some bullshit," Zeke grumbled. "I called before we drove all the way the hell out here. Now if they don't have my shit, ain't no telling how hard I'm gonna go off in this piece."

"Calm down, Zeke. They're just sneakers. You'll get them somewhere else. It's no big deal," Jonah said, then started nodding to the UGK song that had just started playing.

The girl came back out and said, "My manager is talking to someone on the phone in the back. It'll just be one moment. I'm really sorry about this confusion, but I'm sure we can figure it out. Sir, is there something I can help you with while we wait?"

Jonah rapped along with the beat of the music:

She be cross country, givin' all that she got.
A thousand a pop, I'm pullin' Bentleys off the lot.
I smashed up the gray one, bought me a red.
Every time we hit the parkin' lot, we turn head.

"Sir?"

"J, man, she's talking to you!"

He was so into the song that he didn't even realize Zeke and the cashier were talking to him. *"Huh?"*

"I'm sorry for interrupting your groove." The cashier smiled at him, and he blushed. *"I was just making sure there wasn't anything I could help you find while we wait for my manager to come out."*

"Naw, I'm cool," Jonah said.

"Yeah, you are," she replied.

Jonah noticed a small birthmark on the side of her neck when she pulled her shoulder-length hair back. Something inside made him want to reach out and touch it. There was something familiar about her. Then he realized she looked just like one of the lead actresses in the cheerleading movie Bring It On, *which his younger sister used to watch over and over when they were teenagers.*

"Soooo, Lydia, what seems to be the problem?" a tall guy, who was dressed in a paisley button-down shirt and the tightest jeans Jonah had ever seen, came out and asked.

"This gentleman says that he called and spoke to someone about holding some Yeezys. I told him that we don't hold specialty items but—"

"Ohhhhh, yeeeeees! You're the man I talked to a little while ago. I remember! You told me if I held them you would, I believe you said, 'make it worth my while.'" The man batted his eyelashes at Zeke, who was standing like he was caught in the middle of a bad dream he couldn't get out of.

It took everything within Jonah not to laugh. Zeke prided himself on being a ladies' man and being able to pull any woman he wanted. He was tall, athletic, hand-some, and charming, everything women gravitated toward, so for him, it was easy. When he called the store and made the offer, Jonah could only imagine what his friend was plotting when he was on the phone with who he thought was a woman.

"Wait, you are who he talked to?" The woman whose name he now knew was Lydia giggled. "Okayyyyyy."

"I have your kicks, just like I promised. Let me get them for you." The guy gave Zeke a wink, singing as he walked off, "'I choose you, baby.'"

"I am so sorry." Lydia shrugged. "When you said you talked to a woman, I just thought—"

"It's all good," Zeke said and leaned on the counter. "You can make it up to me."

"Really? And how's that?" Lydia asked in a manner that let Jonah know she wasn't too excited by his friend's suggestion.

"How about you give me your number and we talk about it over dinner tomorrow night?" Zeke smiled.

"I'm flattered," she said flatly. "But I really don't think you're my type."

"Why not?" Zeke stood up straight.

Jonah could no longer hold his laughter, and a slight snort escaped. Zeke turned and gave him an ugly look.

"Here you go!" The tall guy came back, carrying the box of sneakers. "Size thirteen, right?"

"No! I said eleven, and you said you had them. I asked like five times." Zeke shook his head.

"Calm down, boo. I got you." The man laughed.

"Stop playing, Ricardo!" Lydia took the box from him. "They are an eleven. Is this all for you tonight?" Lydia opened the box and took out the red sneakers, passing them to Zeke, who inspected them all over.

"No, that's not all," Zeke said. "I'm still tryin'a figure out why you say I'm not your type."

"I guess I kinda know what I like," Lydia told him, then gestured toward Jonah.

For a moment, Jonah was confused and made sure she wasn't talking about someone behind him.

"You're kidding, right?" Zeke laughed. "Him?"

"What? He's cute, and he's different."

"He's corny and white!" Zeke turned to Jonah and said, "You know you're my boy, no offense."

"None taken," Jonah said, still shocked at what was taking place.

"Trust me, she likes corny," Ricardo told them. "Now the whole white thing is kinda shocking to me. But whatever floats your boat."

"That will be twenty-eight seventy," Lydia said.

"Wow, I thought they would be way more than that. I can maybe swing that. Do you have any in a ten and a half? I got thirty bucks." Jonah stepped up to the counter next to Zeke.

They all laughed, and Jonah blinked, confused.

"I told you he was corny." Zeke shook his head. "These kicks are way more than thirty damn bucks."

"I thought she said twenty-eight seventy," Jonah responded.

"Twenty-eight hundred, sweetie!" Ricardo said.

"Dollars?" Jonah was shocked. "For some gym shoes?"

"They aren't gym shoes, man," Zeke said, taking out his credit card and handing it to Lydia.

Jonah glanced up, and his eyes met hers. She smiled. He looked down again, hoping she didn't see him blushing.

"Really, at the end of the day, that's what they are," Lydia said. "Gym shoes."

"No, they aren't," Ricardo said. "They are limited-edition classics and a rare collector's item. They are more than gym shoes, don't get it twisted. Why do you work here again? Oh, that's right, because your daddy knows the owner."

"I think it's because of her amazing customer service skills and her gorgeous smile." Jonah shrugged.

They all turned to him, and this time when he looked up at Lydia, he didn't look down. The energy between them was so intense that he knew it had to be love.

"Well, damn. Maybe he ain't so corny after all," Ricardo said. "I think they may be a match made in heaven."

Ricardo was right. For Jonah, Lydia was heaven-sent just for him. They began dating, and it was as if he had known her his entire life despite their many differences. He grew up in the suburbs of Anne Arundel, Maryland, and she was from the inner city of Baltimore. He graduated from high school and immediately entered the police academy while being a Navy reservist, and she was working on a master's degree in education. He was a corny white guy who loved animals, and she was a beautiful black woman who enjoyed running and was afraid of dogs. His family loved her, and even though her family didn't feel the same, they made it work. He proposed to her a year and a half later, and she said yes. They were preparing to move in together when his reserve unit was activated. He was being sent to Afghanistan for six months.

"I want to marry you before I leave," he told her. "Let's go to the courthouse tomorrow."

"No. I want us to have a wedding, baby. A beautiful church wedding with all of our family and friends and my dad walking me down the aisle." Lydia leaned into his chest. They were lying on the sofa, trying to figure out their living situation.

"Do you think your family will even come to a big church wedding? Your dad technically didn't even give me permission to marry you."

Jonah and Lydia were visiting her parents' home one Saturday evening when he hinted to her dad that he wanted to marry her. He didn't get the chance to ask his permission because her father immediately went into a lecture about how Lydia had an amazing future ahead of her and other goals to accomplish before she was tied down to be someone's wife. He then continued to say how he and his wife had sacrificed to make sure that Lydia had everything she needed to accomplish her goals without the help of a man, especially one who wasn't educated or headed in the same direction of success as his daughter.

Jonah's first instinct was to respond by telling her father that he had his own goals, but somehow becoming a K-9 specialist in the police department didn't seem as impressive as he thought it would. He wanted to say that he wasn't trying to tie Lydia down, but he loved her and wanted to spend the rest of his life with her and wanted her to be the mother of his children. There was so much he wanted to say, but he didn't. He figured he would save it for another time.

"My dad is just trying to be intimidating like he does to all the guys I've dated. You're not gonna let him scare you off, are you?" Lydia teased.

"I ain't never scared! I ain't never scared!" Jonah said in his best Bone Crusher impersonation.

Lydia laughed. "And that's what made me fall in love with you. You remember that day you and Zeke came in the sneaker spot? I saw this cute white dude with swag, nodding to the beat."

"Swag?" Jonah laughed.

"Yeah. The fact that you knew all the words to UGK's 'International Players Anthem' let me know that you had swag. Plus, you were with Zeke, so I knew you couldn't be that bad."

"Zeke just knew he was about to make that move on you until you shot him down!"

"I told you on that day that I knew what I wanted, and I got it!"

Jonah kissed her and said, "I want to marry you tomorrow. You know I'm about to leave, and just in case—"

"I don't want you to marry me out of fear."

"It's not out of fear. It's because I love you and I want to make sure—"

"Just make sure you bring your ass back here in one piece so we can have a huge church wedding. Trust me, I'll have plenty of planning to keep me busy while you're gone. Now promise me you're gonna do that when you get back!"

"I promise as long as you promise to give me a baby as soon as we get married!"

"I promise!" she said, and he kissed her again.

Jonah's deployment went by quicker than they both anticipated. He hoped that by the time he returned, her father would have had a change of heart. However, things were no better when he got back. Jonah knew it couldn't have been his race, because Lydia's older sister had married an Asian guy and he and her father got along exceptionally well. There was just something about Jonah that her father did not like. Things didn't get any better once the two of them decided to move in together before the wedding.

"So you're just going to move my baby girl all the way out here and shack up, huh? You think that's appropriate?" her father asked while he was moving some of Lydia's things into Jonah's apartment, which she'd moved into once he'd returned home.

"No, sir, not at all," Jonah told him. "It's just temporary until the wedding in four months. I would marry Lydia tomorrow if she would let me."

"So you don't think she deserves the wedding of her dreams? You just wanna take her to the courthouse without any of us being there, huh?" Her dad frowned as he fired off the questions.

It was a no-win situation, and Jonah was glad when Lydia's mother came in and said, "Leave him alone. He loves her, and she loves him. They are saving money to close on their house. It's happening. Let it go."

"I just think she deserves better. She's a good girl," her dad mumbled, walking back out to the moving truck. Still, Jonah could make out the words "broke," "struggling," and "hopeless."

"Thank you," Jonah said to Lydia's mother. "And you're right, I do love her more than anything in this world."

"I know you do," her mother said. "Just promise me you won't let anything happen to my baby."

"I promise," Jonah said, and for the first time since they had met, she hugged him.

Jonah kept his promise, and he and Lydia were happily counting down the days to the wedding. One evening, she met her mother and picked up her wedding gown. She came back exhausted and fell onto the couch.

"Did you get the dress?" he asked her. "How does it look? Let me see."

"It's gorgeous, and no, you can't see it. It's not even here, so you can't even sneak and take a peek. It's at my parents' house, safe and sound."

"Oh, I definitely won't be going over there to see it," he told her. Her face was flushed, and her eyes weren't as bright as they normally were, so he asked, "Are you okay? What's wrong?"

"I'm just tired. This wedding is taking its toll on me a little."

"You're not getting cold feet, are you?"

"Of course not, baby. I love you, and I can't wait to become Mrs. Jonah Harrington."

"That sounds so sexy," he said. "Come on, future Mrs. Harrington. Let's go to bed and practice making this baby you want."

"Give me a minute, honey. I'll be right up."

Jonah went upstairs, took a shower, and climbed into bed, waiting for his fiancée. He didn't even realize he'd fallen asleep until he woke up and it was two in the morning. Lydia still hadn't come upstairs. He went back down and saw that she was lying on the sofa. Walking over, he tried to wake her. Then he saw she wasn't breathing.

"Lydia! Lydia!" he called out. He began CPR on her but was so confused. He didn't know whether to stop and call for help or keep going in an effort to save her. Finally, he grabbed her cell phone from the coffee table and dialed 911.

Arf! Arf! Arf! The noise coming from the backyard brought Jonah back to reality. He took off his headphones and heard his dogs barking incessantly. Something was wrong. He hopped off the treadmill and rushed out the back door to the kennels. All eight of his German shepherds were jumping, trying their best to get his attention.

"Calm down, guys!" he yelled as he walked into the backyard. His nose filled with the smell of smoke, and his eyes began to burn as he saw exactly why his four-legged friends were barking.

Chapter 5

Micah Burke

The Guesthouse

1547 Harrington Way

"So when do you leave, and when are you coming back?"

"The conference starts next Thursday, so I fly out Wednesday afternoon, and I will be back on Saturday evening," Micah said, fighting sleep. He and Adrienne had been on the phone for almost thirty minutes: the exact number of minutes since she'd left his house. He was tired, but he knew he had to stay on the phone until she made it home.

"You know we are supposed to attend the dinner for Deacon Garrison and his wife's anniversary Saturday night. We discussed this months ago, and I already sent the RSVP in."

Micah laughed. "Yes, sweetheart, I know."

"Why are you laughing?" Adrienne asked. They had spent most of the day together, ending the evening having dinner at his place while they watched two movies on Netflix until she left just before midnight, as she always did.

"Because you are already sounding like a minister's wife, that's why. Is this what I have to look forward to?"

"Yes, it is. And I'm just wondering why you keep taking on more and more of these conferences with your schedule already being full."

"I'm not taking on more conferences. You already know this one wasn't even scheduled. It's one I agreed to do at the last minute because Dad volunteered me."

"You mean he 'voluntold' you to do it."

"Pretty much. Should I tell him you said I can't go?" Micah asked, laughing at her attempt to sound like she was joking but knowing there was some truth to her statement.

He met Adrienne soon after her parents moved to the area and joined the church. He had just begun working as the youth pastor of Greater Works Assembly of Faith. Micah loved being a youth pastor because he had a sincere love for kids. But he knew this position was only a temporary assignment and a part of his being groomed to someday take over his father's ministry.

He and his twin brother weren't even in elementary school when their father started the church. It was all Micah could remember: sitting in the pews beside his mother and brother while their father preached. Unlike his twin, Micah loved church. He loved the people, the music, the spirit, the emotion he felt as his father bellowed out a sermon. He knew he had been called to the ministry like his father. It was inevitable.

"I didn't say you couldn't go. I'm just hoping you know I'm not planning this wedding by myself." Adrienne sighed. "I put in some applications online for a night job so I can—"

"Night job? For what?" Micah sat up in his bed and turned on the lamp sitting on his nightstand. His drowsiness suddenly disappeared.

"This wedding is going to be costly, Micah. You already know that. The guest list already includes my family, your family, the church members and staff you know we have to invite, and don't forget the people your parents are probably inviting. There's no way my family is gonna be able to foot the bill on this one. I have to be able to help them pay."

"Adrienne, no one expects you to pay for the wedding. My mother has already started setting things in motion. I heard her talking to someone earlier about hiring a wedding planner." He laughed. "Baby, we got this. Trust me. Your family doesn't have to do anything except show up."

"Micah, that's not right, and you know it. There is no way my father is going to just let you all pay for the wedding," Adrienne told him.

"There is no way I'm gonna let you get a night job. With my hectic schedule, we don't get to spend enough time together as it is. Don't do it. Everything will work itself out. I promise," Micah said to reassure her.

"Okay, Pastor Micah, I'm home now. Thank you for keeping me company," she said. "I love you."

"I love you too. I could really show you how much if you would've listened to me and stayed the night," he told her.

"Now you know that wasn't gonna happen when you asked me."

"Come on, Adrienne. You know there would not have been any funny business. I wouldn't do anything you didn't want me to do," Micah pointed out.

"That's the problem," Adrienne giggled, "what I would've wanted you to do to me. Besides, how would that look? Me spending the night at the bishop's house?"

"You wouldn't be spending the night at the bishop's house. You would be spending the night with your fiancé, in your future home, which is separate from the bishop's house. And no one would even know that you were over here."

"Your parents would see my car. And besides, the Bible says, 'flee the appearance of evil.' It's not what we would have been doing if I stayed over there, but what it appeared that we were doing. Why do we keep having this same discussion?" Adrienne asked.

"Because you never give in and spend the night like I ask you to," Micah groaned.

"I love you, your ministry, and your immaculate reputation too much to even give in to that temptation. Just think about this: in a few months I will be spending the night with you in our home every single night."

"I can't wait." Micah's voice was deep and seductive.

"Me neither. Now get some sleep and dream of me."

"That would be easier if you would send me a pic to look at before I close my eyes," Micah said, making a last-ditch effort to at least get his fiancée to give him a glimpse of what he had to look forward to.

"Good night, Pastor Micah," was Adrienne's response.

"Good night." Micah didn't even try to cover his disappointment.

Neither one of them were virgins, but they had been celibate since before they met almost two years ago. Micah was instantly attracted not only to her athletic, toned body and beautiful smile, but he was also drawn to her humble spirit and quiet demeanor. He was surprised, a few weeks later, when he arrived at one of the local homeless shelters to find that she was volunteering as well. As they sorted donated canned goods and served food to those in need, he enjoyed talking with her, so much so that he invited her to join him at his parents' house, where he was headed for dinner, hoping to continue to know her better.

His family immediately liked her as much as he did, and they began dating. A year later, after receiving her father's permission, along with seeking the nod of approval from his own father, he proposed in front of 4,000 members of the church congregation in attendance one Sunday. Micah was happy that he was able to make his parents proud and distract them from the stress and strain that they had been dealing with caused by Malachi and his antics. Micah had lived his entire life being good: a good student, a good son, a good friend, a good boyfriend, and soon, he would be a good husband. Micah could not imagine doing anything other than living out his purpose by serving God, serving in his father's ministry, and serving the youth and the people who needed him. Doing the right thing just came naturally to him.

The only thing he could see Malachi serving was time. His brother was always up to no good and had been for years. Growing up, he was constantly suspended from school, getting in fights, and causing trouble. And it didn't change as they got older. Micah had lost count of how many times Malachi had been to rehab, and his last little run-in with the law had landed him in jail. The more successful and famous their father became with preaching all over the world, appearing on television, and even being beside the president of the United States, the more Micah did to cast a shadow on their family. He was the bad seed, a thorn, and a test from the Lord that Micah had yet to pass.

He was actually relieved that his brother had been residing in the penitentiary for the past eighteen months. Not only did it give him the satisfaction of knowing that his brother was safe and far from the trouble that he seemed to find in the streets he ran, but also because they were free from him doing anything to put their family or the ministry in any further negative light. He prayed that this little "hiatus" behind bars would allow his brother the time to think and reevaluate his life and make some much-needed changes. Micah knew he should have taken the time to visit, but his busy schedule really didn't allow it. He did put money on his brother's books every month though, and he made sure that the church administrator sent him copies of their father's sermons weekly along with the monthly edition of a magazine the ministry put out called *Greater Life*. He hated to admit it, but things for the family just seemed to be a little easier with Malachi not being around.

Micah put his phone on the charger, cut the light off, and closed his eyes, drifting off to sleep. A few hours later he heard an inner voice telling him to wake up. Micah recognized and knew that this had to be the Holy Spirit. He opened his eyes, checked the time, saw that it was almost two in the morning, and then closed them again. A little while later, the voice came to him, stronger this time, and commanded him to get up.

He sat up and walked into his bathroom. The cool marble floors sent a rippled chill through his body. He stood over the commode and relieved himself, then walked over to the sink. As he washed his hands, a sharp, burning sensation shot through his arm. He looked down, expecting to see steam coming from the sink because he thought he had accidentally turned on the hot water, but there wasn't any. He turned the water off and stared in the mirror. The pain continued through his arm, and he rubbed it as he walked back into his bedroom and sat on the side of the bed. His arm was killing him, and he didn't know why.

The same voice that told him to wake up now told him to get on his knees and pray. He immediately did what he was told to do. As he folded his hands and closed his eyes, preparing himself to pray, he saw the vision of someone in his head.

"*Pray for him now. He needs you,*" the voice told him.

Micah peered at the vision in his mind, trying to see who it was he was supposed to be praying for. This wasn't the first time he had been awakened to intercede on someone's behalf, but the person's face was always revealed. For some reason, this person's face was blurred. Micah tried to focus harder, and the pain worsened in his arm. Suddenly, he realized who it was, and he jumped up.

"No!" he said aloud in the empty room. He rubbed up and down his arm, trying to soothe the pain. As he paced back and forth, he tried to get the image of the person out of his head. He went back in the bathroom and put cold water on his face, hoping that would help. He caught a glimpse of himself in the mirror and looked away, again saying, "No. I can't and I won't."

"Pray for him now!" the Spirit told him. *"He needs you."*

"He doesn't need me to pray for him. Hell, he doesn't even want me to pray for him," Micah said, shaking his head and rubbing his arm.

He remembered the last time they had seen one another. It was on a Wednesday afternoon, and Micah had been preparing the sanctuary in their new, state-of-the-art building for Bible study. He had been surprised to turn around and see him standing there. It was always strange because it was like staring at himself in the mirror. As much as their lives contrasted in every other aspect—personality, spirituality, and behaviors—they were still identical in looks.

"I'm sorry this had to happen to you," he told him. "You know, your having to go . . . um . . . away."

"Well, it is what it is. You know. Shit happens."

Micah shook his head. "Can you have some respect for where you're standing, please?"

"My bad," Malachi said, looking around. "This place is big enough to hold a concert."

"We do hold concerts here."

"*How many people can fit in here?*"

"*About six thousand in this sanctuary. There are also two smaller ones. One for youth church and another one for private prayer.*" Micah beamed with pride.

"*Remember the first church Dad started in that little-ass . . . I mean, small building that was a Chinese restaurant before he bought it? That place smelled terrible, like old shrimp fried rice and cat litter.*" Malachi walked down the aisle and into the pulpit.

Micah couldn't help but laugh.

"*He only had about ten people in that jank.*" Malachi stepped behind the huge podium embossed with the church logo where their father preached every Sunday. "*Now look at all of this! The bishop done came up for real! He is the poster child for 'started from the bottom and now we here,' huh?*"

"*Dad has grown his ministry tremendously over the past couple of decades. Everyone knows that.*" Micah wondered why his brother was even at the church. He was surprised he even knew where it was.

"*Yeah, good ol' Walt has done good for himself. Where is he?*"

"*If he's here, he's in his study, preparing for service tonight. Do you want me to walk you over there?*" Micah offered.

"*Naw, I'm good. I just wanted to check things out before I left. I'm just amazed,*" Micah told him.

"*God is amazing. Look at the number of people Dad has blessed over the years, the souls he's delivered, the lives he's changed, the impact he has had not only in the church, but on the world. He's written books, stage plays, traveled the world, and now he is about to produce a movie. Man, he's scheduled to be on* Oprah, Dr. Phil, *and* Jimmy Kimmel *next month! That is unbelievable.*" Micah smiled. "*Especially for a black man from Detroit.*"

Malachi stared at him and shook his head. "You sound like you've been drinking the Walter Burke Kool-Aid a little too long, bro."

"What is that supposed to mean?" Micah walked up to the pulpit and stared at his brother.

"Nothing," Malachi said, looking around. "To think he got all this now. Well, I gotta get out of here."

Micah watched his brother jump from the pulpit and into the aisle, heading toward the door. "Chi, wait!"

Malachi stopped and turned. "What?"

"Look, man, while you're here . . . I mean, I know you leave tomorrow for, uh . . ." Micah paused.

"Jail," Malachi finished for him with a shrug.

"Hey, why don't you let me pray for you at least? We're right here," Micah offered.

"Naw, I'm good. I don't need you praying for me, especially not here. You keep right on doing what you're doing, and I'll be fine."

"Why do you act like you don't belong here? Like you're too good for this place? I know you love God and you love Dad, so—"

"You don't know anything about me, Micah. The only thing you know is that you came out of the same twat I did two minutes later, but you don't know me for real. It's a whole lot that you don't know!"

Micah was hurt by his brother's words. Although they had the same face, it was as if he no longer recognized him. There was so much anger and animosity in Malachi. Micah didn't know if it was the result of the drugs, the alcohol, or if his brother had just turned evil over the past few years.

"Everything that our parents have done for you—private schools when you got kicked out of public ones, counselors, rehab programs, lawyers—and you still acting like an ingrate. They deserve way better than

*what you been doing, Malachi. Way better and you
know it."*

"Fuck . . . forget you, Micah."

*Micah could feel anger rising within and decided to
try a different approach so that things wouldn't get
worse. Although it hadn't happened very often, Micah
and his twin had gotten into some serious physical
altercations when they were younger. No one ever
truly won, but they both suffered bruises and black
eyes back in the day. This wasn't how he wanted
things to go, especially since, in less than twenty-four
hours, Malachi was going to prison for over a year.
Ultimately, this was his brother, and despite their dis-
connect, he was concerned.*

*"I don't know why you think I'm your enemy, but I'm
not. I am asking to pray with you because I love you,
Malachi."*

*"I don't need shit from you, Micah. Don't pray for me.
Pray for yourself and your father . . . and all of this!"*

*Malachi turned and rushed out of the sanctuary.
Micah started to chase after him, but instead, he let
him go. He tried reaching out and making himself
available, and not only was he turned down, but he was
disrespected. There was no hope.*

He hadn't tried to reach out since that day. The only
time Malachi was even talked about was when his
mother brought him up or invited him to come and visit
with her. Micah gave the excuse that Malachi told him
he didn't want anyone to see him in that situation, so he
was respecting his brother's wishes. Their father never
even spoke about Malachi when they were together, and
Micah knew that his father was just relieved. His father
no longer had to worry about phone calls in the middle
of the night telling him his son was in trouble or arrested or in the hospital. They didn't have to worry about

photos in the tabloids of Micah partying at the clubs with some random athlete or celebrity. Both the bishop and Micah could focus on building the ministry for the Kingdom of God without the distraction of Malachi.

Now, here God was waking him out of his sleep, telling him to pray for a man who didn't even want to be prayed for. Although he was spiritual and normally welcomed the opportunity to intercede in prayer for those who needed it, when it came to praying for Malachi, he didn't have that same propensity. Praying was intimate time between him and God that he enjoyed. He and his brother were disconnected in so many ways, and the frustration of their relationship caused him to be hesitant. It didn't have that same sense of enjoyment, and he didn't feel fulfilled like he did when he usually prayed.

"Pray for him. He needs you." The Spirit's voice was loud and clear.

"God, he doesn't need me. He needs you. You are the only one that can fix whatever it is. Me praying ain't gonna help that fool." Micah shook his head and went to lie back down in his bed. The pain in his right shoulder got worse and worse until he couldn't take it anymore. He knew he had to do what he was being told to do. He kneeled down and began to pray for his brother. For nearly thirty minutes, he asked God to handle whatever it was that Malachi needed, and he also asked for his own forgiveness for being disobedient when told to pray for him.

When he got up, there was still a dull aching in his arm, but the shooting pain was gone. He walked over to the window of his bedroom and looked out into the dark night. Flashes of red and orange in the near distance caught his eye, along with gray smoke. Micah grabbed his shoes and threw on a T-shirt, rushing to check on his mother next door and now praying that everything was okay.

Chapter 6

Lisa Wells

6524 Harrington Crest

Lisa Wells walked over to the stainless-steel oven of her dream kitchen and peeked in on the latest masterpiece that she was baking. The idea came to her in the middle of a dream. After being woken up by the constant barking of their nearby neighbor's dogs, she got up out of bed, careful not to wake her snoring husband, and went downstairs to begin baking. The scent of freshly baked apples and peaches wafted through her nostrils, and she smiled. She knew it was going to taste even better than it smelled.

She closed the oven and wiped down the marble countertops. As she looked around, she still wondered if she was living in a dream and would indeed wake up. Never in a million years would she have imagined being able to wake up and immediately put a recipe into action without a thought of not having the ingredients she needed or the money to buy them.

Now here she was able to just walk into the fully stocked pantry and refrigerator of their home, get whatever she needed, and have at it. She had the same mixing bowls used in the kitchens of five-star restaurants, state-of-the-art appliances, and every baking pan she could ever think of. Baking had always been her passion, and now she was able to do it whenever she felt the urge, which was quite often. There was no worrying about how much the gas or power bill would be because she was up all times of night pursuing her passion. There was no worrying anymore about money, period, because for Lisa and her husband, Marcus, money was no longer an issue.

Life for them was way different than it was almost a year ago. She and Marcus had been living paycheck to paycheck, doing their best to make ends meet and take care of their three kids: 12-year-old Michael, 10-year-old Aaron, and their baby girl Faith, affectionately known as Cocoa, who was 8. Marcus worked in the warehouse of a furniture manufacturer, and she worked part-time at a bakery in a grocery store in their hometown of Bristol, North Carolina.

One day, while on their way to work, Marcus and his brother Sam stopped at the corner store to get a cup of coffee. Marcus waited in the car, but when Sam hadn't come out in ten minutes, he decided to go in and see what the holdup was. Just as he suspected, Sam, who would carry on a conversation for thirty minutes about nothing to anyone who would listen, was talking to the cashier.

"Man, what is taking so long? We're gonna be late for our shift!" Marcus said.

"It's my fault," the cashier told him. "I had to restart the coffee pot. He was just talking to me while it brewed."

"Don't mind him. He's always grouchy in the morning," Sam said. "Hey, why don't you make yourself useful and pick out some numbers for me to play in tonight's drawing."

"It's gonna be a big one," the cashier said. "Everybody's been playing."

"I got more important things to do with my money than to play the lottery," Marcus told them. "And if you don't hurry up, I won't have any money, because I'm gonna be fired. Let's go!"

"Here, pick the numbers while I make my coffee," Sam said, passing him the lottery slip.

"We don't have time for this!" Marcus said.

"Just pick the numbers and hurry up!" Sam walked over to the coffee pot with his cup in hand. "You pick. I'll pay. When we win, we will split it fifty-fifty."

Not wanting to waste any more time, Marcus quickly filled in the birthdays of his wife, the kids, and his mother. He estimated that they would get to work nineteen minutes late if he didn't hurry, so he picked that as his Powerball number. Sam walked up to him and took the paper.

"Let's go!"

Sam paid for his coffee and the lottery tickets, and they headed off to work. The next morning the two brothers woke up $97 million richer. The news spread faster than an untrue rumor throughout the town that the brothers had struck it rich. Marcus and Lisa tried to remain normal. Their first purchases were a bigger and nicer home, a new pickup truck for Marcus, and a luxury SUV for Lisa and the kids. They donated money to the church they grew up in and of course made sure that their parents and close family members were taken care of, including Lisa's younger sister, Shari.

But people continued to harass them for money. Random strangers taped notes to their cars and on the door of their new home, and people approached them at local restaurants. Lisa became stressed with all of the attention, and she no longer felt safe, even with the security system they had installed. They no longer had any privacy. Marcus didn't seem to mind the attention, though.

"We need to move, Marcus," Lisa told him one night after they left the kids' school. "This is getting ridiculous, and I don't like it."

They couldn't even enjoy Michael's band performance because people were pointing and whispering. Some even took pictures with their cell phones. Faith didn't want to get out of Lisa's lap because she was so afraid.

"I don't want to move. This is where we grew up. All of our family and friends are here. This is where we wanted to raise our kids, remember?"

"That was before we had money and didn't have a choice. Don't you want better for your kids?" Lisa asked him.

"My kids do have better. We live in a better house, drive better cars. Hell, they have better parents because we don't have to work. What I don't want is for our kids to think they are better than anyone else. This money will not change us. I said that from the beginning," Marcus argued.

"I wanna move," Cocoa's tiny voice whined.

"Me too," Aaron chimed in.

"Dad, I think you might wanna listen to Mom on this one. Everywhere we go, people try to talk to us," Michael said from the back seat of the SUV.

"You act like people didn't know us before. Don't start tripping. We are the same, and money don't change us." Marcus glared at his son in the rearview mirror. Michael sat back and didn't say another word.

Lisa knew there was no point in arguing any further, so she just turned up the radio. Her husband was determined to remain the same cool guy from the warehouse who everyone knew and loved. The chubby, jovial guy who was on their high school football team for four years, but never even touched the ball during a game. Millionaire or not, he was gonna be everybody's homeboy.

They pulled into the driveway of their home, and just as they got out of the car, they heard someone behind them. "Marcus! Lisa!"

Lisa turned around to see some raggedy guy walking toward them. She quickly closed the back door and told her kids, "Don't get out. Stay in the car!"

"It's me, Los!" The guy steadily came toward them.

Marcus stopped and stared while Lisa jumped back in the car and closed the door, preparing to call the police. "Marcus, get in here!"

"Who are you?" Marcus asked the guy.

"Carlos, Tony's brother."

"I don't know you, man. I think you need to leave."

"Don't be like that. We used to shoot ball together down on Bayou Street. Me, you, my brother Tony and our cousin, Johnny." The guy kept coming closer.

"Marcus!" Lisa screamed out again.

"Mommy, I'm scared," Cocoa whined.

"It's okay, Cocoa. Daddy is just talking to the man," Lisa said as she fumbled with the phone.

"I been trying to catch up with you about this business I'm trying to start, and I think you'd be interested in getting in with me. My boy and I—"

"I'm not looking to invest in anything right now, my man. I need to get my family inside and make sure they're safe. So I'm gonna need for you to leave. It's late, and you shouldn't be on our property."

"I see what you're saying, and I don't mean any harm, but you changed your cell number. I reached out to your brother Sam. He told me over a week ago that he would holler at you about it, so I am just doing what I can to follow up."

"Look, I don't know what you're talking about, and I haven't spoken to my brother. But I'm asking you nicely to please go ahead and leave, now!"

Hearing the tone of her husband's voice, Lisa began to pray that Los or whoever he was would listen, turn around, and leave. Marcus was a gentle giant, standing well over six feet and weighing nearly 280 pounds. He was well liked by everyone, and rarely did he get angry. But when he did, there was no calming him down and no stopping him once he got started.

Either Los must've known Marcus was about to latch on to his raggedy self and fight him like a heavyweight boxer with no one to save him, or God heard Lisa's prayer. Either way, the man quickly ran off into the darkness.

After that incident, it didn't take much more convincing. Lisa finally got Marcus to see the light. He agreed that they had to move somewhere far away and do it discreetly. She had always wanted to live in California ever since she heard the R&B group Tony! Toni! Toné! sing about how it never rained there. She began researching new developments and came across Harrington Point. She and Marcus flew out and met with the developer. After touring the properties and seeing the beautiful land, she knew that it was where they needed to be. Somewhere new, different, quiet, and peaceful.

Moving across the country with her family into their custom-built, multimillion-dollar home was exciting to Lisa. Since moving in eight months prior, most of her time was spent furnishing their house and getting settled in. The kids were enrolled in a private school nearby and her days were filled with meeting designers and decorators, ordering and purchasing home decor, and shopping. At first it was all fun. But more and more these days, she found herself getting a bit bored and wanting to do something more.

"Damn, whatever that is smells good, boo!"

Lisa nearly jumped out of her skin as she heard her husband's voice, and then she felt his arms around her. "Boy, you almost scared me to death!"

"Why? You must be down here doing something you ain't got no business doing." Marcus hugged her close.

"Down here baking this cobbler. That's about it," Lisa said.

"At two in the damn morning? That's a shame," he told her, shaking his head.

"What's a shame? Those barking dogs woke me up. I can't believe you didn't hear them. So I came down here and made the recipe I dreamed about," she explained.

"And that's what's a damn shame. I can think of something else you could be dreaming about and coulda woken up and made." He gave her a seductive look, and she couldn't help but smile.

"Like what?" Lisa put her arms around his neck.

"Come here and let me show you," he said and kissed her.

Lisa felt herself being lifted off the floor and placed on top of the island located in the center of the kitchen. She wrapped her legs around Marcus's body and leaned her head back as she felt his lips on her neck, working their way down her collarbone. She fumbled to take his shirt off and reached for the string of the pajama pants he wore. They fell to the floor, and his hands cupped her ass as she arched her back. He eased off the lace panties she was wearing and spread her legs, not even bothering to take off the T-shirt or the apron she was wearing. She didn't know if it was the coolness of the countertop or the softness of Marcus's tongue as he kissed her inner thigh that caused the shiver to go down her spine. She braced herself by gripping the edge so she wouldn't slip off.

"I'm gonna fall," she moaned just as Marcus began to taste her dripping wetness.

He didn't answer her. Instead, his tongue went deeper into her center, causing her to gasp. She wanted to grab his head, but she was afraid that if she did, she would slide off and cause both of them to fall. Over and over his tongue entered her, teasing and pleasuring her, blowing softly and tasting, causing her center to throb.

"Marcus," she whispered, gripping tighter and tighter. "You've gotta stop."

Marcus continued to ignore her, devouring her as she slid down a little farther so his tongue could hit the spot she knew he was aiming for. The sound of him groaning as he devoured her turned her on even more, and she tensed up in an effort not to climax.

"Not like this, Marcus," she panted and tried to move. His grip tightened on her hips, and he pulled her down farther. She tried telling him again, "I don't . . . I don't wanna cum like this."

Marcus swiftly slid her off the counter and turned her around, bending her over so that he could enter from behind. Her favorite position.

"Tell me you want it," he whispered into her ear.

"Yes." She nodded. "I do."

"Tell me."

"You know I do," Lisa said, smiling over her shoulder.

"Naw," Marcus said. "Tell me!"

"I want it, Marcus." Lisa spread her legs just wide enough to give him access and gasped when the tip of him met her melting center. Marcus held on to her thick waist as his manhood slid in and out of her in rhythmic pleasure. Lisa bit her bottom lip in an effort not to scream and reached across the counter to hold on. Faster and faster, Marcus penetrated her dripping core, driving her into a state of passion that she hadn't felt in a long time. They made love on the regular, but it was routine and typical, always in the safety of their bedroom. This was spontaneous and thrilling. As much as Lisa didn't want it to end, she could feel Marcus getting to the point of no return.

"Oh, shit," he said.

"Wait, Marcus, not yet," Lisa pleaded.

"What the hell?"

"Marcus, please, baby, just a little while longer."

Suddenly, Marcus stopped, and she gasped as he eased out of her. She turned around to see what he was doing. "Marcus, you better not try and stick that thing in my—"

Marcus was pulling his pants up and had a strange look on his face. "Stay here."

"What's wrong?" Lisa asked, wondering what had her husband so spooked to the point that he stopped in the middle of the best sex they'd had since being married. She searched around the kitchen floor, wondering where her panties disappeared to.

"Listen," he said. "What is that?"

"I told you those dogs have been barking nonstop."

"I know, but there's something else going on out there."

Lisa found her panties in front of the stove. She started to open it and check on her cobbler, but then thought about it and quickly washed her hands as Marcus walked over to the kitchen door and opened it. Just as she was about to wipe any residue of their lovemaking off the countertop, she heard him yelling, "Fire! Fire! Oh, my God!"

Chapter 7

Malachi Burke

Malachi sat up, not knowing where he was. Nothing looked familiar. Not the king-sized bed he was lying across, not the seventy-inch TV he was staring at, not the dresser covered in bottles of cologne and watches, and definitely not the mirrored ceiling he saw when he glanced up. He closed his eyes and tried to remember how he even got there. One thing was for certain, he wasn't in jail, and that was the most important thing.

Hours earlier, he'd been released and walked out of the penitentiary, wearing his khaki pants, shirt, and kung-fu shoes, and in need of a haircut. Since he didn't have anyone to pick him up, the jail had given him $25 cash and a bus ticket. In his pocket was his ID and also a check for over $3,000, which was the money he had remaining on his books. His father and brother made monthly deposits into his account, but he had refused to touch the money. He thought about leaving it there but decided to use it to celebrate his release.

Once Malachi had gotten into town, he went straight to the bank, cashed the check, and went to the mall. After purchasing underwear, socks, toiletries, a couple pair of jeans, designer tees, and a pair of Tims and Nikes, he still had enough money left over to purchase a cell phone and check into the Hyatt.

Opening his eyes, now Malichi remembered it all. Last night after checking in, taking a long, hot bath, and having a late supper consisting of a medium-well steak, baked potato, broccoli, and an ice cream sundae, he'd lain down on the bed and had the best sleep he'd had in a long time.

Now, with just a glance at the clock, he could see that it was almost noon. His newly purchased phone was ringing. He had texted only one person since purchasing the phone, because not only was it the only number he knew by heart, other than his mother's, but also because it was the only person he wanted to talk to.

"What up?" he said, rolling over and reaching for the remote.

"Nigga, is this really you?"

"Who else would it be?"

"Man, I thought someone was playing a cruel joke on me. When the hell did you get home? Where you at? When you coming through?"

"Damn, Trey, you acting like you my chick with all them damn questions!" Malachi laughed. "Let me find out you getting soft on a brother!"

"Naw, never that and you know it! Damn, I ain't never been so glad to get a text in my life. What's the deal? You at your parents' crib? I gotta drive way out to no-man's-land and scoop you up from the mansion?"

"Hell no. I'm downtown at the Hyatt. My peoples don't even know I'm out, and I don't plan on telling them."

"Why you . . . You know what? Never mind. A'ight, I'm coming through. We got a lot to talk about. See you in an hour!" Trey hung up the phone.

Malachi enjoyed the comfort of the soft bed and the pleasure of *SportsCenter* for another twenty minutes before getting up and getting dressed. He had just stepped out of the shower when he heard the phone ringing again.

"What room number?" Trey demanded.

"2719."

Within minutes, there was a knock at the door, and Malachi opened it. Trey stood in the doorway, shaking his head at the white terrycloth robe Malachi wore.

"You ain't dressed?" Trey said, slapping Malachi's hand and giving him a semi-hug in true manly fashion.

"You said an hour. It's only been like forty minutes," Malachi said. He was glad to see his friend and confidante, whom he'd met when they were 15 years old and pursuing the same girl, Pamela Jones. She was a thick caramel cutie with the biggest breasts Malachi had ever seen. For nearly a month he pursued Pam. He rode his bike all the way across town to see her and sneaked on the phone late at night to talk to her about TV shows and rap music. He even took her to the movies to see some chick flick he had no interest in whatsoever in hopes that she would allow him to cop a feel or rub those nipples he had been having wet dreams about.

One day, he headed to Pam's house and was surprised to see a guy standing outside the fence just as he rounded the corner. He stared at the guy who was staring at Pam's house. They both then stared at Pam, who was standing on her porch, kissing another guy. That was the day Malachi got his first heartbreak. It was also the day he met Ronald Randall Richardson, who demanded that everyone call him Trey because he hated his entire name. The two of them struck up a conversation about being played by a girl who was clearly a ho.

They walked around the block, shared a joint, and ultimately became friends. Trey was a talented artist who loved writing music and pursued it with a passion. Trey's home life was the total opposite of Malachi's. He grew up in a two-bedroom home with his mom and alcoholic uncle, who sold drugs. The only time Trey saw the inside of a church was when he was meeting Malachi, who was usually sneaking out to meet him.

Trey was a good guy who normally didn't get into trouble unless he was with Malachi. Whereas Malachi stayed high and loved to drink, Trey only smoked when he was stressed. Malachi loved having multiple women to sleep with. Trey was shy, and it took him time to even warm up to talk to a woman. They were even different in looks. Malachi was tall, dark, and athletic. Trey was light, of average height, and stocky. In addition to his gift of songwriting, Trey also had what Malachi called his "instant panty catcher," which he rarely used: his green eyes and curly hair. Despite their differences, the two were closer than brothers and thick as thieves.

Trey looked around the hotel room, which was strewn with boxes, bags, and the remains of the dinner Malachi had the night before.

"Damn, somebody went shopping," Trey said, moving the bags out of a chair and plopping down. "I can't believe you're home. I thought you had like eight more months to do."

"Early release for good behavior or something. I don't know. I'm just glad to be out that bitch," Malachi told him. "The fact that I was in there period was some bullshit, but that's neither here nor there. I see you been eating good."

Trey nodded and rubbed his stomach. "I bulked up a little, but I'm about to start back hitting the gym. Damn, man, you trying to grow dreads?"

Malachi rubbed his hand across his thick, wavy hair, which he'd decided to let grow out once he found out he was going to be released early. "I waited to come home and get a cut from Dre. That's next on my list."

"You gonna be waiting a long time and driving a long ways then, because Dre ain't at the shop no more."

"What? Stop lying. Where he at?"

"He met some chick and moved to Florida. He down there now," Trey said.

"Florida with a chick? What about that crazy baby mama of his?"

"I think that's probably why he moved."

"Damn, I need a cut." Malachi shook his head.

"I got a guy I can call, and he will come and hook you up."

"Where's his shop at?"

"He doesn't work in a shop. He's a personal barber. He comes where you want him."

"Damn, you got it like that now, Trey? Life must be good for real."

"Man, life is crazy, I'm telling you," Trey said, reaching into his pocket, pulling out a piece of paper, and handing it to Malachi. "This is for you."

Malachi opened the paper. His eyes damn near bulged when he saw a check written to him in the amount of $30,000. "What the hell? Where did this come from? Who the hell is Triple Threat Entertainment?"

"That's the name of my company. Remember that song I was working on right before you left? The one you helped me with the arrangement on?"

"Yeah." Malachi nodded, vaguely remembering. Trey stayed in the studio working on stuff so much that Malachi couldn't exactly pinpoint what he was talking about.

"Well, someone at MTV heard the song, and they bought it. It's the theme song for some corny reality show, it's featured on the show's soundtrack, and it has been downloaded more than any other song on their playlist. It's a hit with their audience."

"Man, for real? I don't know what song you're talking about." Malachi laughed.

Trey pulled out his iPhone, clicked something, and the familiar tune began playing. The chords and melodic changes Malachi had suggested to Trey when he first played the song were now recognizable. He nodded and enjoyed the music.

"I'm telling you, this is just the beginning," Trey said. "For years, I was trying to sell my beats and songs to black rappers. Who knew I had a talent for writing songs for white teenyboppers? Well, we have a talent."

"We don't have nothing. I ain't no damn song writer. That's all you."

"Man, listen to me, that check is all the proof you need. You have a talent, even more so than I do because your ass can't read music, don't even like music, but you play a hell of a lot better than anyone out here. This is what you're born to do. It's obvious because of that paper you're holding in your hand."

All Malachi could do was stare at the check.

Trey said, "Tell me this: now that you're out, what's your plan?"

Malachi really didn't have a plan other than to do what he had already done, which was to get some clothes, some food, and some sleep. The only real thing he had left on his agenda was a haircut from Dre, which now seemed impossible.

"Get dressed. We got work to do," Trey told him.

"I have an agenda," Malachi told him. "At least for to-night, and it ain't got shit to do with music. Believe that."

"And what's on your agenda?"

"Some loud, a drink, and some ass. I hear what you saying, Trey. But damn, I just got out yesterday. A nigga need to party first!"

Trey didn't say anything else about music. After Malachi got dressed, they hit the streets. Later that night they ended up at Vixen's, one of the hottest strip clubs, where Trey had become a VIP. The club was packed to capacity with men and women as Trey and Malachi made their way to the roped-off section where several familiar celebrities and athletes were enjoying bottle service and lap dances.

"Whoa, it's the preacher's son!" Hakeem Morgan, an NBA player whom Malachi had partied with, greeted him. "When did they spring you out the joint?"

"What's up, Hakeem!' Malachi laughed. "I just got out."

"Jamaica, a bottle of Henny and a special performance for my man over here!" Hakeem yelled.

"My name is Marley!" The pretty waitress, sporting a bikini top, boy shorts, and double Ds, corrected Hakeem and smiled at Malachi as he took a seat on the white leather sofa, enjoying the scenery. More and more of his friends began to show up, and he realized that Trey must've spread the word and invited people to come and celebrate his homecoming. They popped bottles, smoked hookah, and tipped the dancers generously. Even Trey indulged in a few lap dances to Malachi's surprise.

"Can I squeeze over here?" a female voice asked as she entered their area.

Malachi couldn't help staring. He recognized the woman who was damn near sitting in his lap as she tried to sit on the sofa beside him.

"Damn, baby, of course you can!" Hakeem said, trying his best to shift his six foot nine frame over so she could have room, though she seemed to be content on Malachi's lap.

"Hey, sexy." She smiled at Malachi, and her hazel eyes and dimpled smile were as perfect as her body. Her hair was pulled up on top of her head, and the tight black dress she wore clung to her like a second skin.

"Hey, Scorpio," Malachi said, trying to remain cool and act like he wasn't fazed by the fact that one of the world's most famous supermodels was inches from his crotch. Although he had seen her everywhere, from the cover of *Sports Illustrated* to strutting on the runway of the Victoria's Secret fashion show, they had never met.

Being around celebrities was nothing new to him, but Scorpio was in a different league. She was the object of every man's fantasy, including his. While he was locked up, he heard that she and her husband had separated and were going through a nasty divorce. Both of them were known to be party animals, and most people, including Malachi, were surprised they lasted as long as they had.

"Can I crash your party?" she asked, her manicured fingertips caressing his face and rubbing his head. He was pissed that he still hadn't gotten a haircut.

"It's not really my party," he told her, placing his hand on her thigh, which was exposed from the short dress she wore. His gaze followed down her long legs to her feet, and he fought the urge to imagine her naked in bed wearing only her red bottom stilettos.

"Really? Someone told me that this was a party just for you, a homecoming party." Scorpio shrugged. "That's not true?"

"If that were the case, you wouldn't be crashing. You would be an invited guest," he said.

She tossed her head back, laughing flirtatiously, and leaned over, giving him a sneak peek at her ample cleavage. Deciding to take a chance to see if she was really coming on to him, Malachi moved his hand a little higher up her thigh. Scorpio didn't move him away and began swaying to the beat of the song that was coming through the speakers.

"I love this song. Let's dance," she said.

"Naw, I'm good," Malachi told her. "You want something to drink?"

"Did you even have to ask?" Scorpio took the glass he was holding and drank all of the brown liquor.

"Damn." He laughed.

"Can I get a refill?" Scorpio said, looking around for the waitress. "So how long were you in the joint?" she asked him.

"About a year and a half."

"A year and a half with no women? Hmmmmm." She gave him a seductive look.

"What's that supposed to mean?" Malachi asked.

"Scorpio!" an older woman said, attempting to get into the VIP area. The large security guy near the entrance stopped her before she could get any closer.

"Oh, goodness, here comes the party crasher for real." Scorpio sighed.

"What are you doing? I've been looking all over for you. We're ready to go!" the woman said, glaring at the group of men in the reserved area, including Malachi. Two other girls appeared next to her along with a skinny guy who was clearly gay. Malachi recognized one of the other girls as a swimsuit model as well, but he couldn't remember her name.

"So go, Dina! I'm not ready. We just got here!" Scorpio said. "I'm not leaving."

"See, Marcelo, this is why I told you and Dina I didn't want to come with her. She never knows when it's time to go. I'm leaving. I have a shoot in the morning I gotta get ready for," the model chick said.

"Come on, Scorp. We can come back tomorrow night. We've gotta go," Marcelo pleaded.

"You guys go ahead. I'm good," Scorpio told them.

"Fine," the model chick said and turned to walk off.

"Wait, Natalie! We can't just leave her," Dina told them.

Natalie Kincaid! That's her name, Malachi thought as he continued watching the drama.

"Why not?" Natalie said. "She's grown, and she drove."

"But she's drunk," Marcelo said. "Do you think that's safe? This is why I told you to call Cheddar."

"Fuck Cheddar! And carry your asses!"

The four-person entourage shook their heads and departed, leaving Scorpio on Malachi's lap, requesting a refill of what was now her drink.

"We need to take some pics! Oh, damn! My phone is dead. Lemme see your phone!" Scorpio leaned over and yelled at Hakeem, who seemed to be impressed with the petite, big-busted stripper who was rubbing on his chest. He reached into his pocket and handed Scorpio his iPhone. She held it up and commanded Malachi to pose.

"I don't do pictures, ma." Malachi shook his head and tried to block the phone. Scorpio pressed her body against Malachi and kissed him fully on the mouth, gently sucking his bottom lip in such a manner that he didn't even care that she was taking a picture of them as she did so. Afterward, she smiled and said, "Say cheese."

He stared at her, eyebrows raised, and said, "Cheese."

They continued drinking, laughing, and feeling on one another until Malachi's hard-on was no longer caused by the strippers they came to see.

Scorpio leaned over, stroked his crotch, and said, "Let's get out of here. Take me home?"

Malachi shook his head. "Sorry, ma. I ain't drive."

Scorpio reached into her cleavage and pulled out a Porsche key fob. "That's not a problem."

"I can take her home if you want me to," Hakeem offered.

"I don't want you taking me nowhere," Scorpio snapped. "I want Malachi! It's his night."

Malachi considered her surprisingly bold and appealing offer. His ego quickly told him the chances of him ever getting the opportunity to sleep with a supermodel again would be damn near nonexistent, so if ever he wanted it to happen, he'd better do it now.

It didn't take him long to decide, especially with Scorpio whispering in his ear what she wanted to do to him. He told Trey and his boys he would catch up with them later, before he gathered up his newly acquired date. As they stood up, Scorpio stumbled, and Hakeem helped Malachi walk her out of the club. Her custom-colored pewter four-door Porsche was parked right near the door, and Malachi helped her inside before sliding into the driver's seat. The feel of the leather, the sleekness of the steering wheel, and the enticement of the glowing dashboard was almost too much for him to take. He hadn't been behind the wheel of a car in almost two years. He inhaled the scent and looked over at Scorpio, who was so drunk that she was already nodding off.

"I'm staying at the Hyatt. Is that cool? he asked her.

"No, take me home!" she told him.

"I don't know where you live. I can take you home in the morning," Malachi said.

Scorpio hit some buttons on the screen of the dash, typed, and then loudly said, "Home." The GPS map appeared, and the computer voice instructed him.

He saw that it was a forty-five-minute drive and started to suggest again that they go back to his room at the Hyatt, but decided against it and just headed to where she wanted to go. Scorpio reached under the seat and pulled out a plastic bag containing what looked like five or six perfectly rolled joints, and she lit one up. After taking a puff and inhaling, she passed it to him. He held it to his lips, taking a pull and allowing the smoke to fill his lungs.

"Good stuff, huh?" Scorpio smiled.

Malachi just nodded and passed it back to her. She turned on the radio, and old-school rap serenaded them while he drove. They made small talk until Scorpio fell asleep. When he finally arrived in her neighborhood, he pulled in and noticed that although there was a security booth, no one was in it, so he proceeded. There were still houses being built, but the ones that were already completed were huge. He continued until he got to the one that the GPS told him belonged to Scorpio.

"Hey, we're here." He nudged her, but she didn't move. "Scorpio, we're at your crib. Come on. Wake up!"

Scorpio held her head up for a second, pointed to a black plastic square over the visor, and mumbled, "Garage."

Malachi was confused until he saw that on the other side of the circular driveway there was what looked like a four-car garage, and he drove over. He hit the plastic remote, and the garage opened. He pulled inside and parked beside a large SUV and a motorcycle. He tried once again to wake Scorpio, but she was beyond wasted. He knew he would have to carry her.

He got out and walked to the passenger's side of the car, lifting her out and tossing her over his shoulder. The short skirt of her dress rose all the way up, answering the question he had been pondering all night long: she did not have on any underwear. Her perfectly shaped derriere was fully exposed, and he bit his lip in excitement. There were two doors, but one didn't have a window, so he knew that door led to the inside of her home. He then realized he didn't have a key.

"Scorpio, you gotta wake up. Where is your house key? How are we gonna get inside?"

Scorpio awakened but didn't answer. She just pointed to the door and laughed.

"The key," Malachi said again, trying not to get frustrated. He turned the doorknob, expecting it to be locked. Instead, it easily turned, and he pushed the door open.

Once inside, he heard a beeping sound and panicked. "Scorpio, the alarm."

Scorpio wiggled out of his arms and stumbled over to a nearby wall, where she punched in a code. The beeping stopped. Relieved, Malachi closed the door as Scorpio turned on a light.

"Come on," Scorpio said, pulling him down the hall and into the foyer, where there was a huge double staircase. She tried to make it up a few steps but nearly fell, so again he picked her up into his arms and carried her. When they got to the top, she pointed to a door at the end of the hallway. He entered through the darkness into what he assumed was her bedroom and placed her on the huge bed in the middle of the floor. She scrambled out of her dress and lay naked across the black duvet, wearing only the red bottoms.

Malachi looked up at the ceiling and mouthed, "Thank you, God." He took off his own shirt. Just as he climbed beside her, Scorpio jumped up and ran out. He was confused until he heard her heaving and gagging. He waited until it stopped and called out, "Scorpio. You okay?"

When he didn't get an answer, he walked into her bathroom and found her lying on the floor beside the commode, her face covered in sweat. He sat her up, found a nearby washcloth hanging on the rack, wet it with cool water, and then gently washed her face. Lifting her up, he carried her back to the bed, took her shoes off, and put her under the covers.

From the minifridge in the corner, he got a bottle of water and made her drink some. She tried to resist but finally took a few sips.

"Thanks," she smiled and whispered just before closing her eyes.

Moments later, he heard her snoring. He lay across the foot of the bed, falling asleep himself. He stayed there until waking up and wondering where the hell he was. Recollecting what had happened a few hours before, he looked around for Scorpio, but there was no sign of her. He went into the bathroom, but she wasn't there either.

"Scorpio?" he called out. Hearing a noise coming from outside the open bedroom door, he went to try to find out where she could have gone. He walked down the staircase and suddenly smelled smoke.

He called out again, but there was no answer. The smell of smoke was getting thicker. Malachi knew that he had to find Scorpio and get them out of there quickly. He searched the massive home in the darkness caused by the combination of smoke and night, going in and out of doors, trying to breathe. "Scorpio!"

He finally heard coughing from nearby and ran to the cracked door of what he remembered led to the garage. He opened it, and flames came shooting out at him. He could make out a shadowy figure crawling toward him. *Scorpio!*

He reached for her, the fire searing his arm and his eyes tearing up from both the pain and the smoke. Malachi stretched his arm farther until he felt her hand in his, and he yanked her body to him. She cried out as he lifted her through the door and headed to what he hoped was safety.

Chapter 8

King Douglas

"Oh, my God! Okay, I know I'm not supposed to do this, but can I please have your autograph?"

King Douglas looked up from the receipt he was signing and smiled at the young girl behind the counter of the rental car agency. He had just come off a four-hour flight from L.A. and was jetlagged, but he always made time for his fans. Even if he didn't have time, he would have made an exception for her. She was just his type: young, vibrant, and sexy. Even in the collared shirt and fitted black pants she wore, he could make out her curves. Her cute face was set off by long locs, and her thick-rimmed glasses couldn't hide her dark, seductive eyes.

"Of course," King told her. "Do you have something for me to sign?"

The woman reached into the drawer and handed him a piece of paper. "You can sign this. I can't believe this."

"What's your name?"

"Nikita. N-i-k-i-t-a."

"That's pretty, like you," he said and slid the paper back to her. "Tell you what: since you're so pretty, do you have a cell phone?"

"Yes." She nodded.

He looked around to make sure there was no one else around and said, "Grab it. We can take a selfie if you want to."

She squealed and ran through a door behind the counter, returning within seconds, iPhone in hand. "This is un-freaking-believable. My friends are going to die! I'm about to die."

"Please don't do that," King laughed and posed with his arm around her as they both smiled for the camera.

"Thank you so much, Mr. Douglas. I have you all set in one of our premium vehicles, a BMW X5. Here is the key, and if you take a right out the front door, you should see it right there," Nikita said.

"Thank you, Ms. Nikita."

"Actually, my friends call me Niki."

"So can I call you that?" King gave her one of his intense stares, a look that said, "I want you. I need you. And I will have you." It was the same look he would give the camera when he was singing one of his platinum love ballads while filming a video or singing center stage to some lucky fan who was pulled on stage during a sold-out concert.

That was back in the day when music had meaning and music videos had storylines, love interests, and dancing. Nowadays, all a song had to have in order to be a hit was a hot beat, a rapper with what was called "swag," and a record label willing to put millions behind pushing nonsensical words to whoever would listen. Nowadays, it didn't take hard work, endless nights in the studio, and months and months of touring and talent to become a platinum artist. All it took was a hook, a YouTube channel, and enough followers on Instagram to get people's attention.

It was nothing like when he and his boys dedicated their lives to their craft and became R&B icons the Hot Boyz. From the time they were signed at sixteen, King, along with his boys Steve, Kazz, and Tony, worked diligently to create music, produce songs, hit the road, make appearances, and perfect everything needed to become true artists.

And that was why, more than twenty-five years later, he was able to have young tenderonis like Nikita ask for his autograph, stare back into his eyes, and tell him, "You can call me whatever you like as long as you call me."

King laughed and watched as she wrote her name and number on the back of the business card for the rental car company. He told her not to be surprised if he did call later on, and she said she would be waiting.

Then, even though it was late at night, he put on his Salvatore Ferragamo sunglasses, grabbed his Louis Vuitton duffel bag, and headed out to the dimly lit parking lot.

Once inside the luxury SUV, he tried to decide what to do next. The sole purpose of this last-minute trip back to his hometown of Norfolk was because Melissa, the mother of his son, told him she had an emergency and needed to talk to him face-to-face. The two of them had a cordial relationship, and she never put any unreasonable demands on him, mainly because he took great care of their 14-year-old son, Knight. He loved her, but their love affair ended almost four years after Knight was born, especially when it was discovered that King was the father of a 2-year-old: the result of a one-night stand backstage with a groupie named Portia, whom he could not stand.

He dialed Melissa's number to tell her he was on his way.

"Hey," Melissa said as she answered the phone.

"Hey, I'm here and on my way to your house," King told her.

"Wait, I don't want you to come here." Melissa paused. "We need to meet somewhere else."

"Melissa, it's almost midnight. Where are you trying to meet?"

"Where are you staying?"

"At the Westin at Town Center in Virginia Beach. You coming to the room?" King asked, excited because this was definitely not what he expected. For years he had tried over and over to get back with Melissa, whom he considered the closest thing to the love of his life if there was such a thing. She, of course, denied him continuously. Now he wondered if maybe there was a slight chance of him getting some ass from her since she was coming to meet him in a hotel room late at night.

"Hell no. I'm not coming to a hotel room with you. Are you crazy?"

"Why not? You scared of King D, Melly Mel? You know you still miss him after all these years!"

"Boy, please. I'll meet you in the bar. See you in twenty minutes," Melissa said, then hung up.

King got onto the interstate and headed toward the hotel. He was tempted to call his uncle Matt, the only living relative he had since his mother passed away two years ago. King never knew his father, but Uncle Matt and Melissa were close. He swore he looked out for Melissa on King's behalf, but it was more likely the other way around.

Melissa made sure she checked on Uncle Matt and brought Knight over to spend time with him on the regular. Seeing that it was now after eleven, King knew his uncle was probably asleep, and he decided that he would drive over to see him the next morning.

Once he checked into the hotel, he freshened up, then headed back to the bar to wait for Melissa. As he suspected it would be, the hotel bar was fairly empty, but he was surprised to see her waiting for him when he arrived. She looked amazing as ever. His heart began racing as he walked toward her. Melissa was the most gorgeous woman in the world to him. At five foot seven and nearly

190 pounds, she was a thick girl, but she carried it well. Her hair, which was normally long and wavy, was now in a chic, chin-length bob, and he liked it.

"Look at you!" he said.

Melissa stood up from the stool, and they embraced for a few moments before he kissed her cheek. The familiar scent of her perfume filled his nostrils, and he couldn't help but feel the fullness of her chest as he held her tight. He was tempted to let his hands linger below her hips, but he knew better.

"You like it?" Melissa asked, shaking her hair as she took her seat.

"I do." King nodded, reaching out and stroking her bob. "You always stay fly, though."

"What can I get you?" the bartender came over and asked.

"I'm fine," Melissa said, pointing to the bottle of Perrier in front of her. "Do you want anything?"

King gave her a look up and down and smiled. "What are you offering?"

"I'm offering you a soda or some water, whichever you choose." Melissa smirked.

"Naw, I'm good then," King told the bartender. He then turned to Melissa. "You know how to tempt a brother, don't you?"

"You're fine. How long is it now?"

"A while."

"What's a while?"

"Drugs, almost two years."

"And alcohol?"

"Other than a beer I drank to celebrate the Giants' Superbowl win, it's been a little over nine months." King shrugged. Sobriety was a daily challenge, especially since most of his life had been spent indulging in marijuana, alcohol, and even the occasional hit of cocaine. For him, it was all a part of being a member of the group. King was the one member who could perform during a concert, party until noon the next day, arrive in the studio and lay down a track, and be ready to perform again. Unlike the R&B legends King grew to love, like David Ruffin, Rick James, and Gerald Levert, he didn't succumb to the lifestyle and lose himself to it. He thrived while intoxicated. It made him a better performer and did wonders for his songwriting.

What it didn't do was wonders for was his reputation or his relationships. On more than one occasion, he was accused of being a womanizer and philanderer and fathering numerous children. Most of the accusations weren't true. People just didn't understand him, which angered him at times. The fact that he would throw items across the room when he got frustrated, or throw a punch at a guy who disrespected him, just showed how passionate he was. And passion was what music was all about.

He had one failed marriage and was in the process of ending his second one, both in the ten years since he'd broken up with Melissa. Losing his mother had been the one sobering factor in his life. Her death was a shock, and it sent him into a state of depression that landed him in rehab. It was there that he realized he did have some anger issues and emotional baggage from his childhood, and it was there that he got clean. He vowed to stay clean as a legacy to his mother.

So far he had kept his promise. It wasn't easy, especially with the messy divorce he was dealing with. Having people in his corner like Melissa, his group members, and his manager helped out a lot.

"I'm proud of you," Melissa told him.

"Proud enough to go upstairs with me?"

"Hell no, not that proud." She laughed.

"So what's so important that I had to fly all the way to VA to discuss it?" King's curiosity was now piqued.

After a few pregnant seconds, Melissa finally spoke. "I need for you to take Knight for a while."

King blinked for a few seconds. "What? What do you mean?"

"Knight? Your son? I need for you to take him to live with you."

At first he thought she was joking to see what his reaction would be. They sometimes did that with one another: suggest extreme what-if situations to test one another and get a good laugh. But there wasn't a smile on her face or any humor in her eyes. He wasn't sure what to say except, "I'm getting him this summer when school lets out."

King always kept his son for a month during the summer, in addition to seeing him during the major holidays when he wasn't touring. They always had a great time going to amusement parks and movies, and he allowed his son to pick a destination for them to spend an entire week. Knight was adventurous, so they had been everywhere from Hawaii to Brazil. He loved hanging out with his son, but it seemed like Melissa was asking him to do something a whole lot more than jet around for a couple of days.

"No, right now. I need you to take him now," she explained.

King inhaled and then said, "I can take him for a couple of days."

"I need you to take him for more than a couple of days, King. My mother is sick. Really sick. I'm gonna have to go up to Baltimore for a little while," Melissa told him.

King saw the tears forming in her eyes, and he reached for her hand. "Damn, Mel. I'm sorry. What's wrong?"

"Stomach cancer. I don't know how bad it is. I just know she's sick and I need to get to her. But, King, you know I can't take him with me to Baltimore. There's no way." Melissa shook her head.

"But . . . Look . . . What . . ."

"But nothing. There's nothing to look at, and what I need you to do is what I've been doing for the past fourteen years: be a full-time parent. It's not that hard to comprehend. What's the problem?"

Melissa was getting agitated, and he didn't want things to get ugly between them. But this was unexpected. For some reason, he thought she wanted to talk about them. They had been getting closer over the past year, and now that his mess of a marriage would hopefully soon be over, he hoped that maybe there was a chance they could try again. Now here he was sitting there and she was asking him to be a full-time father.

"I'm not saying it's a problem, Mel. But you know I have a lot going on right now. This divorce is crazy—"

"That's because you married a crazy woman. And you told me she moved out and has been gone for months."

"She did, and she has. But I'm still dealing with lawyers and the settlement. And you know the guys and I are touring again, and we're trying to work on this album."

"Your son will be at school during the day when you have your meetings. And you know you aren't on tour. You all are making appearances every now and then. King, I really don't care what you have going on in your life. I just told you my mother is sick. I am leaving to go and take care of her and my father, who you also know has Alzheimer's. Now, you and I have always had a great relationship, and we have an amazing son. Even when you've messed up, I've always had your back. Now I'm gonna need for you to have mine for a little while."

"I do have your back, Mel. I'm sorry you gotta deal with all of this. Trust me, I know what you're going through. It's hard being the only child when something happens to your parent. You know I know that. Why don't we talk to Uncle Matt and see if he can—"

"You can't be serious, King." Melissa's voice was filled with disappointment. "You want to leave your teenage son in the care of your seventy-year-old uncle who has health issues of his own?"

"First of all, Uncle Matt is fine," King pointed out. "He may have a little high blood pressure—"

"The man had bypass surgery last month and wears a heart monitor," Melissa hissed at him.

King could see her anger rising, but he continued trying to reason with her. "But he's fine now. If Knight stays with him, he can stay in the same school with his friends, and we won't have to disrupt his life. Let's just try it out and see."

"King Jabari Douglas, I'm not gonna sit here and argue about this, because now you sound real stupid, and you're not a stupid man. You will be taking your son back to California to live with you until I am able to come and get him," Melissa stated as she stared at him.

King knew he had lost the fight, and an hour later he was back in his hotel room, trying to figure out how he was going to handle his new responsibilities of being a full-time dad once he and Knight went back to California in two days.

The conversation with Melissa and his newfound responsibilities made him want to go back down to the bar and get a drink. He was stressed and needed to do something and do it quick.

His eyes fell on the business card on the nightstand, and he dialed Nikita's number, inviting her to his room. She didn't hesitate to tell him she would be there within minutes. He was slightly relieved, hoping that she would provide a much-needed distraction from his urge for libations. He decided to change shirts and was going through his suitcase when he got a call from an unfamiliar number. Thinking maybe it was Nikita calling from another number, he answered.

"King! So you 'bout to let Knight come and live with you in Cali?"

Immediately King regretted answering the phone as he heard Portia's voice yelling at him. "Hello to you too, Portia."

"Yeah, whatever. Knight 'bout to be living wit' you now? PJ came in and said Knight just put on Instagram that he was 'moving in wit' Pops.' I knew this shit was gonna happen. My mama told me you was always gonna favor him over my son, and she was right!"

"That's a lie, and you know it. I love both my sons equally. I always have."

"Now that's a lie! It's always been all about Knight. He's the one you take on fabulous trips and shopping sprees. My son gets nothing."

How Portia considered the $8,000 a month he paid in child support nothing, King didn't understand. He also didn't understand why his son would put that information out on social media without even speaking to him first. He had some choice words for his son and grabbed his iPad to pull up Instagram. He searched his son's page and was relieved not to find a post even remotely saying anything like she said.

"Portia, I'm not having this conversation with you. I have to go," he said when he heard the beeping on his line. He switched to the other caller and asked, "Where you at, sweetheart?"

"Getting on the elevator," Nikita told him.

He gave her the room number, and when he opened the door and found her standing there wearing a trench coat and heels, he smiled.

"Darling Niki."

Hours later, they were both exhausted and lying in bed when his phone rang again. Thinking it was Portia, he tried to ignore it, but it kept ringing.

"Don't you wanna get that?" Niki asked, turning over and facing him.

He brushed one of her long locs from her face. "Nope. I got something else I'm trying to get."

She giggled. "Well, before I give it to you again, can you at least put your phone on silent?"

King nodded, climbed out of bed, and walked over to the nearby desk where the phone was lying. He picked it up and saw that the missed calls weren't from Portia. They were from Leo, his business manager. King hoped his psychotic baby mama hadn't gone and done anything stupid. He dialed Leo's number, glancing over at Nikita lying in the bed. He prayed Leo didn't answer the phone so he could go ahead and get started on the round two he was looking forward to.

"Man, you need to get on the next flight and get back home," Leo said, having picked up before the first ring was finished.

"You're crazy! I just got here a couple of hours ago. I'll be back tomorrow." King told him.

"You need to get back now. It's an emergency."

King knew something was wrong by the tone in Leo's voice. The last time Leo sounded like this, the father of one of the other group members had been killed in a car accident.

"What's going on?" King asked, praying that someone wasn't dead.

"I just got word that your house is on fire."

"What?" Next to his sons, his Grammy awards for his solo albums, and his custom motorcycle, King's house was his most prized possession.

"They just called me. Hell, I think it's on the news."

King reached for the remote and turned to CNN. Sure enough, there was a shot of his house with smoke billowing out of it. At the bottom of the screen were the words HOME OF FORMER R&B STAR SET ABLAZE.

"What the hell do they mean, 'former'?" King asked, sitting on the end of the bed.

"Wow! Is that your house?" Nikita asked.

"Who is that?" Leo questioned. "I know that ain't Melissa. Is that why you had to fly to meet her?"

"Hell no!" King told him. "I can't believe this." He turned up the volume and tried to think of what to do next.

"Folks, what you're seeing is live footage from the mansion of former R&B singer King Douglas. The recently built mansion is the location of a four-alarm fire, and firefighters are trying to contain the flames and minimize the already-severe damage to the property. We have a reporter headed to the scene, but we have just received word that Mr. Douglas's estranged wife, supermodel Scorpio, was in the home when the fire started. She has been taken to a local hospital."

And just like that, when King thought his life couldn't get any worse, it did.

Chapter 9

Bishop Walter Burke

Walter Burke sat at his mahogany desk and stared at the open Bible in front of him. He was trying to put the final touches on the sermon he had prepared for Sunday, but he couldn't focus. His thoughts were jumping from one subject to the next, and he was tired after being up for almost twenty hours. It was time to go home.

Going nonstop was nothing new for him. The day before had started with his normal routine of waking at six in the morning and spending prayer time with his wife, followed by an hour-long workout with his personal trainer. He then had multiple meetings and conference calls regarding church business, television appearances, the next book he was scheduled to write, and the script for a film project he had just secured that he was excited about. Later yesterday evening, he preached at a revival service at one of his outreach churches, which was followed by another meeting.

After the long day he'd had, all he wanted to do was spend some intimate time with his wife, preferably in their marbled dual shower, and then go to bed. After sweet-talking her on the phone, his plan seemed to be in motion. He'd turned his cell phone off and sat back in the passenger's seat of his black Escalade, hoping to catch a quick nap during the drive. He knew he was in capable hands. Frank had been by his side for years. A longtime member of the church, he was more like a son than an employee.

"Bishop, something's going on." Frank's voice startled him out of his sleep.

Walter sat up and saw that they were approaching Harrington Point, the posh community where his family now resided. Walter rubbed his eyes, confused because there was a line of cars trying to turn into his neighborhood, causing a massive traffic jam. It was the first time since moving there that Walter had seen more than two cars at one time. The area was so secluded and newly constructed that most people didn't even know it existed.

Now, there were news vans and reporters on the side of the road. Frank eased onto the main roadway leading to the entrance of the neighborhood. Fire trucks, police cars, and emergency vehicles lined the streets.

"I'm sorry, emergency vehicles only," a police officer told them after Frank rolled down the window.

"Officer, I am a resident here. I live around the corner, and this is the only way I can get to my home. What's going on?"

"I'm sorry, gentlemen, but there is a massive fire in one of the homes," the officer told him.

Walter panicked, and he began to pray while he searched for his cell phone. He dialed both Olivia's and Micah's numbers, but neither his wife nor his son answered.

"Which house? Where is it?" Walter asked.

The officer didn't have to answer because Walter suddenly noticed the smoke in the distance. It was near his home, but he could tell it was on the opposite side. Nevertheless, he needed to make sure his wife and son were okay.

"Here is my identification, sir." Walter grabbed his license from the wallet in his back pocket and passed it to Frank, who passed it to the officer. "I need to get through and make sure my family is okay."

"I'm sorry, sir, but we can't let any vehicles back there," the officer said, taking the small square of plastic and shining his light on it. "Wait, you're Bishop Walter Burke! My wife watches you on TV, and she has all your books! Man, you saved my marriage," the short, blond white guy said all in one breath.

Frank looked over at the bishop and shook his head. They were used to this kind of reaction once people actually realized who he was.

"I'm glad to hear that, young man. Now I'm sure you can understand why I need to get home and make sure my wife and son are okay," Walter told him.

"I do, but there is no way I can let you through. We were given strict instructions that we can't allow any vehicles anywhere near the area. The press and paparazzi are clamoring to get in." The officer shrugged.

"What if we park the truck and walked to the bishop's house?" Frank asked.

The officer tilted his head to the side, and Walter could tell he was thinking for a minute.

"My house is right around the corner. I just need to get to my home, Officer . . ." He leaned over to see if he could read the name badge.

"Ford, sir," the officer offered.

"Officer Ford." Walter nodded.

"Okay, pull the vehicle all the way to the side, out of the street, and make sure it's not blocking anything or anyone," the officer finally told them.

"Thank you, Officer Ford. God bless you, sir." Walter barely got the words out as the officer flagged them through, speaking into the walkie-talkie on his shoulder and alerting his fellow officers about Walter and Frank.

Frank pulled near an empty lot near the entrance, which held a FOR SALE sign. They quickly got out of the truck and maneuvered their way through the emergency vehicles, rushing toward the bishop's home. The thick smell of smoke filled the air, and Walter almost had to stop and catch his breath, but he persevered and continued until he finally made it to his house. He was relieved to see Olivia and Micah standing out front along with a few other people he didn't recognize.

"O'la!" he called out to his wife.

Olivia turned around and started running when she saw him. She didn't seem to mind that she was dressed in only a bathrobe and some slippers, and neither did he. He swept his wife into his arms and held her tight.

"Are you okay?" he asked her.

"I'm fine. I was worried that they weren't going to let you get in and come home. Someone said they have the entrance blocked off and people couldn't get through," Olivia said.

"They do. But you know there was no way they were gonna keep me from making sure you were okay." Walter rubbed the side of her face and kissed her forehead.

"Hey, Dad, you know I made sure she was fine," Micah said, walking up and putting his arm around his father. "I'm glad you're home, though. I figured if anyone was gonna get you here, Frank was."

Walter turned and nodded at Frank. "Yeah, Frank and his quick thinking got us through."

"Walter, look. Can you believe this?" Olivia pointed to the nearby house that was surrounded by fire trucks and ambulances.

"Is anyone hurt?" Walter asked.

"We don't know yet," said a pretty, Hispanic girl standing nearby. There was something very familiar about her, but Walter couldn't remember where he knew her from.

"They won't let any of us near the area to find out anything," a tall black guy added.

"I believe there were two people inside," a rugged-looking white guy told him. "That's all I know."

"I believe that's King's house!" announced another guy, who was fashionably dressed in blue and white silk polka-dot pajamas and blue slippers.

"Who is King?" Micah asked.

"Do you mean King Douglas, the singer from the Hot Boyz?" asked an attractive, full-figured woman standing with her arm around the tall black guy. Seeing the rings on both of their fingers let Walter know they were married.

"The one and only." The pajama-clad man nodded.

Walter looked at the small group gathered in his front yard. "I'm going over to make sure no one is injured."

"Walter, no! Stay right here. What is going over there gonna do? And if someone is hurt, what can you do to help?" Olivia said, grabbing his hand.

He looked down into his wife's eyes and told her, "Pray for them."

"I'll go with you, Dad," Micah said.

"No, you stay here with your mother." Walter gave his son a knowing look.

Walking over to the house with Frank by his side, Walter prayed that no one was injured or, even worse, dead. He saw a stretcher being brought around the side of the house with someone on it. The rescue workers barked orders as the doors of a waiting ambulance were opened and they placed it inside. Walter walked faster as the sirens wailed and the vehicle drove past them. He made his way over to another waiting ambulance where the doors were open, and he peeped in.

"Can I help you?" one of the attendants asked.

"I'm here to see if everything . . . I'm just . . . I . . ." Walter stared at all the chaos around him and tried not to become overwhelmed. Firefighters were running, hoses in hand, and police officers were roping off the area and calling out instructions.

"Sir, we're gonna need for you to move back out of this area," the EMT told him as he brushed past him and climbed into the ambulance. "Is he breathing better? What are his stats?"

Walter did what he was asked and back up some, but he angled himself so that he could get a better glimpse inside the emergency vehicle. He saw a young man sitting up on a stretcher, his face covered with an oxygen mask.

Another EMT, who was bandaging the man's arm, said, "Pressure is still elevated, but his pulse ox is good. His arm is pretty bad, though. We need to transport him."

The man on the stretcher shook his head.

"You need to go to the hospital," the EMT told him. "You've inhaled a lot of smoke, and your arm is severely burned."

The man shook his head harder, using his free hand to remove the oxygen mask from his face. "No . . . hospital. I'm . . . fine," he managed to get out before he started wheezing and coughing.

"We have to take you. You don't have a choice," the EMT told him, attempting to put the mask back over the man's face.

The man moved his head back and forth. He tried to take the blood pressure cuff off his arm and get up. "Said . . . I'm . . . good."

Walter took a step forward, thinking that maybe he had inhaled some smoke and that was causing him to hallucinate. He felt Frank moving right behind him as he moved closer to the ambulance.

The two EMTs struggled with the man in an effort to get him to calm down and lie back on the stretcher. Walter continued walking toward the vehicle until he was right in full view.

"Sir, please move back." The EMT who had spoken to Walter before looked up and yelled, "Move away, now!"

Walter and the young man locked eyes. Walter saw the look of recognition across his face, letting him know that he wasn't seeing things.

"Officers, please come and get this man out of the way!"

A nearby police officer ran over. "We need you to move out of the way," he said to Walter. "This area is off-limits."

Walter ignored the officer and continued staring at the man on the stretcher, who was now sitting down and staring back at him. "How? When? What?"

Frank walked closer and was now staring as well. "Bishop, is that . . ."

The officer asked both men, "Do you know this man?"

Walter nodded. "Yes, this is my son!"

"Fine, they are taking him to the hospital. Are you riding with him?" the officer asked.

"No! No!" Malachi tried to yell, but he began coughing so bad that he started gagging.

Walter just nodded and climbed into the back of the ambulance, still confused by what was happening.

"I need to accompany the bishop," Frank told them.

"Only one person can ride," the EMT said.

"Go get Olivia and Micah. Tell them what's going on and bring them to the hospital!" Walter yelled just as they closed the doors.

The EMT signaled to the driver that they were ready to go. The van jerked and the sirens wailed as they pulled off. Walter was still confused, but now he was more concerned as he watched the technicians put the mask back over his son's face, grab bags of fluids, and put an IV in his arm. Malachi coughed and gasped as he struggled to breathe. His eyes met Walter's once again before fluttering closed.

"Malachi! Malachi!" Walter called out.

Malachi didn't respond. Tears formed as Walter stared at his son's unmoving body. He began praying like never before.

*God, please don't take my son away from me. I know
that I haven't been the best father, and I know that I
dropped the ball when it came to a lot of things, especially when it comes to him, but you know that I love
Malachi with all of my heart. I am pleading with you
right now. Cover him, protect him, heal him. Save him.
His mother needs him, his brother needs him, I need
him. Forgive me for not being there when he has needed
me. Forgive me for failing him and for failing you. Don't
take him from me, God. He has too much more of your
work to do. He has a purpose to fulfill. Spare his life
and heal his body. In Jesus' name, and by His stripes, I
declare and decree right now. Amen.*

For the first time since he could remember, Walter
then did something that surprised even him. He leaned
over, touched his son's forehead, and whispered, "I love
you, son."

When they arrived at the hospital, Malachi was whisked
away. Walter was told to have a seat in the waiting area
and he would be updated on his son's condition. As he
took a seat, he realized that he didn't even have his cell
phone to reach anyone. He told Frank to bring them to
the hospital, but he didn't even know if they knew which
hospital. He could only imagine how his wife was feeling
right about now. Malachi was his mother's heart, and she
was probably just as confused as he was.

*When did Malachi get out? How did he get out? Is he
even supposed to be out? Did he escape? And why was
he in that house?*

Walter's thoughts were interrupted by what sounded
like a wave of people yelling. He looked up to see hospital
security, along with a few police officers, holding back a
small crowd starting to gather near the reception area of
the emergency room. He began to panic and wondered
how people even knew he was there with his son. He

hadn't given anyone Malachi's name yet. He quickly turned away, hoping no one would spot him.

"You all need to get back right now! You need to be at least five hundred feet from any hospital entrance or you will be arrested for trespassing," the hospital security guard's voice boomed over the crowd. He was a huge guy who looked more like a linebacker for an NFL team.

"Can you just confirm if the woman brought here from the fire is Scorpio?" a man yelled.

"I can't confirm anything," the guard said. "What I can confirm is that you need to get out or you will be escorted out in handcuffs."

"Was Malachi Burke brought here too?" someone else yelled out. "We were told that he was brought in as well."

"People, please. This is a private matter, and I'm sure the families and the hospital will release a statement," a small, slender police officer standing beside the security guard spoke loudly. He took a step toward the crowd with his hands placed on his hips as if he were Superman.

"A statement? Are they dead?"

"So they are here!"

"Families only make statements when people die!"

The officer turned beet red and started shrinking backward.

"Get back now!" The guard easily moved the police officer aside and stepped forward.

The crowd eased back and slowly dispersed. Walter was relieved that he wasn't recognized and that they didn't mention his son at all, but the suggestion that someone had died caused him to worry even more.

"Excuse me. They say you are the father of the man they brought in from the fire."

Walter glanced up to see a woman dressed in blue scrubs. His heart pounded. "Yes." He nodded. "That's my son."

"I'm Dr. Madison." She stared at him for a moment and then blinked before she continued, "He's stable, and we are still working on him right now. He did inhale a lot of smoke, and he has severe burns on his arm, shoulder, and chest."

"Is he going to be all right?" Walter asked, trying to fight the tears that were threatening to fall.

"He seems to be a fighter." Dr. Madison nodded and smiled. "That's for sure."

Walter managed a slight grin. "He is definitely that. Can I see him?"

"It'll be a little while longer. In the meantime, someone from the administration staff will bring some paperwork that needs to be handled. Um, I'm sorry, and I may be out of line for asking, but . . . are you Bishop Walter Burke?"

"Yes." Walter nodded.

"I thought you were. Considering the sensitivity of the situation and the fact that the press is already looming, I think we should have you wait in another area where you'll have some privacy. Is that okay?" she suggested.

"That's fine. But my wife, I'm waiting for her and my . . . my other son." Walter sighed. He was even more discombobulated than he was earlier. This entire situation had rattled him, and he was not a man who was easily shaken.

"We can let them know where you are when they get here. Do you know if anyone else is here from the family of the young woman who was brought in right before your son?" the doctor asked, looking past him into the waiting area.

"I don't know. I haven't spoken to anyone else other than you. How is she?"

"I really can't say. But I would just suggest that you pray for her. You can follow me, and I'll take you where you can have some privacy along with your family when they get here," she told him.

Just as they were about to head down the hallway, Walter heard his wife's voice. "Walter! Walter!"

He turned around and saw Olivia running toward him. Malachi and Frank were right behind her. She fell into her husband's arms, tears streaming down her face. Walter rubbed her back and whispered in her ear, "It's okay, O'la. It's okay."

"What happened? I don't understand. How did he even—"

"Is it really Chi, Dad? Are you sure it's him?" Micah asked, interrupting his mother's question with his own.

"Yes, it's him."

"Where is he? I want to see him." Olivia removed herself from his arms and turned to the doctor. "Take me to my son!"

"Olivia, you can't see him just yet. They're still checking him out. Calm down," Walter said.

"Mrs. Burke, your son is stable, and the doctors are still with him. As soon as you're able to see him, I promise I will let you know," Dr. Madison said.

"If he's still back there, then where are you going, Walter? We need to stay here and wait!" Olivia snapped.

"The doctor is moving us to an area where we can have some privacy, that's all." Walter put his arm around her.

"That's good. The press is all over this place. Frank had to figure out how to get us in here. Malachi's latest adventure lands the family on the front page once again." Micah shook his head.

"No one even knows that he's here. The press is here because they think someone named Scorpio was brought here from the fire too," Walter said as they followed Dr. Madison down the hall.

"The supermodel?" Micah asked.

"I don't know who she is," Walter replied.

"Doctor, is he talking about Scorpio, the model? Was she hurt in the fire too?" Micah's voice was an octave higher than normal.

Walter slowed down and turned slightly. "Do you know her?"

"No." Micah shook his head. "I know of her. I mean, who doesn't? She's one of the biggest supermodels in the world. She used to be married to King Douglas. He owns the house that was on fire."

"How does Malachi know them?" Walter asked, still trying to piece together how or why his son was even in that house.

"C'mon, Dad, you know I don't know anything about who he knows or why anything, for that matter. Your guess is as good as mine." Micah shrugged.

"None of that matters right now. I don't care who, why, or how come! All I care about is making sure my son is taken care of and alive!" Olivia snapped at both of them.

No one said anything else as they were led into a small private room that held a sofa and matching chair along with a meeting table and a telephone. The doctor promised she would be back to update them shortly, and then she left them to be alone. Immediately after the door closed, the small four-person group grabbed hands and began to pray, not only for Malachi, but also for the young woman who they assumed was Scorpio.

A knock on his office door caused Walter to realize he had fallen asleep.

Brigette, his personal assistant, opened the door and stuck her head in. "Bishop, Mr. Maxwell is here to see you."

"Thanks, Brigette, you can send him in. Tell Frank he doesn't need to come in while we're talking." Walter sat back up and exhaled loudly.

"Do you need anything? Water, coffee, juice?" Brigette asked. She had been his assistant for nearly eleven years and had mastered the job and everything that came along with it, which wasn't easy. With his travel schedule, preaching engagements, personal appearances, business meetings, in addition to the occasional counseling sessions when needed, Brigette made sure he maintained a balanced life and had no problem saying no to anyone, even when he didn't want to. Walter was never overworked, even when he was stretched thin, because she had a way of making sure his schedule had perfect symmetry and was prioritized accordingly.

"No, I'm good for now. I'm heading back over to the hospital once this meeting is over."

"Yes, sir. Let me know if I need to handle anything else while you're gone."

"Thanks again."

A few moments later, Jerry Maxwell, Walter's best friend, walked in and sat down in front of him. Dressed in a red polo shirt, matching baseball cap, and a pair of khaki pants, he looked like he had just finished a round on the green with Tiger Woods and popped by to share the story.

Jerry and Walter had been friends since grade school. They grew up in the mean streets of Detroit and fought hard to survive. On more than one occasion, they had saved one another's lives. Their over-forty-year friendship had been built on survival, brotherhood, and most of all, truth. They had shared so much over the years, and next to his wife, Jerry was the only person Walter knew he could count on for anything, anytime, anyplace.

"How is he?" Jerry asked.

"He's stable. They still have him sedated."

"I saw the fire on the news. He's lucky to be alive."

"He is blessed. That's for sure."

"How's Olivia? I'm sure she was about to lose her mind." Jerry shook his head. "You know how she is when it comes to Malachi."

"She's still at the hospital and hasn't left his side. I'm headed over there in a few." Walter stared at him.

Jerry leaned forward and rubbed his hands together. Walter could tell his best friend knew something was up. Normally Jerry was relaxed and laid-back. Walter watched as he looked around his massive office at the pictures on the wall, specifically one of Micah and Malachi as young boys, about 5 years old, taken one Easter Sunday. His sons were identically dressed in blue shorts, white shirts, and red bow ties. They wore long white socks and white Stride Rite dress shoes. On each of their faces was the same dimpled smile. It was his favorite picture of the twins.

"I can't believe this happened, Walt. But Malachi is like you. He's strong and he's a fighter and he's gonna pull through this. You know that, right?" Jerry asked as his attention turned back to Walter.

"Yeah, I know," Walter told him. "But what I don't know is, why the hell was my son released from prison into your custody three days ago, and you didn't tell me?"

Chapter 10

Marcus Wells

6524 Harrington Crest

"Man, are y'all a'ight?" Sam asked.

After the excitement of the night before, his brother was the first person he called the next morning to fill him in on what happened. Marcus sat in one of the lawn chairs overlooking the infinity pool as he talked on the phone in their backyard.

Even with their sunroom, gazebo, pool, and custom-built barbecue pit, he believed they still had enough room for a half basketball court. He had been trying to convince Lisa that he and the boys needed one, but she insisted that they wait a little while longer.

"Yeah, we're good. It was crazy, though. All the neighbors came out, and cameras were everywhere. They even had helicopters flying out here," Marcus said.

"I know. I saw it on the news. Why didn't you tell me you lived in the same neighborhood as King D and Scorpio's fine ass? You really living it up out there, bro." Sam laughed.

"Man, I didn't know. It's a lot of big-time people living out here. Remember that chick Riley Rodriguez?"

"From *Family Brides?*"

"Yeah, her. She lives right down the street!"

"What? That's crazy! And you didn't know?"

"Naw, I didn't. You know me. I just stay in my crib and mind my business, and I guess everyone else around here does too!" Marcus said. "As much as I hate being so far away from home, the one thing that I love about being out here is that I don't have to worry about folks talking. It's peaceful, for real. Kids go to school, Lisa does her thing, and I got my own space."

"Sounds like I need to come check it out, for real. Besides, I need to holler at you about some other ideas I have for us."

"Ideas like what?" Marcus was almost hesitant to ask. Sam didn't have a wife and kids to take care of. He had a bit more flexibility and freedom to spend his share of the lottery winnings. Whereas Marcus's immediate concern was making sure they had a home, savings for his kids' future, and a cushion for him and his wife to be able to live comfortably, Sam bought a fleet of luxury cars and a spacious condo, and he was always ready to invest in whatever sounded like a good idea. He didn't seem concerned with making sure solid business plans or sales forecasts were in place. As long as it sounded like it was going to make money, he was in it to win it.

"I'll tell you about the ideas when I get there," Sam said.

"Get where?" Marcus asked.

"I figured I would come and hang out with you for a few days. You know, check the area out. You did say that there were a few more lots for sale, right? I'm starting to see that leaving here was a smart thing to do. I can't go nowhere without someone hitting me up, and I got chicks blowing up my spot left and right. It ain't no fun anymore, and I'm bored without you."

"Does this have anything to do with those two chicks at Maxwell's and your windshield being busted out?" Marcus had heard all about two women brawling over Sam at a local nightclub and his car being vandalized.

Sam had always had a reputation with the ladies, but money had made him even more of a womanizer. Marcus had suggested that he take some time and travel, hitting up Miami, L.A., and other locations known for the party scene, but Sam enjoyed being Bristol's bachelor of the year.

"Come on, bro. You know shit like that has been popping off for years. This is me you're talking about."

Sam had a point. It wasn't the first time women fought over him, and it probably wouldn't be the last. Marcus wondered if his brother would ever meet a woman who would be able to tame him enough to finally settle down.

"You're right. So when are you planning on coming?" Marcus asked, now wondering how he was going to explain this to Lisa. Although he knew Lisa loved Sam, he also understood it was because he was Marcus's brother and she felt obligated to do so. The fact of the matter was that she didn't like him very much. Marcus knew that had a lot to do with Sam causing havoc over the years in the lives of so many of her female friends and family members, including her sister, Shari. He was not looking forward to letting her know that Sam would be coming.

"I'm not really sure yet. I will let you know," Sam said. "Where is your ball and chain? I mean, better half?"

"Don't do that," Marcus warned. "She's inside baking, as usual."

"That's one thing I'm looking forward to while I'm there. Some of Lisa's peach cobbler and her blueberry pound cake. That woman can do no wrong when it comes to that oven. I gotta give her that."

"Yeah, you're right." Marcus nodded.

"Well, look, I'ma holla at you later on."

Marcus said his goodbyes and ended the call. He was looking forward to seeing his brother. Although their lives were very different prior to Marcus settling down with Lisa, they were very much the same. Marcus had kept a solid rotation of women and never lacked when it came to dating. When he decided to ask Lisa to marry him, Sam tried his best to talk him out of it, calling him whipped, henpecked, and everything in between. Even after their wedding, Sam had tried to slip a few women Marcus's way.

He remembered one night when, after working a double shift at the plant, Sam suggested they stop at a bar to celebrate with Tina, a female coworker who was having a party. It had been a while since Marcus had hung out, and Lisa was out of town with her mother and their two boys. Cocoa hadn't even been conceived, let alone born.

Not wanting to go home to an empty house, Marcus agreed. When they arrived, the party guests consisted of Sam, Marcus, and Tina's older cousin, Tish, who also happened to be a girl who had a thing for Marcus in high school. Marcus realized it was a setup. His initial reaction was to pull Sam to the side and demand that they leave, but Sam convinced him that he hadn't known they would be the only ones there, and there was no harm in sharing a couple of beers, a basket of nachos, and some cake. Marcus agreed to stay, and the four of them had a few rounds of drinks before eventually, a few more people showed up.

Marcus had played a couple of games of pool and was finally starting to relax and enjoy himself when Tish decided to give Marcus a lap dance to a Ludacris song. As much as he didn't want to enjoy the sight of Tish's perfectly shaped, curvaceous ass bouncing to the beat in front of him, along with the sight of her D-cup breasts bulging from the tight, low-cut shirt she wore, Marcus did. He ignored any thoughts of walking away, pushing her away, or leaving altogether. And somehow, he easily convinced himself there was no harm in looking.

Like any good husband, though, once the song ended, and Tish put her arms around him, trying to kiss him, he excused himself and told Sam it was definitely time to go.

Marcus forced that incident into the back of his mind and had almost forgotten about it until a few days later, when he came home from work and found a cake sitting in the middle of the kitchen table. He didn't think anything of it because Lisa always brought goodies home from the bakery. He'd taken off his work boots, plopped down on the sofa, and was watching TV when 4-year-old Michael walked in and climbed beside him.

"Dad, who is Tina?"

Marcus continued staring at the television screen and said, "I don't know."

"Mommy said to ask you who Tina is," Michael repeated.

Marcus frowned and looked at his son. "What are you talking about, Mikey?"

"Mommy brought home a birthday cake, and it says, 'Happy Birthday, Tina,' and when I asked her who is that, she said ask you."

Marcus moved his son so he could stand up, and he rushed into the kitchen. He opened the pink cake box. Sure enough, there was a large, round cake with "Happy Birthday, Tina" written on it.

His heart began pounding, and he closed his eyes, knowing that somehow he had been caught. He closed the lid on the cake box and slowly walked into their small bedroom where he found Lisa sitting on the bed, flipping through a magazine.

"Hey, baby. How was your day?" he asked, leaning over to kiss her.

She moved out of the way and didn't say anything, continuing to flip the pages.

"Lisa, let me explain. I promise nothing happened. It was after work on Friday, and Sam wanted me to come with him to this get-together Tina was having for her birthday. I had no idea Tish was even gonna be there. Sam didn't even tell me. All we did was have some drinks."

"And?" Lisa looked up from the magazine and stared at him.

"And we had some nachos," Marcus added.

"And?" Lisa continued to stare.

"And we played pool."

"And?" Lisa said, her voice rising as she put the magazine down and folded her arms.

"And we danced together."

"Just danced?"

Marcus closed his eyes and finally said, *"Okay, she was grinding up on me. But I swear, I didn't touch her."*

"And?"

"And she tried to kiss me. But, baby, that's when I got up and told Sam it was time to go and we left. Sam brought me home, and that was it. Nothing else happened. I swear! I don't know what else you heard, but anything else is a lie, baby. I promise."

"You know what I heard, Marcus? I heard that skank Tina who works with y'all had a party at the club and the cake was whack and had people known that my husband was gonna be there, they woulda just had you bring the cake! That's what I heard, until you told me all the other stuff just now!"

Marcus hung his head in shame. He was busted, but he made his own situation worse.

"The cake I made was a joke to let you know that I knew about you being at the skank's party. But now I know why you were there!"

"Lisa, baby—" Marcus reached for her, but she snatched away and stood up.

"And you wonder why I can't stand your bitch-ass brother," Lisa said and walked out of the room, leaving him feeling even guiltier than he had on Friday night.

It took some time and a whole lot of begging and pleading, but Lisa forgave him. Eventually, she forgave Sam, but she never forgot. His wife remained cordial with his brother, and things had gotten slightly better after their lottery win, but Marcus still wasn't sure if Lisa was open to Sam visiting their new home just yet.

He walked back inside the home and found his wife pouring batter into what looked like dozens of cupcake pans. The kitchen counters were covered in ingredients. Reggae music was blaring through the surround-sound system into the kitchen.

"What in the world are you doing, woman?" he asked her.

Lisa swayed to the beat. "Making cupcakes."

"Whose class is having a bake sale and needs cupcakes now? Didn't you just make some last week? And why does that school keep needing to have bake sales anyway if we are paying all that damn tuition?" Marcus asked, trying to dip his finger into the bowl of chocolate.

"Stop it, Marcus!" Lisa used her hip to move him out of the way.

"That's not what you were telling me last night while you were baking," he teased.

"I'm not making these for the school. I'm making these for dessert baskets."

"For who?"

"For our neighbors."

"What?" Marcus was confused.

"I'm gonna make baskets of goodies for all of our neighbors and use them as invitations," Lisa told him.

"Invitations to what?"

"A barbecue!"

"A what?"

"How does this sound? 'This basket of sweets is just to say you're invited to a barbecue next Saturday!'"

"What are you talking about? When did we decide to have a barbecue and why?" Marcus leaned against the counter.

"Marcus, I realized last night that we don't know our neighbors."

"Okay, and our neighbors don't know us either. I think we should keep it that way."

"No, we shouldn't."

"Isn't that why we moved all the way the hell out here, Lisa? To get away from people, especially nosy-ass neighbors."

Lisa rolled her eyes at him. "It's different out here. These people ain't begging, and they don't care about how much money we have because they got money of their own. It shouldn't take a tragedy like what happened last night to bring us together."

"So you think these people are actually gonna come over for a cookout? These people are millionaires, Lisa. Actresses, preachers, and God knows what else. They don't go to backyard bashes and pig pickins. This ain't Carolina!" Marcus shook his head.

"They are people just like us. And I'm sure they will come if they're invited. I'm proud to be from Carolina. I ain't ashamed. I'm inviting them. If they come, fine. If they don't, that's fine too. At least they'll know that we are nice enough to invite them over," Lisa said. "Besides, you had that barbecue pit custom built in the backyard, and you haven't fired up the grill not one time since we've moved here."

Lisa was right. He hadn't used his prized pit. Grilling was something he loved to do when they lived in North Carolina. As broke as they were, they always seemed to be able to throw a great backyard get-together. All they needed were a pack of hotdogs, some buns, and a bag of charcoal for the small grill they had. Friends would bring side dishes and coolers of beer, and everyone would have a great time. He wondered if his wife understood that it wouldn't be the same. He couldn't imagine Bishop Walter Burke and his wife dancing to *Maze Featuring Frankie Beverly,* their favorite cookout CD.

"I'm proud of where we're from, and you know that. You wanna have a cookout, fine. We'll have the best damn cookout this neighborhood has ever seen. Hell, it will probably be the only cookout this neighborhood has ever seen." Marcus pulled his wife to him and looked at her.

He was still in love with her now as much as he was in high school. His brother and his boys had teased him when he started dating her because she was, as they called her, a big girl. But for Marcus, she was the most beautiful woman he had ever seen. He still couldn't believe that she married him. He loved her full breasts and thick waist and her smile that lit up a room. She just made his life better. Lisa had stuck with him when he barely had anything to give, and now he wanted to give her the world.

"I love you," he told her.

"I love you too." Lisa smiled and kissed him.

"Let's have another baby." Marcus surprised himself when the words came out of his mouth.

"What did you just say?" Lisa looked just as shocked as he felt.

"I want another baby."

"Marcus, you're joking, right?"

He loved his three kids more than anything in the world, but in reality, none of them were planned. Marcus and Lisa were barely 19 when Michael was born, and protection wasn't anything either of them was concerned with at the time. Aaron unexpectedly came two years later, and Faith three years after that, again unplanned. Standing there in their dream home, with his wife in his arms, Marcus realized that this was their chance to decide and plan to have another child.

"I'm serious. It's not like we can't afford it. Let's have a baby."

Lisa looked at him and said, "I have to think about that one. Right now, I just want us to have a cookout."

The next day the kids were playing in the backyard, and Lisa headed out to deliver her goody basket invitations. Marcus was in the theater room, munching on popcorn and watching his favorite channel, Animal Planet, when he heard the doorbell ring. He made his way down the staircase and through the long hallway. Opening the door, he blinked, wondering if he was seeing things.

"What's up, bro. I decided not to wait and hopped on a flight this morning. You surprised?" Sam stood grinning on the doorstep.

Marcus looked down and saw the Louis Vuitton luggage on the steps next to him. He realized that he'd been so busy planning a cookout and a baby with Lisa that he forgot to tell her his brother was coming to visit.

Chapter 11

Sarena Powell Douglas (Scorpio)

Everything on Scorpio's body hurt: her face, her arms, and her legs. It even hurt to breathe. She could hear people talking in the distance, but even the thought of opening her eyes hurt. She tried to focus on what they were saying so she could figure out exactly where she was, how she got there, and most importantly why she was hurting so badly. Her mind was groggy, and she couldn't tell if she was dreaming.

"Right now we have her intubated to keep her airway from closing due to swelling."

Intubated? Swelling?

"The worst of the burns were suffered on her legs and right foot, which we have treated. It doesn't appear as if she will need plastic surgery right now, but time will tell."

Burns? Surgery?

"She's a very lucky woman to have survived that fire."

Fire?

The last thing Scorpio remembered was being in Vixen's with her friends. Was there a fire at the strip club? Were her friends all right? Where were Marcelo, Dina, and Natalie?

"Thank you so much, Doctor. We appreciate everything you all are doing."

Scorpio realized she had to be dreaming when she heard the familiar voice. It was a voice she hadn't heard in months and one she didn't want to hear. Her heart began pounding, and as much as it hurt to open her eyes, she did so in an effort to wake up. She glanced around the room, blinking as she tried to focus. She could see a blurry figure standing nearby talking to a man in a white coat, which let her know that she had to be in a hospital.

"The main thing now is that she must continue to get as much rest as possible. The next couple of days will be critical, which is why we are keeping her in ICU. But I'm confident that she will be fine," the doctor told the blurry figure.

"Thank you again," the blurry figure replied. There was no mistaking the voice. The heaviness of the tone, the crispness of the words—it was a voice that made even the toughest of men stare and stand at attention. That voice had put the fear of God into Scorpio for the slightest infraction as a toddler, a child, and a teenager. It was the voice that she escaped years ago and dreaded hearing on the other end of the phone when she saw the name on her caller ID. It was the voice of Yolanda Powell, her mother. Scorpio was not dreaming. Her worst nightmare had come true.

She tried getting up out of bed, but pain shot through her body, and although she tried to talk, she couldn't. A beeping sound filled the room, and she realized that it was coming from one of the machines connected to her body.

"Mrs. Douglas, don't move!" The doctor came over quickly.

"Sarena! Sarena! Do what he says," her mother warned.

Stop calling me that! Scorpio yelled in her mind because she was unable to do so with her voice. She settled down as the doctor told her that she couldn't talk because there was a tube down her throat to help her breathe. He then went on to tell her that she was heavily medicated, so moving was not possible.

Scorpio was dazed, and everything was obscure. The more she tried to think, the more confused she became. Her body continued to ache with each breath she took.

"Sarena? Do you understand what he's saying to you? Please nod if you understand."

Scorpio looked over and saw her mother standing beside the bed. As usual, she was impeccably dressed in a pantsuit and matching heels, not a hair out of place on her perfectly coiffed head. With a touch of rouge on her cheeks and her favorite shade of Fashion Fair lipstick perfectly applied to her lips, her mother looked the exact same way she did four years ago when she made a surprise appearance at Scorpio's wedding. Not thinking that her mother would even show up, Scorpio sent her an invitation because Marcelo, who was her makeup artist and one of her best friends, told her it was the right thing to do.

"What's that?" she heard her mother asking the doctor, who was now injecting something into the IV in Scorpio's hand.

"Just something to settle her down and make her rest easier," the doctor told her. "Her blood pressure is elevated, probably due to the trauma she's sustained and the pain she's in."

"I don't need for you to give her anything that will make her a junkie. The last thing I want is for my daughter to end up addicted to narcotics as a result of this ordeal. She is strong. She knows how to handle pain." Her mother shot him a warning look.

"Ma'am, your daughter has been through hell and back in the last forty-eight hours. The fact that she is even conscious at this point is a miracle. I am going to do whatever and give her whatever she needs to feel comfortable, rest, and begin healing," the doctor responded.

Thank God, Scorpio thought as she looked over at the doctor and wondered if he could read the gratefulness in her eyes. She knew if Yolanda had her way, Scorpio would be given two aspirin and told to get up out of bed and shake it off.

"I will be back in a couple of hours to check on her. Why don't you leave and let her get some sleep? You look like you can use some yourself," the doctor told Yolanda.

"What's that supposed to mean?" Yolanda snapped.

"I'm just saying that you've been here all day and haven't left this room. You should take some time, get some food, and come back in a little while," the doctor said.

Scorpio knew before her mother even responded that he probably pulled a trigger. She hated being told what to do, even if it was only a suggestion. That's how much of a control freak she was. The look on Yolanda's face told it all, and as much as Scorpio wanted to giggle, the pain wouldn't allow her to. Instead, she closed her eyes and drifted off to sleep, praying that when she woke up, her mother would not be anywhere in sight.

"Sarena . . . Sarena . . ."

Scorpio drifted into a deep sleep, her mother's voice becoming fainter as she did.

Yolanda Powell was smart, educated, well raised, successful, attractive, articulate, and talented. She was an amazing seamstress who had a natural eye for fashion. She dreamed of becoming a successful designer and was pursuing her goal when she met Howard Crawford, a tall, athletic, handsome lawyer who taught part-time at the college Yolanda was attending.

As soon as Yolanda laid her eyes on Howard, she knew he was special. The first time she held a conversation with him, she knew she liked him. The first time she kissed him, she knew she was in love.

For months, he shared stories with her of cases he was working on, while she shared sketches of her latest de-

signs in between classes at a small sandwich shop near the college. It was innocent at first, but the more time they spent together, the more intense their relationship became. Soon they no longer met at the sandwich shop to swap stories, but instead, they shared afternoons full of passionate lovemaking in the bed of her one-bedroom apartment.

Howard fulfilled her. He was everything she had ever wanted in a man. Not only did he satisfy her mind, but he took her body places that she never dreamed possible. He savored her, touched and tasted every part of her. She couldn't get enough of him. It was as if he had her vexed on every level.

After the sex, he would hold her naked body close to his and whisper in her ear about how much he enjoyed her. They would lie there for hours, laughing and talking.

Then, one Saturday morning when Yolanda was looking for inspiration for a design she was working on, she decided to venture out to a local flea market. Normally, she slept in on Saturdays, but she was just getting over the flu and decided the fresh air would be good. While walking through the crowded booths, she was bumped by the cutest little girl she had ever seen.

"Oops, sorry." The little girl smiled at Yolanda.

"It's okay, sweetheart," Yolanda said, reaching down to pick up the teddy bear the little girl dropped. She passed it to her.

"Monica, didn't I tell you to stop running?" the little girl's mother called out.

"It's okay, she's . . ." Yolanda stood up and couldn't finish her sentence. In front of her was a pretty woman reaching for the little girl . . . and standing alongside Howard. Yolanda's first instinct was to look at the woman's left hand. To her heart's disappointment, there was a wedding ring. Her glance quickly flew to Howard's hand, where there was now a gold band.

"What do you say to the lady?" The woman nudged the little girl.

In an effort not to look at Howard, Yolanda stared at the teddy bear in the tiny arms of the girl.

"Thank you."

"You're welcome," Yolanda managed to say before rushing off, hoping the woman and little girl didn't see the tears that had formed in her eyes. She barely made it to the car when she allowed herself to break down. For nearly fifteen minutes, she cursed and screamed at the steering wheel, angry that she had allowed herself to be used, to be played, but more importantly, to fall in love with a man who did nothing but lie.

There was a tapping on the car window, and she looked up to see Howard.

"Get the fuck away from me!" she hissed at him.

"Yolanda, please open the door. Let me explain," Howard pleaded.

"Get away from me, Howard! I mean it!" Yolanda started the ignition and put her foot on the brake. She was about to put the car in gear when a wave of nausea overcame her. She quickly opened the car door and vomited. Howard jumped back, barely escaping the yellow liquid pouring from her mouth.

"Sweetheart, are you okay?" he asked.

"Please don't act concerned. I will be okay when you get the hell away from me," Yolanda told him, reaching into the glove compartment and grabbing a napkin to wipe her mouth.

"Just give me five minutes, Yolanda, please," Howard said.

Yolanda shook her head in disgust. She slammed her door and pulled away. For days Howard called and begged for her to talk to him, even stopping by the apartment various times throughout the day and night, knocking on the door. Yolanda continued to ignore him. Every time she thought about him, she would vomit and feel ill for hours afterward. It was as if his existence was making her physically sick.

Almost two weeks went by with her barely able to eat, drink, or get out of bed. Finally, she went to the doctor, who confirmed that it wasn't Howard who was making her physically ill. Instead, it was the child he had fathered that she was now carrying.

Now, she had no choice but to speak with him. Refusing to allow him back into her apartment, she agreed to meet him at the sandwich shop where their friendship began.

"How are you?" Howard asked when she sat at the table across from him.

Yolanda looked at him and hated herself when she felt her heart race as she stared at his handsome face. She realized she missed him, and that angered her because she didn't want to miss him. She wanted to feel nothing for him.

"I'm pregnant," she said icily, her heart pounding as tension filled her body.

His eyebrows rose in surprise. Yolanda had prepared herself for his reaction, ready to go word for word and cuss him out.

"Okay." Howard nodded.

"I'm keeping it."

"Okay." Howard added a shrug to his nod.

"That's all you have to say? Okay?" Her voice cracked slightly and her brows furrowed.

"Yes, and to tell you I'm sorry."

This was not the reaction Yolanda was expecting. She had imagined him lecturing her about her decision being unreasonable and a bad one that he didn't agree with. The truth was she really hadn't decided whether she would be keeping the baby. She was only six weeks along and still had a month to make a decision. However, she wanted Howard to sweat and be afraid the same way she had felt the past few days. She figured that her telling him that she was having his baby would be the last thing he wanted to hear and cause him to panic. Instead, here he was sitting across from her, acting as if she'd made some minuscule confession, and being calm about it.

"I don't want your apologies." Yolanda shook her head.

"I love you." Howard reached across the table and took her hand.

Yolanda snatched it away from him. "I'm having this baby."

"Okay, I love you. If that's what you want to do, then that's what we will do."

"'We'? Who might that be, Howard? Me, you, and your wife?"

"Yolanda, please, it's not what you think."

"Are you married?"

"Yes." He nodded.

"Then it's what I think it is. You're married. You have a child. It's not that hard to comprehend. I am your pregnant mistress. Well, correction, I used to be your mistress. I just didn't know it. I'm no longer willing to hold that title. I hold a new title: the mother of your illegitimate child." Yolanda had told herself that she wasn't going to cry, but she couldn't stop the tears that were now falling.

"That's not what you were, and that's not what you are now. You are so much more than that to me. I need for you to believe that."

"I don't know what to believe. Really it doesn't even matter. I have to go. The only reason I agreed to meet you was to tell you about the baby, that's it. Goodbye." Yolanda stood up. Before she could walk off in the

*dramatic exit she had planned out in her head, Howard
grabbed her and pulled her to him. His hand cupped her
face, and he leaned down and kissed her so passionately
that she nearly lost her breath. Without saying another
word, they walked hand in hand and exited the café
together.*

*An hour later, they were lying naked in her bed, a res-
idue of sweat from their satiating lovemaking covering
their bodies, and Howard quietly told her the truth.*

*The truth was he was married and had been for the
past eight years. The truth was the practice he worked
at was owned by the father of his wife, who was an
only child. The truth was he was being groomed to take
over the thriving practice because his father-in-law was
dying from cancer. The truth, Yolanda knew, was that
he was not going to leave his wife.*

*Eight months later, Yolanda gave birth to a beautiful
baby girl, whom they named Sarena, after Howard's
mother Sara, whom Yolanda had never met. Howard
was an excellent provider for them, though the two
transitioned from lovers to friends. He never promised
to leave his wife, and Yolanda never asked him to.*

*She graduated with her degree, but instead of fol-
lowing her dream of becoming a fashion designer, she
chose a more practical career for a single mother: a
sewing teacher at a local high school. Although she
loved Sarena more than anything in life, she raised her
with an uncompromising level of discipline, grooming
her to be resourceful, be independent, and succeed at
whatever it was she wanted to do: dance, gymnastics,
academics, anything. Sarena excelled at it all. Yolanda
made sure she positioned her daughter to never need or
want a man for anything.*

*After Howard, she never dated anyone else. Whenever
Sarena tried to bring up relationships or love, Yolanda*

told her to focus her energy on things that were more important and sent her off to her room to study. "Love will do nothing but hold you back from your dreams," her mother constantly told her.

Growing up, Sarena was teased relentlessly. She was blessed with every good characteristic of both parents that God could have given her. She had their good looks, their powerful minds, their charm, and unfortunately, their height. In elementary and junior high Sarena was taller and thicker than most of the girls in her school. She was called everything from "Sarena the Hyena" to "Sarena the Slug." By the time she was in high school, although she had lost nearly thirty pounds, the teasing continued because now because she was tall and slender. It didn't seem to matter to those who bullied her that she was a straight A student with the potential to be a track Olympian. They weren't drawn to her long black hair, which reached the center of her back, or her dark hazel eyes, which were framed by the exotic features of her beautiful face, the product of her half-Persian, half-Nigerian mother and Italian father. She became a recluse and closed herself off from everyone because no one seemed to like her.

That was until she met Bilal Mauldin her senior year.

Bilal was a transfer student who was also in all the honors classes along with Sarena. She really didn't pay him much attention until one day, while they were both attending an SAT prep class after school, he asked her if she was a model.

"No." She looked at him as if he were crazy. She thought he was trying to be funny like all of her other classmates had been over the years.

"Really? That surprises me," he told her. "You're very pretty, and you're tall. You should try it."

"Thank you, but I don't think I'm cut out for that kind of stuff." She tried not to blush.

"I think you'd be a natural at it." Bilal smiled at her. "You're beautiful."

She floated home and thought all night long about what he'd said. No one other than her mother had ever called her beautiful. She wondered if he was serious or setting her up for some cruel joke, like in the horror film Carrie. She was tempted to tell her mother what he said and ask her thoughts, but she knew better.

"Hey, were you serious yesterday?" she asked him the next day.

"About?"

"What you said when we were talking."

Bilal put his finger on the side of his face and pretended to be deep in thought. *"What were we talking about?"*

Sarena suddenly felt embarrassed for asking. There was no hiding the blushing today. She turned away and said, *"Forget it."*

"Stop being so sensitive. Yeah, I was serious. I think you're beautiful." Bilal laughed, sending shivers down her spine. She looked at him out of the corner of her eye. They were the same height, both standing at about five eleven. Bilal was stocky, but he had a sense of style and personality. They were both quiet and unassuming in class, but unlike her, people gravitated toward him. When Bilal spoke, people listened. She didn't even think he even noticed her.

"Thank you." She smiled back at him.

"The question is, do you think you're beautiful?" He leaned against the lockers. The hallway was crowded and filled with loud students, but to her, it was as if they were the only two people in the world.

"I guess." She shrugged.

"Come talk to me when you know, so then maybe we can make something happen." Bilal slung his backpack over his shoulder, winked at her, and left her standing in the hallway.

For the first time ever, she felt self-conscious about her looks, and it wasn't in a negative way. That night when she got home, she stared at herself in the mirror, paying attention to exactly what she saw. Her eyelashes were long and curved, and her eyebrows were thick and naturally arched. Her nose was keen like her mother's, and her plump, slightly puckered lips were exactly like her father's. Although she'd never seen him in person, she'd seen a few pictures her mother thought she kept hidden in the bottom of an old jewelry box.

She removed her clothing and looked at her naked body. She was slim, and her breasts were small but perky. Her arms and legs were long but fit her frame. She turned and admired her hips and butt, and she thought, not bad. *Then she did something she had never thought of doing before. She snuck into her mother's bathroom and grabbed her blush, mascara, and lipstick, the only makeup Yolanda owned. Carefully, she applied them to her face, and she smiled, suddenly seeing for herself that maybe Bilal was right.*

"Is that lipstick?" Bilal asked her when she saw him.

"No," she lied. "It's lip gloss."

"Fine, lip gloss." He smiled. "It looks nice, cutie."

"Don't call me that." She wrinkled her nose and shook her head.

"What? Cutie? What's wrong with that?" Bilal frowned.

"I'm not a cutie."

"So, tell me, what do you think I should call you?" He took a slight step back and waited for her answer.

She flashed the smile she perfected the night before in the mirror and told him, "Call me beautiful because that's what I am."

Chapter 12

Eden Rodriguez

Eden was sitting in the sunroom enjoying brunch with Riley and Peri when they heard the doorbell ring.

"Are you expecting anyone?" Eden asked her sister.

"The only person I was expecting is sitting here with us, and he wasn't even invited." Riley nodded toward Peri.

"At least I brought good champagne and fresh-squeezed orange juice, heffa. If I hadn't, we woulda been sitting here sipping on Andre and Tropicana." Peri rolled his eyes and poured himself another mimosa.

"You're so bourgeois," Riley told him.

"I'll take that as a compliment." Peri smiled, holding up his glass.

Eden shook her head at the two of them and hurried to answer the door. She was praying that it wasn't anyone from the media. Although the police had been doing a pretty good job of patrolling the area and keeping the paparazzi away since the recent fire, there were a few who had gotten past and tried to sneak pictures and get information. She peeked out and recognized one of the neighbors they met the night of the fire.

"Oh, hello," Eden said, opening the door.

"Hi! Eden, right?" the woman asked. She wore a simple black Nike sweat suit and matching sneakers. Her hair was pulled back, and she looked like she was about to enjoy a midmorning stroll.

Eden felt overdressed in her long black maxi-dress and heels. She nodded. "Yeah. Lisa, right?"

"Yes. I'm sorry to bother you, but I wanted to give you this!" Lisa handed her a large decorated basket with an envelope attached.

"Wow! Thanks!" Eden took the basket and smiled. "Come on in."

"Um, sure. Why not? Can I leave this here?" Lisa pointed at a red wagon at the edge of the entrance steps, which held more baskets.

"I'm sure it will be safe." Eden nodded.

The two ladies entered the house. Riley's and Peri's laughter drifted through the rooms as Eden led their guest to where they were.

"Who was it, Eden? Please don't tell me the Jehovah's Witnesses have discovered where we are!" Riley cackled.

"I hope they have. That's the only way you'll get some Jesus in your life—if they knock on your door and hand Him to you in one of those pamphlets!" Peri responded.

"Oh, my goodness, why do y'all have to be so loud?" Eden asked as she walked into the room with Lisa behind her. The two of them instantly seemed embarrassed as they realized their conversation was overheard. Peri nudged Riley, who was leaned over and giggling.

"Why didn't you tell me we had a guest?" Riley said, quickly straightening up in her seat.

"Yes, why didn't you tell her?" Peri added, placing his hand on his chest dramatically as if he were clutching a pair of imaginary pearls.

"That's what you get for being ignorant," Eden scolded the two best friends. "I keep warning you about being loud and inappropriate. Now here this woman is, coming to visit and share the Gospel with us, and look how you all are acting."

The two of them looked down in shame and began apologizing until they saw Eden and Lisa smiling at one another.

"You play too much!" Peri snapped.

"You guys remember Lisa from the other night. She lives down the street with her husband, uhhhh . . ."

"Marcus," Peri volunteered, causing everyone to stare. He shrugged and said, "What? He looks like he could be a tight end in the NFL. Of course I'm gonna remember his name!"

"Peri!" Riley gasped.

"She knows her husband is fine. Don't you?" Peri turned and asked Lisa.

"Yes, I do know that." Lisa laughed. "And thank you."

"Please, sit down, join us. Peri, pour her a drink. We were just having brunch. Grab a plate," Riley told her. Unlike her sister, she was casually dressed in a pair of cutoff jean shorts, a T-shirt, and a pair of Ugg boots.

"Thanks," Lisa said, sitting in the empty chair beside Peri, who was now pouring orange juice and champagne into an empty glass and handing it to her.

"Your husband is fine, though," Riley teased. "I remembered his name, too!"

"I can't believe you." Eden shook her head and placed the basket in the middle of the table. "Lisa came bearing gifts!"

"Really? Awww, that's so sweet!" Riley whined. "You didn't have to do that."

"Well, I wanted to do something for the neighbors, and I also wanted to invite you to a cookout we are having next Saturday," Lisa told them.

"A cookout? I haven't gone to one of those in years!" Eden laughed.

"We used to have them all the time back home, and I figured it would be a great way to get everyone in the neighborhood together. Well, I guess the eight house-holds who are here," Lisa said.

"I'm sure now that the neighborhood is all over the national news, all of the lots are gonna be sold, and those three houses that are already built are gonna go even faster." Peri passed the glass to Lisa.

Eden took the envelope off the basket and read, "'This basket of sweets is just to say you're invited to a barbecue next Saturday!' That is soooo cute! Well, I know I will be there!"

"That is cute! Who do have catering?" Peri asked.

"I don't have a caterer." Lisa shrugged.

"Do you need me to help you find one? I know an amazing barbecue master from Texas who does a great job if you need his number. He and his staff are impeccable! What's your theme?" He reached into a leather bag on the floor beside him and pulled out an iPad.

"I don't have a theme." Lisa laughed. "It's a cookout!"

"I told you. You are so bourgeois, Peri! OMG!" Riley giggled.

"I can't believe you're gonna do all the work by yourself!" Peri said.

"It's not that much work. We're only inviting people in the neighborhood. Heck, those are the only people we know really, and we just met you guys the other night. We've only lived here for about two months."

"Where are you from originally?" Eden asked, opening the basket and taking out what looked like a blueberry muffin.

"We're from a small town called Bristol, North Carolina," Lisa told them.

"I knew I recognized that accent." Peri smiled. "I love Southerners! They are so hospitable!"

Eden bit into the muffin, and it tasted like heaven in her mouth. It was slightly thicker than she expected, but the buttery flavor and sweetness were unimaginable. "Where did you get these? They are freakin' amazing!"

"I made them," Lisa replied.

"You lie!" Eden said, taking another bite. "I have never tasted a blueberry muffin like this!"

"Well, technically it's not a muffin. It's a pound cake, but I put it in muffin pans to kinda make it easier to pass out. They are bigger than regular muffins. I figured that was better than putting slices of cake into the basket. That seemed kinda tacky," Lisa explained.

Eden and Peri reached into the basket and started pulling out items. There were additional flavors of the pound-cake muffins that she made: strawberry, chocolate, and peach. The three of them sat at the table and tasted each one. There were also cookies and brownies as well.

"These are the best muffins . . . cakes . . . whatever they are . . . I've ever had. Jesus, I'm gonna have to be on that damn elliptical for two hours tonight, and I don't care because it's gonna be well worth it," Peri announced, reaching and taking another muffin.

"Stop it! You're not gonna eat up all our goodies!" Eden smacked his hand.

"Don't worry, you have your own basket, Peri. Had I known you were here, I would've brought yours in!" Lisa told him as she stood up. "That reminds me, I need to go complete my deliveries. I hope no one has stolen them, or one of those dogs across the street hasn't gotten to them. I'm saving that house for last."

"Those dogs stay barking!" Riley shook her head.

"I hate dogs. They scare me." Lisa sighed.

"Are you sure you don't need help with anything for the soiree next weekend, Lisa?" Peri offered.

"No, my sister is actually coming to visit, so she will be more than enough help. And my husband will handle the grilling. The only thing I need is for you all to please come and have a great time," Lisa said as they all walked through the foyer and toward the front door.

"Marcus on the grill? Oh, I am there!" Peri nodded, giving Riley a high five.

"He wouldn't happen to have any brothers you can invite, would he?" Riley asked.

"He does have a brother, but he's definitely not invited." Lisa laughed. "He's more trouble than you two combined would be able to handle."

"I doubt that," Peri said. "Especially if he looks anything like your husband."

They walked Lisa out, and she gave Peri his basket of goodies along with his invitation, and he promised to see her at the cookout.

"That was so nice of her," Riley said when they went back inside.

"Yes, it was. She is a sweetheart. I love her Southern accent." Peri nodded.

Eden's cell phone rang, and she excused herself. She knew if Riley saw who it was, she would be pissed.

"Hello," Eden said, walking up the steps and into her bedroom.

"How are you?" he said.

"I'm fine."

"And how is she?"

"She's fine."

"Are you sure? The last time you told me she was fine, she was headed to rehab."

"That was because she was using to cope with the fact that you walked out on her," Eden said.

"That's not fair. You can't blame that on me."

"No, what isn't fair is you were her best friend who abandoned her when she needed you the most. You said you loved her."

"I did love her. I still do. But I wasn't in love with her. I was and am in love with you."

Eden ended the call without responding. She didn't want to hear anything else. Her phone began vibrating, and she hesitated before answering it again.

"I can't deal with this," she told him.

"You can't deal with the truth? Eden, you know how I feel about you."

"You can't have those feelings for me. They aren't right. I shouldn't even be talking to you right now. If Riley knew—"

"I don't have a problem with her knowing. You do."

"That shows how little you care about her. You know she's still in love with you," Eden hissed into the phone.

"She's not in love with me, Eden. We weren't in love. Your sister and I were codependent on one another. There's a big difference. She needed a superhero in her life, and I needed someone to save. We fed off one another's insecurities. But you and I, what we have—"

"We don't have anything! Stop it!"

"No, you stop it. Stop denying that you feel the same way I do. Stop forcing yourself to believe that your sister and I had some fairy-tale romance when it wasn't. Stop making me feel like my falling in love with you is something horrible. Stop acting like when we were together, it didn't feel like magic."

"It wasn't magic. It was wrong, and you know it. That's why you walked out and left me here to pick up the broken pieces of my sister's life, because you know what happened was wrong. You put a ring on her finger, and she was planning a wedding. "

There was a brief silence.

"I couldn't marry her, Eden. Not after everything that happened. It just wouldn't have been right for any of us."

"But she loved you. I could have left, and you could have stayed. Things would be different."

"All of us would be miserable. Hell, I'm miserable now. I miss you, and I want to see you more than anything. Come and meet me—"

Again Eden ended the call. This time when it rang again, she didn't answer it. She should have never answered it in the first place, but the truth was, she wanted to and needed to hear his voice. It had been a few months since they had talked. The last time was when Riley had checked into rehab. He was furious that she hadn't let him know what was going on. She didn't feel inclined to let him know because in her mind, had he stayed, Riley wouldn't have been on the downward spiral that she was now on.

Cornelius Baker was Riley's entire world, and now because of Eden, he was gone.

Cornelius was a cameraman who met Riley while she was filming some low-budget commercial for a new fad diet pill. Eden didn't understand why Riley even took the job, because she had never needed or taken diet pills in her entire life. But Riley was convinced that being on screen for a cheap commercial was better than not being on screen at all.

They filmed for two days, and by the time they wrapped, all Riley could talk about was someone named "Neil," whom she had met on set and who had caught her eye.

"Eden, did I tell you what Neil said to me when I walked on set this morning?" Riley gushed through the phone.

"Yes, Riley, three times already," Eden said. She had never heard her sister so giddy over a guy. Most of the time Riley was unimpressed by the men she came in

contact with. Neil was different. He wasn't in awe of her being the infamous Riley Rodriguez, nor was he intimidated by her cocky attitude. When it came to Riley, he seemed unbothered, and for Riley, that was a turn-on.

"I want to go on a date with him," Riley whined.

"Then ask him out," Eden told her.

"Nooooo, I can't do that. That's rude."

"This isn't the nineteen-hundreds, Riley. Women ask men out all the time. Men like confident women."

"That's not true. Men like the thrill of the chase. That's why women are supposed to play hard to get. Men are natural hunters," Riley told her matter-of-factly.

"When is the last time you've been on a date?"

"Sheesh, a while," Riley replied.

"Exactly."

"But we've wrapped filming, and I don't know how to get in contact with him." Riley sighed.

"I'm sure the director can tell you how to find him," Eden said. "Sometimes you have to go after what you want! Make it happen instead of waiting for it to happen!"

"You sound like a motivational speaker. Have you been watching Tony Robbins?"

"No, I haven't. Now stop wasting time with me and go get your man!"

Eden's speech worked, and before she knew it, Riley chased Neil down and proudly showed him off on her arm. The two of them were truly an odd couple. Riley was loud, outspoken, and the center of attention. Neil was quiet, observant, and laid-back. Unlike all of her other beaux, Neil seemed to be able to handle Riley's partying and wild streak, until about a year after they had been dating.

"Eden! Are you home?" Riley's voice came bellowing from outside of Eden's apartment, which was an hour

away from where Riley lived. She had been in her living room preparing lesson plans for the kindergarten class that she taught.

"Riley?" Eden jumped up and ran to the door. She opened it, and Riley almost fell in, drunk. She looked around to see if someone had driven her, but no one was there. "How did you get here? Please don't tell me you drove."

"Yes. I'm a grown-ass woman. I know how to drive," Riley said, pushing past Eden into the living room and falling onto the sofa.

Eden grabbed the books and papers she was working on out of the way. "You're in no condition to drive. I'm surprised you made it here."

"I had to drive myself. Neil left me all alone."

"All alone where?"

"We were at this party downtown. A friend of mine just got a spot on a sitcom, so we went to celebrate. Everyone was having a great time, but you know how Neil is. I was dancing, and he got all upset. Why does he do this? He gets mad over the dumbest stuff," Riley said, slumping over onto her side. The tight sequined dress she had on rose over her hips and Eden could see that she wasn't wearing any underwear.

"I doubt that he got mad because you were dancing." Eden shook her head. She went into her room and grabbed one of her oversized T-shirts and a pillow for her sister.

"We were dancing," Riley repeated.

"Who is we?" Eden said, now pulling the dress over Riley's head and helping her into the shirt.

"Some guy. He said he was my biggest fan."

"All guys say they are your biggest fan, Riley. Sit up so I can pull this down."

*"He asked me to dance. You remember that video I
was in by Moby D? The one where I had on the mermaid
outfit? Mom was mad because I was topless?"*

"We all remember that one." Eden sighed.

*"The song came on. Here I was talking to my biggest
fan, and the song comes on where I starred as the love
interest in the video. It was fate. I had to dance with
him!"*

*"I think saying you were the love interest is a stretch,"
Eden said. The way Eden saw it, it was more like a
bunch of thug-looking rappers standing over and looking at a topless Riley dressed as a mermaid, splashing
in a bathtub and mouthing the words to the chorus. The
song was offensive, sexist, and misogynistic, but it was
melodic, and the video was borderline pornographic. It
was an instant hit, to their parents' and a whole lot of
other people's dismay, including Neil.*

*"He pulled me up, and we were jamming. Everyone
was crowding around us. Then out of nowhere, here
comes Mr. Spoilsport, grabbing on me and yelling for
me to stop! So the guy gets mad—"*

*Eden's cell phone began ringing. As if he could sense
them talking about him, Neil was calling.*

"She's fine," Eden said without even saying hello.

*"Where is she? Did she tell you what happened? Your
sister is crazy!" Neil snapped.*

*"She told me she was dancing with some guy and you
got upset," Eden told him.*

*"Did she tell you he had her dancing on top of a table
to that song in front of a whole bunch of other guys who
were with him? Did she tell you she ain't have no draw-
ers on and they were taking pictures with their phones?"*

Eden sighed. "No, she didn't tell me all that."

*"Is that him? Is that Neil? Give me the phone!" Riley
jumped up and snatched the phone from her. "What the*

fuck do you want? You always ruin it when I'm having a good time! You always get mad!" Riley yelled into the phone.

"Riley, calm down. I have neighbors," Eden warned her.

"You knew what the deal was when we started dating! Guys are gonna approach me, Neil! What? I don't give a damn! I'm Riley Rodriguez! Fuck you!" Suddenly, Riley took Eden's cell phone and threw it across the room, breaking it into pieces and scratching the paint on the wall.

"Riley! What is wrong with you?" Eden yelled.

"I hate him! He makes me sick! All I want is someone to love me, and he can't even do that!" Riley cried.

"He does love you, Riley. That's why he is so protective of you. Hell, he needs to be here now because I'm about to fuck you up. You broke my phone, and look at my wall." Eden picked the broken phone up off the floor.

"Why can't he just love me?" Riley bawled.

Eden stared at her sister and shook her head. Not only was Riley an angry drunk, but she also turned into a crier. She went into the hallway closet, handed her a blanket, and went into her bedroom, closing the door behind her.

The next day, while her kids were at recess, the office called and told her she had a visitor. She was surprised to see that it was Neil. Eden winced when she noticed his black eye and swollen jaw. He followed her into her empty classroom.

"She didn't tell me about that."

"Of course she didn't. You know your sister has selective amnesia when it comes to these incidents. I turned my back for two minutes to go to the bar and grab a beer. Next thing I know, she's at the back of the club, dancing on a table with some guy who's groping her

*in front of his friends. Her dress is rising over her ass,
and she is up there laughing like it's okay. What was I
supposed to do?"*

"I understand." Eden nodded.

*"I love Riley. She's always been fun and vivacious. Her
energy is infectious. That's why everyone loves her. But
lately, she's just become . . ."*

*"What?" Eden knew her sister's out-of-control behav-
ior had been bothering him for a while.*

*"Reckless. The projects she's been taking, the partying,
the drinking. Don't get me wrong, I don't mind her
drinking, but your sister is getting out of hand. And I
think it's because of me," Neil told her.*

"What do you mean? What are you doing to her?"

*"I am there. I pick her up when she calls because she
can't drive from a bar or club. I come over when
she doesn't want to be alone in the middle of the night.
I make sure she's safe. And lately, I am fighting off
goons who disrespect her," Neil said, looking as if he
was about to cry. "I've never been a partier or a drink-
er, and I damn sure was never a fighter. I'm not myself
anymore. I feel like I'm turning into someone else, and I
don't like that person."*

*"Neil, I get it. I promise I will talk to her. Riley gets like
this when she gets stressed. She'll snap out of it. I hear
you loud and clear," Eden said. She liked Neil, especially
for Riley. He balanced her out, and she knew how much
her sister loved him. She had never seen Riley so gung
ho for a guy before.*

*"Career Month?" Neil said, pointing to a flier on the
bulletin board in her classroom.*

*"Yeah, you should come and talk to my kids next
month," Eden told him. "Bring your camera. Teach them
how to shoot commercials!"*

"*Let me know when. We can make it happen.*" *He smiled.*

And he did. The following month Neil came and spoke not only to her class for Career Month, he actually let them create their own video for the PTA program to promote the school literacy program. The kids enjoyed it, the parents enjoyed it, and the principal enjoyed it. The problem was that Eden and Neil more than enjoyed it. The countless hours they spent together working with the kids on the project, along with the long evenings spent at the studio where Neil worked editing the project, allowed them to get to know one another. They laughed and swapped stories of growing up with famous siblings. Neil had two younger brothers who were actors. He understood, like Eden, the feeling of being in the shadows while trying to find your own sparkle.

Eden felt comfortable with him. At first, she didn't even realize Neil had become attracted to her. It came so naturally.

"I don't know how to thank you!" she told him the night of the PTA meeting as they walked in the school parking lot.

"I know exactly how," he said and stopped walking.

Eden was still excited from the accolades of their well-received video presentation. "You name it!"

Neil took her hand, and before she knew it, his mouth was on hers. She closed her eyes, savoring the moment and putting her arms around his neck. She became lost in the kiss. It wasn't until minutes later that she realized that she was in love with her sister's fiancé.

Chapter 13

Lisa Wells

All except one of Lisa's goody baskets had been delivered, and she was proud of herself. To her delight, the neighbors were really open and friendly for the most part, including Jonah, the white guy who owned the clan of dogs that continually barked. She was tempted not to even go to his door, but she gave herself a pep talk and forced herself to get out of her comfort zone.

Jonah's house seemed slightly smaller than the other ones in the neighborhood, if one considered what appeared to be about 6,000 square feet small. The front lawn was still perfectly manicured, it was a custom-built brick home like all the other ones, but his just seemed simpler. There was a black pickup truck and an older Honda parked in front, along with a trailer of some sort. The closer she got to his door, the louder she heard the barking coming from the backyard. Her heart began pounding, and she hurried and rang the doorbell before she could run off. She waited a few moments, and just as she was about to leave the basket on the steps, the door opened.

"Hello," he mumbled. He was dressed in a T-shirt and basketball shorts and had a towel around his neck.

Lisa wondered if he had been working out, but then she saw he wasn't wearing sneakers. "Oh, hi! I didn't think you were home," Lisa said. "I'm Lisa. I live down the street. We met the other night."

Suddenly, a huge German shepherd walked up and stood beside him in the doorway. Lisa stepped back, praying she wouldn't faint.

Jonah calmly said, "Dash, inside."

The dog walked away, and Jonah stepped out, closing the door behind him. "Yeah, I remember. How are you?"

"I'm fine. So I'm out delivering goody baskets to all the neighbors, and this one is for you." She handed him the basket. The look on his face let her know he was wondering what the hell would make her randomly show up on his doorstep with a basket of treats.

He paused for a few seconds, then finally took it from her hands. "Um, thanks," he told her. "That's really nice."

"There's also an invitation attached. We're hosting a cookout on Saturday, and we would love for you to come." Lisa smiled.

"I really don't do crowds, but I appreciate the invitation," Jonah said halfheartedly.

"It's not gonna be a crowd, trust me. The only people we know in this entire city are the ones who stood in that front yard the other night." Lisa pointed to the yard of the home up for sale where they'd gathered the night of the fire. "And that was the first time we met. Don't get me wrong, I was glad to finally meet everyone, but I wish it had been under better circumstances."

"True." Jonah nodded.

"This is just a way of kind of getting everyone together in a positive setting, so to speak. You know, some food, music, conversation. Oh, and we have a pool if you want to swim," Lisa added.

"That's cool," Jonah said.

"So hopefully you will come over, and you can bring someone if you like. Your wife or girlfriend . . ."

"I don't have either."

"Or boyfriend, that's fine too. We don't judge." Lisa held up both hands and waved them.

"I don't have one of those either." Jonah laughed.

"Well, feel free to bring whomever you like other than your dogs."

"What's wrong with the dogs?" he asked.

"I don't do dogs."

"Don't tell me you're afraid."

Lisa nodded emphatically. "I am."

"Aw, come on. Don't you know dogs are a man's best friend?"

"I'm not a man, and I have a sister who is a great best friend. So I'm good," Lisa said. As if he could feel her talking about him, the dog began barking incessantly, and Lisa jumped. "Well, that's my cue to go. I will see you next Saturday, alone."

"I'll make sure it's okay with Dash. She doesn't like when I go out without her. She has a jealous streak." Jonah laughed.

Lisa waved and walked off, pulling the wagon behind her.

"Marcus! I'm back!" Lisa called out when she returned to her home. She walked upstairs into the theatre room, expecting to find him there, but he wasn't. "Marcus!"

"Hey, baby, you're back already?" Marcus's voice came from the opposite wing down the hallway. She was surprised because, since that area of their house only held the two guest bedrooms and another unfinished room, he rarely ventured to that side.

"Yeah, everyone was so nice and seem excited to come. I told you this cookout was a good idea. Oh, and guess what? I think Peri has a crush on you." She was just about to walk out of the theatre room when he came rushing in.

"Who?" Marcus asked.

"Peri, the gay guy who had on the polka-dot pajamas."
Lisa laughed.

"That's not funny. You play too much."

"I took it as a compliment. But if it's any consolation,
Riley Rodriguez thinks you're cute too," Lisa told him.

"I got something to tell you," Marcus said.

"Me first. I talked to Shar this morning, and she is
gonna come and help me with the food and hang out for
a couple of days."

"Your sister? She's coming here?" Marcus seemed
bothered all of a sudden.

"Yeah. I told you the other week she was coming for a
visit." Lisa raised an eyebrow and peered closer at him.

"You didn't say when."

"I didn't know exactly when. But since we're having this
cookout, I figured it would be a good time. What's the
problem?"

Marcus sighed and folded his arms across his chest.
"It's not a problem. I just didn't know she was coming for
the cookout. I wish you woulda mentioned it, that's all.
You coulda told me."

His expression, his body language, his words—something was bothering her husband.

"I'm telling you now. Marcus, what the hell is wrong?
Why are you getting an attitude because my sister is
coming?" She snapped at him.

"I don't have an attitude because your sister is coming!"
Marcus snapped. "I have an attitude because you're
yelling at me for no reason!"

"Hey, hey, hey! What's all this about? Is that how y'all
act when company is in the crib?"

Lisa looked at the doorway and had to blink to several
times to make sure she was seeing correctly. She couldn't
believe Sam was standing there grinning at them.

He and Marcus looked very much alike, only Sam was younger and shorter. Their similarities stopped at their physical looks. Dressed in jeans, an Armani Exchange T-shirt, and Gucci loafers, he looked like a rapper about to take center stage at a concert, complete with the platinum and diamond chains around his neck and huge studs in his ear. Sam took the term "flashy" as a compliment. Everything about him—his dress, his attitude, and his demeanor—screamed, "Look at me," and Lisa couldn't stand it. Instead, her eyes turned to her husband.

"Baby, when I told you I had something to tell you, this was it. Sam is here."

"What's up, Lisa Lisa?" Sam walked over and hugged her tight, kissing her on the cheek while doing so. "You surprised? I told Marcus I been dreaming about your blueberry pound cake for weeks. You gotta hook me up."

"Uh, bro, it's some already made downstairs in the kitchen. It's right on the counter. Help yourself." Marcus pointed toward the door.

"Sure thing. Lisa, you are looking beautiful as always. I'm so glad to be here, and I hear we planning a cookout, too. Perfect timing, huh?" Sam hugged her again before walking out.

"Where are my kids?" Lisa asked.

"They're in the backyard," Marcus said, then nervously asked, "Why?"

"Good," Lisa told him, closing the door so they would have privacy. She was glad her children were outside. Even though she knew the custom-built room was soundproof, she wasn't sure if it would be able to drown out the yelling that she knew was about to take place.

"Lisa, let me explain. Sam and I were talking yesterday. You know, about the fire. He called to make sure we were okay," Marcus said.

"And?" Lisa put her hand on her hip.

"And he mentioned that he wanted to come for a visit sometime soon."

"And?"

"And I was like, cool. Let me know when you wanna come."

"And?"

"And he said he would check the flights and let me know."

"And?"

"And that's it. That's all he told me. I didn't know he was coming today until he showed up!"

"And?"

"And what?" Marcus seemed confused.

"And now I have a reason to have an attitude since a few minutes ago you accused me of having one for no reason!" Lisa snapped and walked past him, slamming the door behind her as she left. She was furious, and he knew better than to follow. She entered into their bedroom and slammed that door as well. She wanted to make sure Marcus knew how pissed she was.

She paced the floor, trying to get her mind together and calm down. Sam's sudden appearance complicated her life in so many ways. Had Marcus told her he was coming, she would have prepared her mindset to deal with him and his ignorance, made plans to stay gone from the house. But now she was in an impossible situation. She had to call Shar and tell her. There was no way her sister would even consider coming to visit once she found out Sam was at the house.

For a brief moment, she wondered if she was making a big deal out of nothing. Maybe Shar wouldn't have a problem with Sam's being there as much as she thought she would. Then Lisa remembered the last time the two of them had been in her house at the same time.

It was at the last cookout that Lisa and Marcus hosted at their small house before the lottery win. Marcus was in the backyard, firing up the grill and entertaining their guests, who had arrived with numerous stories about his short-lived career as the star of the high school basketball team. Lisa was inside the kitchen prepping the food when her sister walked in.

"Those look good," Shar said, pointing to the tray of deviled eggs Lisa had just taken out of the refrigerator.

"You look like hell." Lisa frowned. Shar looked as if she hadn't slept in days. Her short hair, which was normally curled to perfection, was slicked back on her head, and she had on a tank top, jeans, and a pair of sandals. Shar prided herself on being stylishly dressed, even when she was going to Walmart, so Lisa knew something had to be wrong.

"I know. I've been at the hospital all night and day," Shar said as she sat in one of the kitchen chairs.

"Hospital? For what?" Lisa became alarmed. "What's wrong? Why didn't you call me?"

"Girl, you know if something was wrong with me you would be the first person I call. It's Kendra," Shar said. Kendra was Shar's best friend and had been since elementary school. And unfortunately, she was also Sam's pregnant girlfriend.

"What's wrong with her?" Lisa asked, assembling the eggs on a tray as she talked.

"She called me yesterday morning because she was having really bad cramps. I drove her to the hospital, and turns out she was having contractions." Shar sighed.

"Oh, no, it's too early for that. How far along is she?" Lisa stopped arranging the eggs and focused on what her sister was saying.

"She's only five months."

"Were they able to stop them? She's probably gonna be on bed rest until she delivers," Lisa said.

"She delivered this morning." Shar's voice cracked.

"Oh." Lisa's heart sank, and she hoped her sister wasn't going to say what she was thinking.

"The baby died."

Shar's words caused Lisa to gasp. She gabbed a paper towel and wiped her hands as she walked over and hugged her sister. "Oh, Shar. I'm so sorry. That's terrible. Oh, my God."

Shar cried in Lisa's arms, her tears wetting her shirt. Lisa held on, comforting her.

"I was right there with her. I held her hand and tried to tell her it would be okay, but as soon as I saw that little boy, I knew it wasn't. He didn't even take a breath. He was so tiny." Shar cried even harder.

Lisa was heartbroken. She knew how much her sister's friend had been looking forward to having the baby. They had already started planning her shower and designing the cake.

"It's okay, Shar. She's gonna be fine. I know Sam was probably crushed," Lisa said. She wondered if Marcus knew any of this was going on, because he hadn't mentioned it to her.

"That bastard didn't even come to the hospital. She called him over and over. He kept telling her he would get there when he could. I got fed up and called him myself, and he told me he was tied up and wouldn't be there. He is so trifling!" Shar said.

"You're lying. Please tell me you're lying, Shar." Lisa could feel herself getting angry. She knew Sam was an asshole, but this was inexcusable.

"I wish I were. I don't even think he knows she lost the baby yet. When it was all over, Kendra didn't want me to call and tell him. She said he had made it clear that he didn't care. I hate him. He is the worst!"

"Who's the worst?"

Sam's voice caught both of them off guard. Lisa looked up and saw him standing in the doorway of her kitchen.

His arm was around a woman who was scantily dressed in a pair of too-tight shorts and a shirt that barely covered her breasts.

"I don't believe this," Shar said, standing up.

"Believe what?" Sam laughed.

Lisa couldn't believe it herself. Shar had just told her the devastating news, and here he was standing in her house with a new chick on his arm as if everything were fine.

"I should fuck you up right here, you trifling bastard!" Shar took a step toward Sam.

Lisa reached out and grabbed her sister's arm. "Shar, don't!"

"Yo, you better listen to your big sis, Sharlise." Sam smugly called Shar by her full first name, which people rarely used. "I don't know what your problem is, but you need to calm down, for real."

"You know what my problem is! How dare you come waltzing in here with another bitch like you don't know what's going on with Kendra!" Shar yelled, tears still streaming down her face.

"I thought you said you broke up with her," the girl snapped at Sam.

"We did. Don't listen to her," Sam replied.

"Can you excuse yourself, please?" Lisa directed at the girl, who hurriedly went back out the door.

"Look, I don't have time for no drama. Marcus invited me over for a cookout and told me it was cool if I brought a date. Now here y'all go tripping." Sam frowned.

"Marcus! Marcus!" Lisa yelled for her husband.

"You came over to a cookout when Kendra has been in the hospital since yesterday? You ain't go check on her. You ain't go be with her. You just came to a damn cookout?" Shar shook her head.

"What's up, baby? What's wrong?" Marcus came through the back door and into the kitchen. His eyes went from Lisa to Shar then finally to Sam, and he slowly asked, "What's wrong now?"

"Man, I brought a date. But you told me I could." Sam acted as if he had done nothing wrong.

"I thought the date you were bringing was Kendra." Marcus shook his head.

"I never said that. You assumed it," Sam told him.

"Shit," Marcus said. "Baby—"

"Don't nobody give a damn about his whack-ass date!" Shar yelled. "Ask him where Kendra is and has been since yesterday morning."

"Where is she?" Marcus looked confused.

Sam took a few moments and then said, "She went to the hospital. You know how she is. Her stomach was hurting again. It's been hurting since she got knocked up. Do you know how many times she's been to the doctor and the hospital and nothing's been wrong? She is being dramatic as usual. Hell, she must not be that sick, because you sitting here chilling at the cookout, eating deviled eggs."

"Her stomach hurt because she was in labor, asshole!" Lisa was so mad that her voice was an octave higher than normal.

Sam's eyes widened, and his head snapped around to look at Lisa. "Labor?"

"Yes, labor. She kept calling you. I kept calling you, but you were busy, remember? Well, you were so damn busy that you missed the birth of your son! It's a boy, bitch!" Shar spat the words at him.

"What? What are you talking about?" Sam's eyes widened, and he took a step closer toward Shar.

"Kendra had the baby earlier today." Lisa directed her words toward Marcus.

"Isn't it too soon for her to deliver?" Marcus looked to his wife to explain.

"Yes." Lisa nodded.

"What are you saying?" Sam asked.

"Your baby is dead. That's what she's saying," Shar cried.

The room became completely silent, and no one moved. It was as if no one knew what to say.

Finally, Sam spoke, "I ain't really think that baby was mine anyway."

Shar moved so fast that Lisa didn't even realize what was happening. Her sister's fist connected with the side of Sam's face with a force so hard that he stumbled. As he was steadying himself, she kicked him in the stomach, and he stumbled back again.

"Sharlise!"

"Shar!"

Marcus and Lisa yelled at the same time. Hearing the commotion, people rushed inside to see what was going on.

Sam charged at Shar, but Marcus grabbed him before he could reach her.

"I'm gonna kill her! Get off me!" Sam yelled. "You betta watch your back, Shar, because I'm coming for your ass. Believe that. I'm coming for you!"

"Let him go!" Shar demanded.

Lisa pulled her sister by the arm into her and Marcus's bedroom. "It's over, Shar. Calm down."

Shar's bottom lip trembled, and she could barely talk. "I h . . . hate h . . . him!"

"I know you do, Shar. You're right. He's the worst. But you've gotta calm down."

Lisa had never seen her sister so angry. Shar was normally the cool, calm, collected one who got along with everyone. It was the first time Shar had ever physi-

cally put her hands on anyone, let alone a man. Lisa sat on the bed and pulled Shar's head into her lap, rubbing her back. "Calm down, Shar. It's gonna be okay."

Shar continued to cry, but her breathing slowed, and the trembling stopped. "I told Kendra not to mess with Sam. We all told her. She knows how he is. But she . . . she really loved him . . . and he treats her . . . treated her like shit."

Lisa heard the door creak, and Marcus stuck his head in. "Is she okay?" Marcus asked.

"Is he gone?" Lisa responded.

Marcus nodded and motioned for Lisa to come into the hallway. She eased Shar's head off her lap and said she would be right back.

"I feel horrible, baby," he said when the door was closed and they were out of earshot.

"Your brother is horrible. You didn't do this. He did," Lisa said.

"I told him he needed to get over to that hospital now and check on Kendra. He's going. I think we need to go over there too, but all these people are here," Marcus said. "I don't want to tell them to leave and then they ask why. It ain't their business."

"You're right. But I don't even feel like entertaining anyone. Let's just let everyone know they can eat, but we have a family emergency to deal with." Lisa sighed.

"Okay." Marcus nodded, then pulled her close and said, "I love you. I didn't know he pulled a stunt like this."

"I know you didn't, Marcus. But I need him to stay away from me, for real. I need some time to deal with all of this." Lisa shook her head.

"I know what he did is messed up but, Lisa, he's still my brother. We work together. Hell, he's my ride to work," Marcus told her.

"*Then you need to work on finding another ride,*" Lisa said. "*Brother or not, there are just some things that are just wrong, and I'm not gonna deal with.*"

Marcus didn't say anything else, and she went back in to check on Shar, who had drifted off to sleep. Their guests ate and were understanding when they explained the cookout would be ending early.

That night, Lisa and Marcus went to the hospital to check on Kendra and pay their respects. Sam still hadn't made it to the hospital or called when they got there. Later, as they drove home, Lisa reminded Marcus that she wanted his brother to stay away.

"I understand, and I'm gonna respect what you're asking. But again, realize that he's still my brother. He's not perfect and neither is this situation, but that's my family. You gotta respect that. There's going to come a time when we're all gonna have to heal from this, put it past us, and move on. Trust me, that's how God works."

"I can't think of any situation that God will put us in where I have to deal with getting along with your brother after this, Marcus," Lisa said matter-of-factly.

Ninety days later, the two brothers walked into a convenience store, and the next day they woke up millionaires. Marcus was right. They had no choice but to deal with one another, but Lisa still could not move on, and she knew neither could Shar.

Chapter 14

King Douglas

"What are you doing here?"

King entered Scorpio's hospital room and immediately stopped. He had been confused by so many things that had happened over the course of the past two days that nothing should have surprised him. Not the sight of his newly built home now roped off by yellow crime scene tape and police officers, not the overly protective hospital security staff who gave him a hard time when he arrived to visit, not even the look of shock on the face of Scorpio's personal security guard, Cheddar, who was posted outside of her hospital room door. But the sight of Yolanda Powell, sitting at Scorpio's bedside, came as a surprise to him.

"I, uh, I came to see Scorpio?" His words came out sounding more like a question than a statement. He walked a step closer and stared at his soon-to-be ex-wife lying motionless in the hospital bed, an IV in her arm and tubes coming out of her body. There were all sorts of monitors connected to her.

"Well, you see her. You can leave now," Yolanda told him.

He had only met her one time, and that was when she came to his and Scorpio's wedding. They were introduced briefly before the ceremony, and she hadn't seemed any happier to see him then than she did now. Scorpio told him that her mother was her least favorite person in the world to deal with. She didn't care for her very much, and he was starting to see why. She was cold and callous.

"I don't think so," King told her, walking closer to Scorpio's bed. "I'm not leaving."

"I'm asking you politely to leave my daughter's room now. You haven't been here all this time. Now all of a sudden you're concerned?" Yolanda stood up.

I could say the same thing about you. "I was across the country when all of this happened. I flew back as soon as I heard, but I had to take care of the house and make sure it was secure," King said.

"So the safety of your property was more important than the safety of my daughter."

"That's not what I'm saying." King tried to remain calm, but she was making it difficult.

"That's what you said," Yolanda snapped. "I don't have to do this. This is why we have security in place. Young man, please come and escort him out of here!"

Cheddar walked into the room, looking and sounding very much like Ving Rhames with a beard. "What's the problem?"

"I don't have a problem, Cheddar. You already know. I just came to be with Scorp, that's all, man. She seems to be the one with the problem, not me." King nodded toward Yolanda.

Cheddar looked like a child who had been asked to choose between both parents, and he didn't know which one to choose. He was saved by the doctor who came in.

"Mr. Douglas, I'm Dr. DeWitt, Mrs. Douglas's doctor. Nice to meet you."

"Her last name is Powell," Yolanda offered.

"Nice to meet you too, Dr. DeWitt." King ignored her and extended his hand to the doctor. "How is she?"

"She is coming along nicely. We have started weaning her off the sedation medication, and she has been alert at times. The most important thing is that she remains calm," Dr. DeWitt said. "She did inhale a lot of smoke, which was a major concern. That is why we have her under the constant flow of oxygen, but there doesn't seem to be any lung damage, which is a good thing. She suffered some burns to her right leg, ankle, and foot, but they will heal over time."

"We already know all of this." Yolanda seemed frustrated. "This is no concern of his. She needs to be taken off the drugs completely, and when are you taking the tube out of her throat?"

"Soon, Mrs. Powell," Dr. DeWitt said.

"Miss Powell," Yolanda corrected him.

He pursed his lips. "I apologize, Miss Powell. I will have the nurse come in, and we'll do some more blood work and check her levels. If they're good, then we'll see about taking out the tube," Dr. DeWitt told them.

"More pricking and prodding." Yolanda rolled her eyes. "And no progress."

King turned back to Scorpio and noticed her eyes open for a moment. She looked at him, then looked over and saw her mother and quickly closed them again.

"Dr. DeWitt, is there any way I can have some privacy with my wife?" King asked.

"I don't think so!" Yolanda said. "Absolutely not! And stop calling her that!"

"Well, we are still married. Right, Cheddar?" King asked.

Cheddar nodded slowly.

"I am her next of kin, and any medical decisions really should be made by me," King informed them.

Dr. DeWitt seemed happy to agree with King's revelation. "Yes, sir, that's correct. I think we should leave them alone and give them some privacy."

"No! I'm not going anywhere!" Yolanda hissed.

"Cheddar, can you escort her out, or do I need to call hospital security?" King smiled.

"I'm sorry, Mizz Powell. You're gonna have to leave the room for a little while," Cheddar said.

"This is ridiculous. That's my daughter! I'm calling my attorney to see what can be done about this," Yolanda said and stormed out of the room.

King shook his head and thought for a moment. The last thing he wanted was for things to get worse than they already were, and he didn't want to run the risk of having any more of their personal drama leaked to the press.

"I'll be right back," he told Cheddar and went into the hallway. "Miss Powell, wait!"

Yolanda turned around quickly. "What?"

"Look, I don't want things to get ugly. I don't . . . we don't know one another very well, but we do have something in common. We both love your daughter. Yeah, I know the marriage is over, but despite what you may think or what you may have heard, I still love her. And at the end of the day, we're still friends. So I'm gonna be here for her, because she needs me. I'm not going anywhere until I know she's good or she tells me to get the hell out," King told her. "I'm sorry if that's not what you want, but it ain't about you. It's about her. I hope you understand and respect that the same way I respect that you're her mother and wanna be here too."

Yolanda inhaled deeply and told him, "I'm staying at the Hilton downtown. If there is any change before I return in a few hours, I expect to be alerted. I also expect the same privacy with my daughter that you do."

"Yes, ma'am." King nodded and walked back into Scorpio's room.

"You good?" Cheddar asked when he returned.

"Yeah, it's cool," King told him. "Thanks."

"That woman is a pistol," Cheddar said as he headed toward the door.

"So is her daughter," King said, pulling a chair closer to Scorpio's bed and taking her small, delicate hand into his. He looked at the beautiful face that he had seen plastered all over magazines, billboards, television commercials, and fashion runways. It was the same face he had the pleasure of waking up next to for many mornings during happier times. "I guess that old saying is true. The apple don't fall far from the tree."

Scorpio's eyes opened.

"Hey, you," he whispered.

Her eyes widened, and she looked around the room wildly.

"She's gone."

He felt her fingers wrap around his, and her gaze softened.

"You're welcome, baby. I got you." He smiled at her. He was relieved to know that she was going to be okay. He spoke the truth when he told Yolanda that he loved Scorpio and she was his friend. They had been so way before they were married.

They had met when she attended one of the Hot Boyz concerts years ago. They had just performed, and he was in his dressing room when Kaz, his bandmate, knocked on the door.

"Yo, you ain't gonna believe who's out here asking for you."

"Is she fine as hell and over twenty-one?" King asked, using a towel to wipe the sweat off his muscular chest and abdomen.

"She is beyond fine, and she's legal. She is dream girl material, way outta your league. I'm tryin'a figure out why she even wanna meet your corny ass, but she does, real bad." Kaz was so excited that he could hardly keep still.

"Yo, if she busted and this is a joke, you know I'ma get you back! I ain't forgot about that other chick in Atlanta with the bad weave and fake ass! She better not be from the Squad, Kaz," King warned his group member.

The guys constantly played jokes on one another while on tour, and sending in a groupie from what they called the Terror Squad, because of how terrible they looked, was one of the most common pranks.

"Naw, son, this chick is glam squad! Naw, she ain't even glam. She is—"

"Man, just bring her in!" King laughed.

"Now? You sure you ready? You might wanna put on a shirt for this one."

King looked down at the six pack that he worked so hard to keep, and he flexed his chest muscles at Kaz, who was on the slim side and who envied King's muscular body. *"Bring her in."*

Kaz rolled his eyes and opened the door slowly. *"You ladies can come in."*

King almost panicked when a tall, stout white woman walked in, smiling at him, wearing a tight, low-cut dress. *"Oh, my God, it's really you!"*

"'Sup." King's voice was flat, and he gave Kaz a look of disgust.

Kaz opened the door wider and in walked the tallest, most beautiful woman King had ever seen. He did a triple take to make sure it was really Scorpio standing in front of him, and he became almost as fidgety as Kaz. Keep it cool, he reminded himself. She may be Scorpio, but you're King!

"Hello." Scorpio smiled slightly.

King smiled and tossed the towel he was holding over his shoulder. *"How are you, ladies? Did you all enjoy the show?"*

"Oh, my God, yes!" the other woman squealed. *"It was amazing!"*

"I'm glad, I'm glad. Have a seat." King motioned to the red leather sofa. *"Well, since you all know who I am, how about you tell me who you lovely ladies are?"*

"I'm Scorpio, and this is my friend, Jewel, your biggest fan," Scorpio said, introducing the woman beside her.

"Nice to meet both of you. I'm sorry I'm a little under-dressed," King apologized but made sure he gestured toward his torso so they would look.

"You're fine!" Jewel gushed. *"I mean, you look fine. I mean—"*

"She's a bit nervous." Scorpio shook her head. *"But it's her birthday, and I promised her front row seats to tonight's show, so meeting you is the icing on the cake, so to speak."*

"What? Happy Birthday, Jewel!" King walked over and gave her a hug, and she screamed.

"Jewel!" Scorpio scolded.

King looked up and winked at Kaz, who just shook his head.

"Can I get a picture?" Jewel took out her cell phone and passed it to Scorpio.

"Sure." King took the phone from her. *"Kaz, can you take this pic of us right quick? Give him the phone."*

Kaz looked like he wanted to smack King.

"Wait, we can't take a pic without him being in it. That's not right. How about if my security, Cheddar, takes the pic of all of us? He's right outside," Scorpio told them.

"Thank you, Scorpio!" Kaz smiled with a vindicated look on his face.

"No thanks needed. You're my favorite Hot Boy!" Scorpio winked.

"What the . . ." The smile on King's face disappeared.

"Too bad you're married," Scorpio teased, and it was Kaz's smile that now dropped. *"Congrats on the new baby!"*

"Uh, thanks," Kaz told her, clearly disappointed. "Lemme get the security dude."

Cheddar came in, and not only did the ladies take pictures with King and Kaz, but the rest of the guys as well. Jewel was ecstatic and became even more so when King suggested they all go out for drinks to toast her birthday.

"I'm sorry. We have an early morning flight to catch," Scorpio explained.

"Damn, too bad," King said. "I was hoping to spend a little more time with you and get to know you a bit better."

"Really?" Scorpio's eyebrows raised slightly, and she tilted her head.

"I would, even though I'm not your favorite Hot Boy." King laughed. "Why does that seem to surprise you?"

"Because I never formally get asked out on a date, I guess." Scorpio shrugged.

"You're lying." King shook his head in disbelief. There was no way he was going to believe that. She was Scorpio the supermodel. What man wouldn't jump at the chance to ask her out?

"Nope, not at all. Guys will send messages through my publicist, and she sets the dates up most of the time," Scorpio explained.

"Well, I'm a real man, so I'm doing what real men do. Would you like to have dinner and drinks with me when your schedule permits?" he didn't hesitate to ask, feeling confident.

Scorpio nodded and gave him a wink. "I would love to. Give my publicist a call and have her set it up."

The room erupted with laughter, and King realized that the private conversation he thought they were having was being heard by everyone. Talking with her *made him feel like they were the only people in the room. It was magnetic.*

"I'm just kidding," Scorpio teased.

They exchanged numbers, and before he knew it, they were in a whirlwind romance, flying into different cities to see one another, taking romantic getaways between his concerts and her photo shoots and runway shows. The moments they spent together were brief and sporadic, but intimate and filled with passion.

King was in love, and so was she. He didn't ask her to marry him. Instead, he called her publicist and had her check Scorpio's schedule and asked when would be a good time to have their wedding. The publicist called Scorpio to confirm. The wedding was planned, and they got married. Their lives continued as they were until the label decided it wanted to go into a younger, different direction, and Hot Boyz was dropped.

Just like that, King's life changed. Instead of being on the road for months at a time, he was now home, and he wanted his wife there with him. Scorpio, however, had no desire to slow down, and when she was home, they usually argued about her schedule. It got to the point where neither one of them was happy with the situation.

Things got worse after his mother's death. Depression kicked in, and he began hanging out on the local club scene, drinking and partying heavy. He was enjoying the attention from other women because he wasn't getting any from his wife. Word got back to Scorpio, who couldn't believe that he had the audacity to cheat on her, the woman who had just been named one of People magazine's Most Beautiful People and one of Time magazine's Most Interesting People in the World. For Scorpio, it was an insult, and her heart was broken. Everyone in the world wanted her except for the man she loved. She wanted King to hurt as much as she did.

Not only did she tell him she wanted a divorce, but she made it a point to make it the worst situation for him ever.

Her demands were over the top. She smeared his name in the media and left the country, refusing to talk to him or his lawyers. It had been months, and King didn't even know she was back in the States until he got the call from Leo telling him about the fire, and that she had been in the house.

King tried not to flinch as the nurse came in and took tubes of blood from his almost-ex-wife. He settled back into the chair and continued to hold her hand. They stared at one another until Scorpio's eyes closed again, and so did his.

They were both awakened a few hours later by the sound of Dr. DeWitt, who came in with the results of Scorpio's blood work and test results.

"Well, it looks like we can go ahead and take the tube out."

"Okay, that's good." King nodded. "I guess I can call her mom and let her know."

Suddenly, Scorpio's grasp tightened on his hand, and he saw the frown on her face.

"Uh, maybe not." King shrugged, nodding to let her know he understood. He stepped away so the doctor and nurses could have room to maneuver. "I should step out so you guys can work."

"You can stay. It'll only take a few moments," the doctor said, putting on a pair of gloves and leaning over Scorpio's body.

King was squeamish, and he hated anything that had to do with blood or any other body fluid. He'd fainted in the delivery room when Knight was born, and he had waited in the lobby of the hospital while Portia gave birth to PJ. He turned his back and closed his eyes, moving closer to the wall. He listened as there was a slight commotion. The doctors and nurses talked, followed by a swooshing sound, and suddenly he heard Scorpio coughing and gagging.

"I'll get her some water," a nurse said.

King's back remained turned, and he closed his eyes tighter like a scared little kid watching a horror movie.

"Mrs. Douglas?" Dr. DeWitt asked. "Is that better?"

"Yes, much." Scorpio's voice was raspy, and she coughed a little more.

"Good, good," Dr. DeWitt told her, then said, "Mr. Douglas, it's okay. You can look now."

King turned around and saw Scorpio staring at him. She smiled weakly and whispered, "Punk."

"I think she's going to be okay."

"Me too." King nodded.

The doctor and nurses made sure she was fine, and then they left the room. King sat back in his seat beside her. Scorpio was holding a small cup with a straw.

"I'm glad you're alive," he told her.

Scorpio took another small sip of water and coughed a bit more. King became nervous until he heard her raspy voice. "Me too." Scorpio passed him the cup.

"Man, this is crazy." King took the cup from her and placed it on the tray near the bed.

"I know." Scorpio nodded.

"You almost died. Your mom is—"

"I know," Scorpio repeated.

"I'm just trying to figure it all out. I didn't even know you were back in the States. When did you get back? You know what? It don't even matter. I'm just glad you're okay."

Scorpio rubbed her fingers along the back of his hand. "I'm sorry."

"It's cool. I mean, we just gotta deal with it as it comes along. What's important is that you're okay," King said.

"Thank you. I look terrible." Scorpio looked down at the hospital gown she was wearing and touched her wavy hair, which was slightly disheveled on her head.

"You look gorgeous as always, especially for someone who just survived a fire."

"Liar." Scorpio smiled.

"I do have one small question though, Scorp."

"What?"

"Why did you burn down my damn house?"

Scorpio began coughing again, and he quickly passed her the water. She slowly drank from the straw, and when the coughing stopped, she cleared her throat and took another sip.

"I didn't." She shook her head at him and frowned.

"The fire marshal told me their investigation is pointing toward arson," King said. He couldn't believe it himself when the investigator told him the news. Although he knew he and Scorpio weren't on the best of terms, the idea that she would actually burn down his house, especially one that she helped design, plan, and was in the process of fighting him for in the divorce settlement, was unimaginable to him. Scorpio loved that house as much as he did.

"It . . . it wasn't me," Scorpio managed to get out.

"Was it the guy you were with? Bishop Burke's son? Why was he even at my house?"

"Gave me a . . . a ride. I was drunk." Scorpio cleared her throat again and tears formed in her eyes. "He pulled . . . pulled me out."

"Are you sure?"

Scorpio nodded, and a tear slid down her cheek. "He saved me."

King could see that she was straining, and he didn't want to upset her. "Okay, it wasn't him, and it wasn't you. Maybe they're wrong. It's a newly built house. Maybe the wiring had something to do with it." He reached over and wiped the wetness from her face.

Scorpio shook her head and said, "Th . . . there was another g . . . girl."

"Another girl?"

"In the garage."

King was even more confused. Neither the fire marshal, the police, not even the media said anything else other than Scorpio and Malachi Burke being in the house when the fire happened. Scorpio must have been mistaken, because if there was another woman, where was she now?

Chapter 15

Malachi Burke

So this is what death feels like, Malachi thought.

Everything around him was completely dark. He couldn't move. He had to admit, he was kind of disappointed. Although he lived a little on the reckless side, he thought he had a couple more years on earth.

"Hey, Dad, how is he? Any change?"

"Hey, Micah. No, not since yesterday."

Shit, this ain't what death feels like. I'm in hell.

Malachi heard the voices of the bishop and his brother. He wondered if he would have rather been dead. He definitely didn't want to be anywhere near the two of them.

"Where's Mom?"

"I'm right here. Hey, baby. Hey, Adrienne," his mother said.

Malachi heard her kissing someone on the cheek. He realized that he could also smell the scent of her latest favorite perfume, Euphoria by Calvin Klein.

"What are the doctors saying?" Micah asked.

Malachi knew his brother was probably hoping he died if for no other reason than to have the satisfaction of saying, "I told y'all he was bad news. The world is now a better place without him."

"They say there really isn't a reason for him not to be awake. Sometimes the body just needs time to heal itself," his mother said quietly.

Wait, I am awake. Well, at least I think I am.

"What's that?" the bishop asked.

"Oh, one of the neighbors brought a goody basket by the house. It has all sorts of things in it, and I figured we would bring it so you can have something to snack on. The muffins are really good," an unfamiliar soft voice said. Malachi figured it must have been his brother's new fiancée, Adrienne.

"That was thoughtful," the bishop responded.

"Try one, Mama," Micah said. "They're the bomb!"

"I'm not hungry, sweetheart. But you can put it over there," his mother said.

"You need to eat something, Mama," Micah told her. "Please."

"I'm fine."

"Mr. and Mrs. Burke?" another male voice said, and Malachi realized someone else had walked into the room. "I'm Detective Adam Frazier with the police department."

"Yes, how can we help you?" the bishop asked.

"I'm sorry about your son Malachi. But we did have a few questions for you. We are investigating the cause of the fire, and it appears to be arson. Now, it seems that your son was released from prison the day before the fire . . ."

Arson! What the hell? Oh, no, I ain't have nothing to do with that fire!

"Leave!" Malachi's mother yelled.

"Ma'am, excuse me?" Detective Frazier asked her.

"I'm asking you to leave. Now is not the time and it is certainly not the place for you to be questioning us about this," she replied.

"She's right. We don't have any answers for you, and my son and his health are the only things we're concerned about right now," the bishop told him. "Now kindly excuse yourself."

"Sir, I don't think you understand the seriousness—"

"You don't understand the severity of my requesting that you leave, sir," the bishop said, interrupting him before he could say anything else. "And anything else can be handled directly though my son's legal counsel."

"We'll be in touch," the detective said.

"The nerve of some people." Adrienne sighed.

"Granted, his timing was not the best, but the man was just doing his job. We don't even know why Malachi was at that house. Something was going on. He didn't even tell us he was getting out," Micah responded.

Leave it to Micah to agree with the white man and accuse me of being the number one suspect.

"Listen, since Micah and Adrienne are here now, O'la, why don't we go ahead and leave? They can sit with Malachi." The bishop sighed.

"I'm not leaving. I'm not going anywhere. Look at what just happened!"

"Mama, you've been here for two days. You need to go home and get some rest," Micah pleaded. "I'll be here with him."

"You can be here with him, but so will I."

"Olivia, I've got to go and get ready for the morning," the bishop told her.

"Walter, what do you mean? I know you're not trying to preach tomorrow!"

"Olivia . . ."

Even in his current state of what he thought was dying, Malachi knew the familiar argument his parents were about to have. It was one that he heard thousands of times before. A major family crisis would take place and yet the bishop would still find it necessary to preach. His father's Sunday presence in the pulpit was more dependable than the U.S. Postal Service. Neither snow nor rain nor heat nor gloom of night would stop *the* Bishop Walter Burke from the completion of his sermon on any given

Sunday. Especially not his son who was in the hospital. Well, not his son Malachi. Had it been Micah, the bishop probably would have shut the whole church down. But one thing Malachi did know was that, for some strange reason, the pulpit was a place of comfort for the bishop, and ministering brought him peace. He also knew that as angry as his mother was, she understood that as well.

"You have an entire staff of preachers, Walter. Your son is lying here in a coma. You need to be ministering to him, not everyone else," Olivia cried.

"Mama, please," Micah said.

"No, I want everyone to leave. Please just go and do what you all need to do. I want to be left alone with my son. So just go!"

Hearing his mother sobbing made Malachi's heart ache. He wanted so badly to wake up and tell her he was fine, but for some reason, his body wasn't listening to his mind and he couldn't.

"Olivia, calm down. Don't act like this." The bishop's voice was strained.

"Listen to me, Mama. We're leaving," Micah told her.

"Good," Olivia snapped.

"But when Adrienne and I come back, I'm gonna have her take you to the house. You need to get some food in you and take a shower, put on some clean clothes. I will stay here with Chi while you do all of that, and she'll bring you back. But you can't just stay in here with him for days at a time. It's not good for you, and you're gonna stress yourself out and make yourself sick," Micah tried to reason with his mother.

As much as Malachi disliked his brother, he knew he was right and was grateful that he was being the voice of calm and reason in the moment. Malachi hoped his mother would listen and agree.

"Lady Olivia, we know you want to be here for Malachi, but you have to keep your strength up if you want to stay," Adrienne said.

"O'la, listen to them."

"We'll be back to get you later this evening, Mama," Micah said.

The room was quiet and for a second. Malachi wondered if they had all left until he heard his mother say, "I'll be ready."

Malachi could sense the relief of all of them. Soon he and his mother were the only ones in the room. He felt her lips kissing him gently on the forehead and cheek.

"Chi, baby, I know you hear all this nonsense going on, but I'm here. Mama's here."

And then she began humming. Even though his eyes were already closed, Malachi felt himself drifting to sleep as his mother sang the lyrics to one of her favorite gospel songs, "My Soul is Anchored." Her talented voice comforted him as only she could.

Though the storms keep on raging in my life,
And sometimes it's hard to tell my night from day,
Still, that hope that lies within is reassured
As I keep my eyes upon the distant shore.

Malachi drifted in and out of consciousness to the point where he no longer knew what day it was or how much time had passed. Sometimes he heard her talking and reading the Bible out loud to him. Other times, he heard Micah and Adrienne talking about their wedding plans. He was never alone.

For the most part, only the immediate family was in the room with him. He knew that members of his father's congregation had been dropping in to check on him, but the bishop made sure that they didn't get past the waiting room down the hall.

A few times he was glad to hear the voice of his boy Trey, who had somehow made it past the bishop's tight security. The few times his mother wasn't by his side, Micah was. Those were the weirdest times for Malachi because he knew his brother would probably rather be anywhere else than stuck babysitting him.

"Excuse me."

Malachi strained to hear who had entered the room.

"Yes, can I help you?" Micah asked.

"I just wanted to see . . . check . . ." The voice was light, barely above a whisper, but Malachi still recognized it.

"Scorpio, right?"

If Malachi could have breathed on his own, he would have let out the biggest sigh of relief. He had been wondering if Scorpio was okay. No one had really said anything, so he wasn't sure.

"Yes. I'm sorry to stare. It's just . . . you look so much like your brother. Are you twins?"

"Yeah." Micah laughed. "How are you holding up?"

"I'm better. It's been a rough couple of days. But I'm finally able to sit up. I had that same tube down my throat until two days ago. My leg and foot suffered the most damage, but I'll be fine."

"That's good to hear and see. I'm glad you are better."

"I had my security guard wheel me down here so I could see him. I hope it's okay," Scorpio told him.

"That's fine. I'm so sorry my brother got you into this situation."

"Got me into it? No, he didn't get me into anything. He pulled me out of it. Your brother saved my life. I wouldn't be here if it weren't for him." Scorpio's voice quivered and then she sniffed. Malachi could tell she was crying.

"Oh, I didn't know," Micah said. "Here take this."

Yeah, you wouldn't know, asshole. Always tryin'a make me out to be the villain!

"Thanks," Scorpio said after blowing her nose, then she continued. "He drove me home from the club because I was too drunk. Later, when the fire started, I collapsed. He found me and got us both out of that house."

Now what you got to say, Micah? I saved her life!

"The police told us they were investigating him because it was arson."

"It was arson, but it wasn't him. I keep remembering seeing a woman right before the fire started. It's fuzzy, but I know she was there, and she was yelling at me about something. Then, she kicked me and ran out right before the fire."

Woman? What woman? Malachi didn't know who or what Scorpio was talking about. As far as he could recall, they were the only two people in the house.

"Wow." Micah sighed.

"Is he going to be okay?" Scorpio sniffed again. "What are they saying?"

"All we can do is wait and pray," Micah told her.

"I really can't help with that."

"With what?"

"Praying. I don't know how. The only thing I know about prayer is it's what some people do before they eat and during church. I don't eat that much, and I can't tell you the last time I've been in a church. I think it was for a bridal photo shoot," Scorpio said. "I'm sorry."

"Don't be embarrassed. I definitely don't judge."

Liar! You've been passing judgment on me since we were in sixth grade! You're the most judgmental, hypocritical man alive. You and your daddy!

"Thanks."

"But prayer is a simple conversation with the Lord. It doesn't have to be deep. He already knows what's on our hearts. He just wants us to be honest with Him and speak it. It's not always asking but simply sharing with Him.

The Bible says, 'Open your mouth wide, and I will fill it.' When we pray, we build a relationship with God. Would you like for me to pray with you?" Micah asked.

"Can we pray for him? He's the one who needs it more than I do. I need you to help me pray for him if that's what they say he needs," Scorpio said.

"We can pray for both of you," Micah told her. "Take my hand."

Malachi then felt the presence of his brother beside him as he took his hand. *What the hell? Is he really about to do this? I don't believe it.*

"Close your eyes. Now, Father God, in the name of Jesus, we come to you right now saying thank you. Thank you for bringing us here together, God, and for sparing these two beautiful lives. God, we know that you will heal Malachi and strengthen him, Father. We are asking that you bring him back whole to us. We cover him and ask that you fall fresh on him and restore him like never before. We ask, God, that you continue to heal Scorpio. Hear her heart and be her comfort right now as she continues to regain her strength. Guide her wherever you would have her to go right now. Direct her path and give her peace in her situation. In Jesus' name, amen."

"Amen," Scorpio repeated. "How did you do that?"

"Do what?" Micah asked her.

"Know to pray for peace in my situation? And that I needed guidance? How did you know to say all of that? Are you, like, psychic?"

"No, I'm not psychic." Micah laughed. "It wasn't what I knew, but it was what the Holy Spirit put on my heart to say. I told you, prayer is what's in your heart, that's all."

"Well, thank you. I guess I should go. I'm sorry. I don't even know your name. I'm normally not this rude."

"You're not rude. And my name is Micah."

"Thank you, Micah."

"You're welcome. I'll keep you in prayer."

"And now that I know how, I will keep praying for Malachi."

Malachi listened and seconds later realized she was gone. He felt Micah's hand on his again and then heard him say, "My brother the hero. Who would have thought? God, heal him, cover him, protect him."

Malachi didn't want to hear any more. He didn't want to feel his brother's hand or accept any prayers from him. Again, he went back into the darkness of what he thought was sleep.

When he woke again, Micah was gone, but there was someone else standing beside his bed talking to him.

"Chi, I don't know if you can hear me, but I want you to know I'm praying for you, son."

It was Jerry, the bishop's best friend, and Malachi's godfather. "You know your daddy is pissed at both of us right about now, but everything is gonna be all right. We just need for you to stick around awhile longer. Man, we ain't even get to celebrate your coming home. I tried explaining to him and your mama how you didn't want them to know—"

"What are you doing in here?" The bishop's voice interrupted what Jerry was trying to say.

"Walt, man, you know I had to come and see him," Jerry said, "I love this boy as much as you do. He's just as much my family as he is yours. I will do anything for this boy."

"Well, we know you'd lie for him." Bishop said, "You've shown us that much. Malachi should have come home when he was released. He needs direction, structure, and some Bible-based discipline in his life. This right here shows that he wasn't ready to handle freedom. He was out of jail how long? Twenty-four hours and look at what happened. I blame you for this, Jerry!"

"It wasn't like that, Walt. You know I didn't want this to happen, and neither did Malachi. You don't give him enough credit."

Malachi was glad that Jerry was sticking up for him. He had always had Chi's back no matter what. It was one of the reasons he was closer to him than to his own father.

"Just get out, Jerry, before I have you thrown out," the bishop said.

"Stop trying to be his bishop and try being his father for a change. I been telling you that for years," Jerry said.

"And how many sons have you raised, Jerry?"

The room got quiet, and Malachi waited for Jerry to say something, but he never did. He realized that he was gone, and Malachi thought he was alone until he heard his father's voice again.

"Malachi, I'm gonna need for you to stop this and wake up. You've always been the stubborn one. I remember the night you were born, they delivered Micah first, and you made your mama labor for five more hours before you came out. You made us wait until you were good and ready. Well, your mother is laboring again for you, and I'm begging you to just come on out so she can . . . we can stop worrying about you. It's been too long since . . . since . . ." The bishop's voice stopped.

Malachi wondered if he had drifted off into the darkness until he heard the voice again, this time, with tears. He had never seen nor heard his father cry before, and it stirred something within him. He wanted to yell for him to get out because he was so uncomfortable.

Malachi tried to force himself back into the darkness. He used everything within him to block out the sound of the bishop's tears. Then he heard his voice, this time in song.

I realize that sometimes in this life
You're gonna be tossed by the waves
And the currents that seem so fierce
But in the word of God I've got an anchor. . .

Malachi's chest became heavy, and he tried to fight the emotions that were erupting inside of him. *Please let him leave, God. I don't want to hear any more. I just want to sleep and be left alone.*

Malachi tried and tried to go back into the darkness that had been comforting him for the last several days. But something was different. He couldn't find it.

"I . . . I love you, son," the bishop told him. Then he softly called, "Malachi? Son, can you hear me?"

Malachi didn't answer. He tried to fight his way back, determined to find the dark tunnel and stay there. Slowly, the darkness surrounded him and he was relieved. He realized that each time he left the darkness, it was becoming harder and harder to return.

He lay in the hospital bed, listening to the sounds of the bishop's crying fade as he slipped back into the coma. Malachi wondered if death really would have been an easier option for him.

Chapter 16

King Douglas

King Douglas looked around the living room of his home and fought tears. It looked as if a bomb had gone off inside. The hardwood floors were soaked with water. The walls were charred. There was a terrible odor. The grand piano, which was the central feature of the room, was unrecognizable along with the furniture, art work, and other decor. The damage in the kitchen was even worse. The garage and the entire left side of the first floor of his home had sustained the most damage. King's motorcycle and custom Suburban, along with Scorpio's Porsche Panamera, were also completely totaled in the fire. His life had been in shambles ever since he got the call that his home was engulfed in flames. For the first time in over two and a half years, King needed a drink. He had finally got the okay from the fire marshall to come inside his home. Seeing the damage was overwhelming in addition to all the confusion behind the entire incident.

"Are we going to the hospital to see Madu when we leave here?"

King didn't respond. He kept looking around at all of the damage. He tried to remember if he had a bottle hidden somewhere in the house and if was somewhere that the fire didn't reach.

"Dad, are you okay?"

King snapped out of his trance and said, "Yeah, son. Just trying to assess the damage."

"Are we gonna see Madu?" His son's shoes made a squishing sound as he walked on the wet floor.

Knight had been asking about "Madu" ever since King had picked him up from the airport that morning. It was the name Knight had affectionately called Scorpio. At first, they couldn't figure out why he called her that, until they realized he was saying "Mom Two" in his own way. King appreciated that his son and Scorpio had such a great bond. He knew Knight was worried about her.

"Yeah, we can go check on her. I just need to check things out," King said as he navigated his way through the watery chaos that was formerly his living room.

"Are we gonna stay here?" Knight asked.

"Naw. Do you see how bad this is? It's not safe right now." King frowned and shook his head.

"Why not? I know it's really burnt down here, but upstairs is fine. Well, my room is, and the studio, oh, and the game room!" Knight said and began bouncing the basketball he had in his hand, causing water to splash onto the matching Air Jordans they both wore.

King jumped back. "Boy, didn't I tell you not to go up there! I swear you don't listen. And stop bouncing that damn basketball in my house. I mean, our . . . well, this house!"

Knight stopped bouncing the ball, which was now wet. "Are we gonna have to move? Are we gonna live in the hotel? That would be kind of cool."

"Hell no, we ain't living in the hotel," King snapped.

"I'm sorry, Dad. Do you want me to go back with Mom?" Knight's voice softened.

King looked up and saw the worry in his handsome son's 14-year-old face. "No. Stop tripping." He reached over and gave him a hug and playfully hit him on the head. "You trying to chuck the deuces on me, kid?"

"No one says that anymore, Dad. I just figured . . . maybe now isn't a good time for me to be here. And maybe you want me to go."

"I don't want you to go," King told him. "Go outside. You can even bounce your ball!"

Knight grinned and went rushing toward the door. "Cool!"

"Be careful!" King called behind him. For a second, he thought maybe his son had a point. Maybe this wasn't the right time for his son to be staying with him. Not that he had a problem taking custody of Knight, but it was all so sudden. Melissa suggested they postpone Knight's arrival to California to stay with King after she heard about the fire, but he told her he could handle it. Now he wasn't so sure. He had to not only deal with the aftermath of the damage to his home, but also make sure that his estranged wife was okay.

The first stop King made when his plane touched down was to the hospital to check on Scorpio. He assured Scorpio that he would make sure she was taken care of and everything was going to be okay. But now, standing in the middle of what used to be his living room, he didn't know what he was going to do.

"Hello," a voice called, and the front door opened.

King turned around and hoped his mind was playing tricks on him. "Yolanda, what are you doing here?" he asked.

"I'm here to see about my daughter's belongings and assess the damage to her home," Yolanda told him.

"You do know she hasn't lived here in almost a year, right?" King asked her. "There isn't much here that belongs to her."

"I know that her name is still on the deed to this property, so everything in here belongs to her as far as

I'm concerned. I don't care how long she hasn't lived here. And she was here when the fire started. Explain that." Yolanda looked him up and down.

King really didn't have an explanation. The fact that Scorpio was here in the house was just as much a mystery to him as the woman who Scorpio said started the fire. King didn't know who the woman could be, and so far, the authorities had yet to find her. He began to wonder if there really was a mystery woman. Scorpio admitted that both she and Malachi had been drinking and smoking weed before the fire. None of it made sense to him.

"Look, Yolanda, there is no need for us to be at odds, especially now when Scorp . . . I mean, Sarena needs us."

"Sarena doesn't need you! What does she need you for? There's nothing you can do for her. You're a washed-up musician with no money, a bunch of illegitimate kids, and a whole bunch of baby mama drama." Yolanda's words cut him like a knife, and he could feel his anger rising.

"I think you should leave," King told her, trying to remain calm.

"I'll leave when you do. This is my daughter's house!"

"I don't have time to deal with you and your craziness," King said, shaking his head. He considered calling the police, but the last thing he needed was even more publicity about this entire ordeal. Instead, he turned, carefully stepping across the charred, wet floors, and headed upstairs in an effort to get away.

There was still a stench of smoke in the air, but the upstairs of his home wasn't nearly as damaged as downstairs. The garage, which was where the fire started, along with the kitchen, downstairs bathroom, living room, and foyer, seemed to have sustained most of the damage. The door to his bedroom was closed, and he took a moment and closed his eyes before opening it.

Relief consumed him when he stepped inside and saw that everything was still intact. His custom California king bed was still made, with the exception of a blanket on top. His bottles of cologne, seventy-inch plasma television, and numerous watches on the dresser were untouched. The high-tech keyboard in the sitting area of his bedroom was exactly as he left it, along with his designer headphones and his Mac computer.

King's eyes spotted a pair of Jordans near the bed that he knew weren't his. Even though Scorpio's feet were a women's size eleven, the sneakers were too big for her. Not to mention, they weren't really her style. They had to belong to Malachi Douglas, the guy who was in the house with Scorpio when the fire started. King looked around, checking to see if there was anything else that didn't belong and hoping to maybe find some clue as to why the famous bishop's son had even been in his home. His estranged wife was not a religious woman, so he couldn't figure out the connection. The only other clothing lying on the floor was a tiny dress, a discarded thong, and a pair of red bottom heels. Those he easily recognized as belonging to Scorpio.

King walked into the huge closet on the right side of the bedroom. When the house was built, they agreed that they would have identical closets that were the same size. For months, Scorpio's had remained empty. Now there were three Louis Vuitton suitcases sitting in the center. There were a few items hanging in the once-empty 350-square foot space. King slowly inhaled her scent, which never left even after she did. Although his own closet was filled beyond capacity, he still never put any items into her space. It was as if he subconsciously wanted her to come home, and with her luggage there, it looked as if she finally had. Maybe, just maybe . . .

"Where are her things? What did you do with them?"

King cringed without turning around. "Right there."

Yolanda brushed past him and looked around the empty space. "Where?"

King pointed at the suitcases and the hanging dresses. "There."

"Where are the rest of her clothes? Her shoes? Her jewelry?"

King didn't answer her. Instead, he walked past her and went down the steps and out the front door. Yolanda was making him more and more upset, and he could feel his stress level rising. He decided it would be best if he just left and came back later. He climbed into his Acura SUV and was about to pull off when he remembered his son. He turned off the ignition and hopped out. He looked around but didn't see Knight.

Damn it, where is he?

Listening for the sound of the basketball, King didn't hear it, and he rushed back inside, yelling, "Knight! Where are you?"

He continued through the house, not caring about the drenched floor ruining his shoes and splashing on his clothes as he stepped. He snatched opened the door leading to the backyard, hoping to find Knight. The yard was empty with the exception of a lone duck floating in the swimming pool. He jogged across the yard into the gazebo, but still, no Knight. King continued calling out his son's name, his voice becoming more and more panicked as he tried to think of where he could be.

"Knight! KJ!" He used variations of the nicknames his son had.

King's heart began pounding as his head filled with thoughts of Amber Alerts, pedophiles, and horror stories of abducted kids. He rushed back through the house and out the front door to his car, where he had left his cell phone. He pondered who he should call first: the police or Melissa. There was no way he could explain this.

"Dad! I'm right here!"

He heard his son's voice in the distance and glanced up. Knight was a little ways down the street, headed toward him, along with a woman and two other boys who looked to be a couple years younger than his son.

King waited until his son got in front of the house before he began yelling at him. "Boy, didn't I tell you to wait for me out front! I been calling your name for the past fifteen damn minutes!"

"You said go outside and bounce my ball. That's what I was doing. Then I saw these guys, and so I walked down there." Knight pointed at the two boys who now stood beside him.

"Hi, I'm Lisa," the woman greeted him as she walked up. "These guys belong to me."

"Nice to meet you. This guy belongs to me!" King affectionately smacked the back of his son's head.

"Dad, this is Mike and Aaron. They live down the street."

"Whoa, my mom has your CDs," Aaron said. He looked to be a little younger than his brother. "She always talks about how the Hot Boyz was the first concert she and my aunt ever went to, and you were her favorite one and the best dancer!"

"Aaron!" Lisa quickly put her hand over her son's mouth, and King laughed at her embarrassment. He could hear the Southern drawl when she talked, so he knew she wasn't from around there.

"It's okay," King laughed. "I was back in the day. Those were the good old days."

"They were." Lisa nodded. "And I am such a fan, but my son didn't have to put me on blast."

"I told them I'm moving here, Dad. Now I have friends in the neighborhood! Well, when we get the house fixed."

Knight gestured toward the front of their home. There was still yellow police tape hanging across the front.

"I'm so sorry about the fire," Lisa told him. "How is your wife, uh, Scorpio?"

"She's doing a lot better. Lucky to be alive, and we're glad that she is," King said.

"Is there a lot of damage inside the house?"

"Not upstairs in my room!" Knight answered. "Or the game room either. We can just stay upstairs and eat out. Dad never let anyone hang out downstairs anyway."

"Boy, be quiet. There's no electricity or running water. We just have to find somewhere to stay temporarily until we get things straightened out. I am meeting with the insurance company this week. We'll probably have to just rent a spot for a minute," King told her.

"What about over there?" Michael pointed to a house down the street.

It was the first house King and Scorpio toured when they first visited Harrington Point. King loved it and had been tempted to purchase it, but he and Scorpio decided to have their home custom built. "That house is for sale, not for rent." King laughed.

"Maybe they'll rent it to us, Dad."

"It has been sitting there for sale for quite some time." Lisa shrugged.

Their conversation was interrupted by a loud thud. They all turned around to see Yolanda standing in the doorway, listening. King didn't know how long she had been there. She bent over to pick up one of the large Louis Vuitton suitcases she had with her. King didn't move, but Knight along with the other two boys rushed over to help her.

"Hello," Lisa greeted her.

Yolanda barely spoke back and gave the three young men a muffled, "Thanks," as they helped her carry the bags to the sedan parked in the driveway. She popped open the trunk of her car, and they hoisted the bags inside.

"I'll be back for the remainder of my daughter's things," Yolanda said just before she climbed into the car.

King just shook his head. He didn't know what things she was talking about and didn't care.

"Who was that?" Knight asked.

They watched her drive off, and then she paused for a second before she continued down the street.

"Nobody important," King told him.

"Dad, Miss Lisa says they are having a cookout for all the neighbors this weekend and we're invited. Can we go?"

"I don't know. We'll see. I gotta figure this living situation out first." King sighed.

"You guys can stay with us. We have plenty of room!" Aaron offered.

"I'm sure he appreciates the offer, Aaron . . ." Lisa shook her head.

"Dad, I'm telling you, call about the house across the street," Knight said.

"It's worth a try." Lisa shrugged. "And you are invited to our home for the cookout this weekend."

"Maybe Knight can spend the weekend," Michael suggested. "Right, Mom?"

"Can I, Dad?" Knight pleaded.

Lisa said, "I don't have a problem with him staying over if it's okay with his dad. I know you have a lot to deal with right now."

King hesitated before answering. Although he didn't have a problem with it, he knew he would at least have to run it by Melissa. Or did he? She had given him full control over their son, so ultimately it was his decision. Still, he did need to think about it. Their new neighbors seemed friendly enough, but they were still strangers.

"We'll see," he said.

"Well, even if he doesn't sleep over, he can come and hang out when he gets out of school on Friday," Lisa offered.

"Shit, school." The words slipped from King's lips before he could stop them. "I gotta enroll him. I don't even know what school is around here."

Lisa laughed. "Well, I don't know about the public school, but my kids go to Wentworth Academy. It's a really good school, and they enjoy it."

"We gotta wear uniforms though," Aaron said. "And we gotta go to church."

"Chapel," Lisa corrected him.

"I'm used to that. My mom made me go to private school my whole life. But Dad said when I get to high school next year, I can go to public and experience real life." Knight nodded at his dad.

"Maybe," King told him. "Wentworth Academy. Okay, I've gotta remember that."

"Why don't you finish up here, then stop by our place when you're done? I can give you all the information on the school," Lisa told him.

"Sounds like a plan. Come on, Knight. Help me grab some stuff from inside before it gets dark. You know our lights are cut off," King said jokingly.

"I'll see you guys in a little while," Lisa told him, then headed back down the street with her sons. There was something about her that made King instantly like her. She was warm and inviting, and her demeanor made him feel better.

King grabbed the basketball from Knight and played keep away for a few minutes before they went back inside to grab a few of King's things. When they finished, he secured his damaged residence as best he could, reminding himself to have the locks and alarm code changed as soon as possible. He had a feeling that things between him and Yolanda were about to get ugly.

When they arrived at the Wells home, they were welcomed with a home-cooked meal of pork chops, macaroni and cheese, yams, greens, homemade biscuits, and peach cobbler. King had the best time laughing and talking with Lisa and her husband, Marcus. They were a great couple. He also met Marcus's younger brother Sam, who seemed to be cool, and there was also their adorable 8-year-old daughter Cocoa. When it was time to go, King was looking forward to returning the following weekend for the cookout. Lisa also gave him an armful of departing gifts, which included plates of leftovers, dessert, and a basket of goodies to take to the hospital for Scorpio, along with the promise to meet him at Wentworth Academy the following morning to assist with getting Knight registered.

"Dad," Knight said as they drove down the street.

"What?" King glanced over at his son.

"Today was a good day. I'm glad I'm here."

"Me too, son." King smiled.

"Call about the house across the street," Knight said, drifting off to sleep.

King promised, "First thing tomorrow. Right after I enroll you in school."

As he looked over at his son, who looked very much like he did at that age, King knew that even with all of the chaos and confusion going on in his life, having his son by his side was the best decision he had made in a long time.

Chapter 17

Marcus Wells

"Man, that dude was cooler than a fan."

"Yeah, he was," Marcus said to Sam. They had just enjoyed dinner with their neighbor, King Douglas, member of the Hot Boyz and R&B superstar. Marcus tried his best to act like it was no big deal when he opened the front door and saw King and his son standing there. The truth was he was starstruck at first. He had gotten plenty of ladies back in the day while listening to the Hot Boyz. Hell, he could even credit them for helping him get as much ass as he did.

Back in the day, Marcus would create "Marcus's Magic Mood Mixtapes" featuring slow jams, most of which were sung by King Douglas and the Hot Boyz. Marcus would set his eyes on a certain young lady at school, flash his smile, flex his pecs, and stare into her eyes, convincing her that the tape he was putting in her hand was made just for her. And just like that, he had her. Within days after listening to the tape, he had the prized possession between her legs, too. The mixtape worked like a charm on all the girls, except one.

"Who woulda thought King Douglas would be chilling at your crib having dinner?" Sam shook his head. "Man, life is good, I tell ya, and it's about to get even better."

"How so?" Marcus asked.

"This meeting I set up for us. I'm telling you."

"What's this all about, Sam? What's the deal?"

Since his unexpected arrival at their home a few days ago, Sam had been talking nonstop about some big meeting he was scheduling, but wouldn't give him any specific details. Marcus knew it had to do with money, and although he told Sam over and over again that he wasn't interested in any investment deals, Sam wasn't trying to hear it. He and Lisa already had a financial planner who dealt with his share of the $97 million lottery winnings that he split with his brother.

Sam was adamant about Marcus coming to the meeting, and Marcus agreed to attend just as a support for his brother. There was no way he was going to be writing any checks though, that was for certain. Sam's unexpected visit was causing enough drama in their house. His wife was barely speaking to him, and it wasn't even his fault. She didn't seem to understand that Marcus was just as surprised as she was by Sam's arrival on their doorstep. Not only did Lisa despise his brother for multiple reasons, Sam's sudden appearance definitely complicated the plans for Lisa's sister Shar and her best friend Kendra to come and hang out for a couple of days, which pissed Lisa off even more.

Marcus was hoping that after the wonderful evening they had with King as their dinner guest, Lisa's good mood would continue into their bedroom. He told his wife not to worry about the kitchen, he would handle it, and after he made sure the kids were settled, he directed her to go upstairs and relax. She didn't have anything smart to say and didn't give him any dirty looks, so Marcus took that as a good sign.

"Have you considered hiring a housekeeper to do that?" Sam asked.

Marcus looked up from the dishes he was loading into the dishwasher. "Do what?"

"Clean, cook, wash dishes, do laundry, sweep, mop. You do know you're a millionaire now. You can afford to pay someone to do that stuff." Sam pointed at the food waiting to be put away and the additional dirty pots on the stove.

"Now you know damn well my wife ain't gonna let nobody come in this kitchen and cook nothing. This right here is her sanctuary, man. I wouldn't even suggest that to her."

"Okay, then the other stuff. You love her so much, you shouldn't want her mopping floors and washing windows. She deserves better than that. And you talking about you want another baby, too? You better hire someone and lighten the load. What's wrong with you?"

Marcus thought about what his brother was saying. Maybe Sam was right. When they first bought the house, Darby, the real estate agent, suggested hiring household staff, but Marcus never considered it. They did everything themselves, with the exception of the pool service. Marcus even did his own landscaping. In the grand scheme of things, their home was so big, it never seemed to get messed up. The kids played upstairs in the game room, and everyone had their own space, which they kept clean. Lisa did all the housework and never complained. Maybe hiring someone to help around the house would be a good idea, especially if they planned on having another baby.

"You have a point." Marcus tossed his brother a dish towel. "But until then we can handle it ourselves."

"Man, I would have a maid and a damn butler up in here. Oh, and a nanny. I wouldn't lift a finger and Lisa wouldn't either. I tell you what: how about I treat you guys to a housekeeper?" Sam offered. "Maybe then Lisa would stop being so damn mean to me."

Marcus shook his head and exhaled loudly. "Sam, we don't need a housekeeper right now, and if we do decide to get one, we can afford to pay for it ourselves. And another thing, I'm going to need for you to please stay out of Lisa's way while you're here at the house. Please."

"I haven't even said anything to her, man. I can't believe she's still tripping. Hell, me and Kendra ain't even together no more. How long is she gonna be mad at me?" Sam took a cigar out of his pocket and was about to light it. Marcus went to stop him, but before he could say anything, he heard his wife's voice.

"What the hell do you think you're doing?"

"Hey, don't do that. You know we don't allow smoking in our house," Marcus scolded his brother while he silently prayed Lisa hadn't heard their conversation before she walked in.

"My bad. Damn, I forgot," Sam apologized as he put the cigar and lighter back into his pocket.

"You forget a lot of stuff, don't you?" Lisa glared at him.

"What is that supposed to mean?" Sam asked.

"You forgot that your brother was married when you invited that ho over to the house that time. Oh, and more importantly, you obviously forgot that I don't like your black—" Lisa was talking so fast that her words were running together, and she looked like she was ready to assault him at any moment.

"Baby, baby." Marcus stepped in front of her just in case she happened to take a swing at Sam, who seemed amused by her anger instead of concerned.

"Come on, Lisa Lisa. Why are you always tripping?" Sam smirked.

"Sam, chill," Marcus said over his shoulder. "As a matter of fact, why don't you head out to the backyard? You can smoke there."

"Fine." Sam shrugged and eased past them as he walked toward the back door leading to outside.

When he was gone, and they were alone, Marcus stared at his wife. "Lisa, baby—"

"Don't, Marcus." Lisa glared at her husband.

"I know, and I'm sorry. I'm gonna talk to him, I promise." Marcus told her.

She continued to stare at Marcus for a second, then without saying anything else, she turned and walked away. He listened to her footsteps as she went up the stairs, and he waited a few moments before finally going out the same door as Sam. Outside, Marcus followed the trail of smoke that was coming from where Sam was seated near the pool, smoking his beloved cigar. The sun had set, and the night sky was clear and full of stars. A slight breeze chilled the warm air, causing Marcus to shudder a little. It was peaceful, and he paused to enjoy the scenery of the landscape before going over to join his brother.

"She still tripping for no reason?" Sam asked.

Marcus took a seat in the chair next to him. "Man, why do you keep doing this? I told you if you stayed here, you'd have to keep a low profile. You promised me."

"I have been keeping a low profile, Marcus. I stayed out of her way like you told me. All I wanted to do was smoke a cigar after dinner, that's it." Sam shrugged.

"In my house though, Sam? Come on, now," Marcus told him.

"I forgot, honestly, and I tried to apologize. It's like I can't catch a break with Lisa. No matter what I try to do, she flips out on me, and you know it. You'd think being a millionaire would've made her ass loosen up a bit." Sam took a long drag and slowly let it out, then he held out the cigar for his brother.

"Nah, I'm good." Marcus shook his head.

"The way she was acting, you woulda thought I was about to fire up a damn blunt." Sam laughed. "Which, by the way, I have upstairs if you need some. Lord knows Lisa does."

"That ain't funny, man." Marcus tensed up.

"Damn, why the hell is everyone so tense around here? You would think we would all be happy as hell right now and enjoying one another. We got more money than a platinum-selling rapper, but we not even enjoying it for real. We won that money together, me and you. And even before we won it, we had each other's backs. You think I enjoyed being back in Carolina without my brother to enjoy? No. That's why I came out here. I miss you, and despite her treating me like trash every time she sees me, I miss Lisa too, and the kids," Sam told him, his eyes now filled with tears.

Marcus felt bad. He didn't realize his leaving even mattered to him. "Sam, come on. It's not like that. I mean, we ain't leave because of you. You know that. It just got real dangerous for my family. You gotta remember it's just you, but I got a wife and kids to look out for, and I had to make sure they were safe."

"I get that." Sam nodded.

"This situation between you and Lisa though, I don't know," Marcus told him.

"Listen, I got a meeting in the city in an hour." Sam looked down at the diamond beveled watch on his arm that Marcus knew he probably paid to much for. "Let's make a deal."

"What kind of deal?" Marcus frowned.

"I agree to go stay at a hotel in the city. But I want you to agree to meet with this guy I was telling you about, the one with the business proposal," Sam told him.

Marcus was so glad to hear his brother offering to leave the house and go stay at a hotel that he would've agreed to damn near anything. "I'll meet with him, but I already told you I'm not interested in investing in any business right now. Lisa and I already have a financial advisor and a plan in place."

"I hear ya, but I'm telling you this plan is brilliant. I just want you to hear this guy out," Sam told him.

"Fine," Marcus said.

"Well, let me get inside and grab my shit before your wife comes out here and complains about me keeping you out here too long." Sam stood up.

"Just hit me up in the morning and let me know where you are," Marcus told him.

"I will. And hey, let Lisa know I'm really sorry I pissed her off. I really just wanted to spend some time with y'all and the kids, that's all," Sam said.

"I know. I'll talk to her." Marcus dapped his brother's hand, and they both walked back toward the house. Marcus hoped Sam's leaving would put Lisa at ease, especially with her sister and Sam's ex scheduled to arrive in a few days. He missed cuddling up to his wife in their California king bed, having her warm body next to his. When she was angry, she made sure there was plenty of space between them. He decided he would tell her Sam's leaving was his idea. Hopefully, she would be so relieved that she would reward him with some good ol' loving that he hadn't had since his brother's arrival two days ago.

Chapter 18

Riley

"Where are you going?" Eden yelled, startling Riley and causing her to jump.

"Oh, my God, don't you ever knock?" Riley gasped and asked, "And why are you yelling?"

"Because you got the music blasting and I wanted to make sure you heard me."

Riley reached for her phone, slightly turned down the music that was blasting from her Bluetooth speaker, then went back to posing in the full-length mirror she was standing in front of. Although she was satisfied with the mixed black-and-white ensemble she wore, consisting of a striped wrap shirt, floral print skirt, and polka-dot pumps, she felt overdressed for where she was going. She slipped out of the skirt and shoes, reached for a pair of black palazzo pants, and pulled them on.

"Does this look right, or do I look like a member of a chain gang?" she asked her sister.

"It looks cute. But you didn't answer me. Where are you going?" Eden asked.

"Out." Riley shrugged.

"Out where?"

"Out of the house."

"Riley, I'm serious," Eden stated.

"I am too." Riley laughed as she walked into her closet and settled on a pair of funky black flats to top off her

Bohemian chic outfit. She grabbed a black clutch and tossed her favorite tube of lipstick, her favorite lighter, and her wallet inside. Taking one final look at herself in the mirror, she exited her room and headed down the steps.

"Riley!"

Her sister was following her so close that when Riley stopped midway down the stairs, she bumped into her. "Eden, damn it!"

"Sorry. But if you would just stop and tell me . . ."

Riley continued to the bottom floor and finally stopped in the foyer. "Oh, my God, I'm just going out for a little while. I'm not going to do drugs, I'm not going to make another porn video, I'm just going out for a little while, that's it."

"How long is a little while?" Eden asked.

"As long as it needs to be. Can you please stop acting like you're my mother? I'm not a kid, and I can come and go as I please. You're worse than those damn wardens at rehab. If they couldn't keep tabs on me, you damn sure can't, and I don't need you to," Riley yelled as she snatched the front door open. Her dramatic exit was cut short by Peri, who was standing at the door, about to ring the bell.

"Am I early?" he asked.

"No, perfect timing," she told him.

He looked past her and waved. "Hey, Eden."

"Oh, hey, Peri. Riley didn't tell me she was going with you," Eden greeted him with a smile.

"I don't have to tell you anything, Eden. I wish you would chill." Riley rolled her eyes at her sister. She knew Eden was only being concerned, and she had every right to be, especially considering Riley's screwups over the past few months, but she was being borderline suspicious. It was getting on her nerves. "I'm going out, and it's no big deal."

"I know it isn't. I was just asking because you didn't mention anything about going out." Eden shrugged.

"I didn't mention it because Peri literally just called me a few minutes ago and told me to get dressed," Riley told her.

"Facts." Peri nodded. "And she's right, it really isn't a big deal. We're just going to a hookah spot a friend of mine owns. You should come with."

"No, I'm good," Eden said.

"You know she's a homebody." Riley shook her head. "Don't turn the alarm on, just lock the door."

"Okay. Have fun and be safe." Eden waved as they walked out the door.

"Don't wait up for me, Mom." Riley laughed.

"Why you do her like that?" Peri asked after they climbed into his Tesla parked in her driveway.

"Like what? I swear, she followed me around the past twenty minutes asking over and over where was I going. I wanted to swing on her," Eden said. "And I ain't had no smoke. She's lucky I didn't."

"Stop it," Peri screamed and cackled so hard that it made Riley laugh along with him.

"This is all your fault."

"Mine?" Peri asked, placing his hand on his chest.

"Yes, yours. I've been begging you to go out all week, and you said no, and now tonight you call and tell me to be ready because you're on your way. What's up with that?" Riley asked.

"Well, if you must know, we are on a mission."

"What kind of mission?"

"I got a call from a friend of mine who told me DJ Avenger is in town, and we're gonna go find him," Peri said.

"DJ Avenger? For what?" Riley looked at him strangely.

"Because I have a client who wants him for her wedding. I've been trying like hell to reach him the professional way, but I can't even get a damn response."

"So you're stalking him? Must be one hell of a client." Riley gave him a side-eye.

"She is. Daddy is an oil tycoon, and money is no object." Peri winked. "My favorite kind of client."

"Liar. I know you very well, Peri, and your sudden urge to find DJ Avenger has nothing to do with a damn client. Now, why are we looking for him?" Riley asked.

"Okay, fine. Because I'm just curious to meet him and find out if he's just as sexy in person as he is in his pics. I know that sounds crazy—"

"Say no more, friend. You know I understand craziness and strategically locating someone." Riley gave him an impressed look. Normally, she was the one having to convince Peri to help her stalk someone she found herself interested in. This was a nice change, and she was excited.

"Strategically locate?" Peri laughed.

Riley touched the iPad screen attached to the dash of the car, then said, "Siri, play DJ Avenger."

The screen lit up, and a song began to play. Riley turned up the volume, sat up in her seat, and loudly sang along with Peri. It had been a long time since she'd been out and had a good time, and tonight seemed like a great night to make up for lost time. By the time they arrived at Inhale, their destination, she was hype. It was an unassuming, low-key spot, and had there not been a simple sign on the door, most people wouldn't have even known it was there. Inside though was a lavish atmosphere of exotic sophistication. Sultry lighting, plush seating, and moody music greeted them. Even the servers were beautiful. The crowd was thick, but it wasn't cramped, and everyone seemed to be relaxed and having a good time. Peri took her hand, and they headed straight for the VIP area.

"What's up, Maurice?" Peri greeted the handsome man who was seated in the booth that was roped off.

"Peri, my friend. It's so good to see you. Come, join me." The man motioned for the muscular security guard to let them in. The two other women sitting beside him moved over, even though there was plenty of room. Neither one of them seemed pleased at Peri and Riley's arrival, but she didn't care. She wasn't thinking about them.

"Maurice, this is my friend Riley," Peri introduced her.

"Ms. Rodriguez, the pleasure is mine. I'm somewhat of a fan," Maurice told her. Riley couldn't help staring at his smooth olive skin, silky hair, and perfect teeth. He was one of the most beautiful men she'd ever seen, and she wondered if he was Persian.

"Nice to meet you, Maurice." She held her hand out, and he kissed it.

Once they were seated, he motioned for one of the waitresses. "What do you drink?"

"Patrón and cranberry," Peri said.

"I'll take a glass of white wine." Riley shrugged.

"Look at you being all classy and shit," Peri teased.

"Bring a bottle of Patrón and Riesling," Maurice instructed. "And your shisha?"

"What do you suggest?" Peri asked.

"My personal favorite is what I call Miami Nights," Maurice told him.

"Sounds good to me," Riley said when Peri looked over at her for her approval.

The waitress nodded and held Riley's gaze for a second. Riley shifted uncomfortably and finally blinked away, relieved when the young girl walked off. She had become accustomed to people staring when they recognized her her entire life. But now she wondered if the stares were because they'd seen the leaked video.

"So, I heard DJ Avenger was coming through, Maurice." Peri leaned back. "I need to holler at him right quick."

"Who told you that?" Maurice said.

"Is he for real? He's coming here?" the two women asked excitedly.

"You know my place is the new hot spot in town, so I wouldn't be surprised." Maurice shrugged and took a pull from the glass canister sitting on the table in front of him. "Everyone wants to Inhale."

"Come on, Maurice. I know his people called and gave you the heads-up already." Peri tilted his head in a knowing manner.

Riley had never seen her best friend so pressed about anything. Granted, DJ Avenger was popping these days, but she didn't understand Peri's sudden interest. Although he said it was for his client, she knew it had to be something more.

"Here you are." The waitress returned, carrying a large tray with their items. She set everything up for them and then placed a shot in front of Riley.

"I didn't order this," Riley told her, confused.

"From the gentleman over there." The waitress motioned toward another booth across the aisle. "He's been asking about you since you walked in."

Riley realized the staring earlier had nothing to do with the horrific video, but because of the man's interest and inquiry. She sat up to get a better look at who she was referring to and saw two men seated. One of them raised a glass at her when he saw her looking.

"What is it?" Riley looked down at the glass. "I mean, I can't drink it, but I'm just wondering."

"Louis," the girl said matter-of-factly.

"Wait, did you say Louis?" Peri sat up on the edge of his seat. Riley couldn't blame him. The guy had sent over a shot of cognac that had to cost at least $125.

"Yep," she said.

"Tell him I said thank you, but I can't drink it," Riley told the waitress. Then she turned and waved at the guy.

"Who the hell is that?" Peri asked Maurice.

"I am not sure who the man is who sent the drink, but the other guy is Bruce Crawford, one of my regulars. He is an investment broker and very successful. I don't know the guy he's with. He's not from around here, but if he's with Bruce, trust me, he's wealthy," Maurice said. "Bruce only hangs with seven-figure associates."

Suddenly, the two women who were moments earlier gushing over Maurice now turned their attention to the other booth. It took everything for Riley not to burst out laughing at their obvious thirst. Although seven figures was impressive to her as well, she would never show it.

The waitress went to pick the drink up, but Peri stopped her and picked it up. "She may not drink it, but I damn sure can."

"So you're just gonna drink in his face like that, Peri? You ain't gonna play it off or nothing?" Riley laughed.

"I sure am." Peri took a swallow and closed his eyes.

Riley looked back over at the two men and noticed they did not seem pleased at all. "Uh, Peri, I think they're pissed."

"No worries, I got this." Peri stood up, adjusted the floral blazer he wore, then walked over to the booth.

"Oh, God. Please don't let them knock him out." Riley's eyes widened, and she watched with anticipation. Maurice poured her a glass of wine, and she took a gulp.

"Bruce is a good guy. He won't beat him up. I'm certain of it," Maurice told her.

A few minutes later, Peri came back with Bruce and the other guy. "Riley, this is Bruce and—"

"Sam, Sam Wells, and I have been dying to meet you," the guy said with an accent that let her know he definitely wasn't from the West Coast. His eyes were mysterious, and he grinned at her mischievously. The look he was giving her screamed trouble. It was one she had given men all the time. But instead of it being a red flag warning her to stay away, it was magnetic and drew her to him. It had been a long time since she'd had fun, and Sam seemed like he was just what she needed.

Chapter 19

Eden

Although her sister's last-minute plans to hang out caused some concern for Eden, it also gave her an opportunity of her own. Neil had asked to see her because he had something to tell her. She'd been trying to figure out an excuse to leave the house herself. The only reason she'd been questioning her sister about where she was going was that she needed to know how long she'd be gone. Once she found out she was going out with Peri, Eden knew she'd have a few hours to spend with Neil. She took a shower, got dressed in record time, then headed to his condo.

"Damn, you look sexy," he said when he opened the door.

Eden glanced down at her outfit, which consisted of leggings, a T-shirt, and sneakers, and she smirked. "You're only saying that because you want me to give you some ass."

"I mean, yeah, I do want that, but that's not why I said it. You do look sexy," he said, then kissed her softly as she stepped through the door. Neil put his hands around her waist and guided her into the living room. The lights were dim, soft jazz was playing, and a bottle of champagne, already poured into two glasses, and a plate of fruit and chocolate were sitting on the coffee table.

"Oh, you really want some ass." Eden turned and looked at him.

"Stop saying that. It's turning me on." Neil laughed and kissed her again. "But, baby, I got some big news. You're not gonna believe this."

"Whatever it is, it must be good because you are damn near glowing. You're not pregnant, are you?" She feigned a shocked look and put her hand on her chest.

It was Neil's turn to smirk as he handed her a glass of the bubbly liquid. "Funny."

"I'm serious," Eden told him. "Okay, so if we're not celebrating your being pregnant, then what are we celebrating?"

"I had a meeting today with a director friend of mine. He just got hired for a major motion picture," Neil told her.

She'd never seen him act like this. Normally he was mellow and laid-back, but tonight he was damn near giddy. His excitement was contagious, and she was now anxious to hear what it was he had to tell her. "Okay, okay. And?" Eden asked.

"And he wants me to be his director of photography," Neil announced.

"Oh, my God. Baby, are you serious? Oh, my God," Eden screamed.

Neil lifted her into his arms and twirled her around, almost causing her to drop her glass. "Baby, I'm serious. Can you believe this?" he said, putting her down.

"Yes, I can believe it. This is what you've been wanting for so long and what you've been working hard for. You deserve this, and I'm so proud of you," Eden told him. Again, he took her into his arms, but this time it was to kiss her fully on the mouth. When they finally pulled away, she asked, "Okay, so what project is it? Tell me more."

He picked up his glass and took a sip. "It's a new movie being produced by . . . you ready?"

"Yes, I'm ready. Tell me."

"Bishop Walter Burke. *The* Bishop Walter Burke. And it's gonna be big, Eden. The movie is a historical fiction project based on this bestselling book called *For the Love of Thomas*. It's about Thomas Jefferson and—"

"Sally Hemmings." Eden finished his sentence and stared at him, her wide smile fading.

"You heard about it? I told you it's big." Neil nodded.

"Yeah, I read it, and so did Riley."

"Riley? She read it?" Neil seemed just as surprised as Eden had been to hear that Riley had read the book.

"Yeah, four times, and she heard about the movie, too. She wants the part." Eden swallowed hard.

"What part? Not the part of Sally. That's already going to Lauren Carmichael." Neil's eyebrows furrowed.

"Are you sure? That's just a rumor and not a done deal yet, right?" Eden asked, hoping that he would say the part was still open, remembering how intense her sister had been when discussing her aspirations to be the lead in the movie. Riley had been through so much over the past few years and seemed to be working hard on her sobriety and getting her life back on track, including her career. Eden was willing to do whatever she could to help her. And even though she was secretly sneaking around with Riley's ex, something that she wasn't proud of, that was still her sister, and she wanted to see her win. "Neil, you have to listen to me. She wants this bad."

Neil took her by the hand, led her to the sofa, and they both sat down. "Eden, baby, I don't think you understand how major of a project this is. We're talking Oscar potential. It's some heavy hitters making this happen. They even got Trey Money doing the soundtrack."

"Neil." Eden sighed, knowing where this conversation was heading. She took his glass from him and placed it, along with the one she was holding, on the table in front of them. "I get it."

"And, Eden, I'm not trying to be funny, because you know I love Riley and I admit she's one of the best actresses out here. But come on, this is a project being produced by a bishop, and Riley's reputation, especially what's going on now with that video—"

"What's going on with that video has nothing to do with her acting talent. It was a setup by that stupid rapper, Touché. And you said it yourself, she's one of the best actresses in the business," Eden responded and stared at him. "She's clean and sober. She's doing good. Neil, please just give her a chance."

"I'm not the director. That's not my call to make." Neil shook his head.

"You're the director of photography. You can make suggestions." Eden was not going to give up without a fight. Feeling the tears beginning to form in her eyes, she whispered, "Riley needs this. And we owe her."

Neil leaned over and pressed his forehead against hers. His fingers brushed the wetness from her cheeks. "Eden."

"Please, Neil," Eden pleaded softly and wrapped her arms around his neck.

"I'll see what I can do. But no promises."

Relieved, Eden closed her eyes and smiled slightly. "Thank you."

"I said no promises," Neil repeated.

The next thing she felt was his mouth on top of hers. They tasted one another for what seemed like an eternity, and she instantly became aroused. He leaned her back on the sofa, and as he pressed his body against hers, she could feel he was just as ready as she was. Her hands traveled under his shirt and along his back. His mouth moved from her mouth to her neck. He sucked on her collarbone gently as he lifted her shirt over her head and caressed her breasts through the lace bra she wore. Between the feel of his hands and the chill of the room, her nipples hardened, and she moaned.

Neil sat up, and for a moment she thought something was wrong, until she saw him reach to the table and grab one of the plump strawberries. He took a bite, then ran it along her chest, leaving a trail of juice leading to her mouth, where he held it for her to bite. She bit into it and savored the taste while enjoying the feel of his tongue that now traced the trail he'd created. He paused, and in one swift movement, removed her bra and freed her full bosom, taking her erect buds into his mouth and teasing them. Eden arched her back and reached between his legs, fumbling to undo his jeans to release his hardness, which she now desired. His hands met hers, and instead of helping her get what she was reaching for, he pulled her to her feet and took her into his bedroom, where he slowly took off the rest of her clothes before undressing himself.

"Damn, you look sexy," he said, his eyes full of lust.

Eden gave him a seductive grin as she played with her nipples and spread her legs so he could see just how wet she was. "You're just saying that because you want some ass."

"Damn right I do," Neil growled, pulling her toward the edge of the bed as he got on his knees. The sound of his moaning as he devoured her with his tongue sent her into another level of pleasure. She reached for something to grab, her hand finally finding a pillow, which she used to cover her face and scream into. Neil gently sucked her swollen clitoris in a rhythm that nearly sent her over the edge. She felt herself begin to erupt from deep within and tossed the pillow and tried to grab his head as she begged him to stop, but he refused. Instead, he continued tasting her until she climaxed, releasing herself onto his face.

"Ohhhhh, my God," she cried out.

"Mmmmm mmmmm good." Neil grinned as he finally removed his now-wet face from between her legs.

"Damn," was Eden's only response as she tried to stop panting and breathe normally. Her eyes went from his face down his chiseled chest and eventually landed on his manhood, standing at full attention in all of its glory. She eased off the bed and stood, now pushing him onto his back and into the position where she was lying moments before.

"Hold up," Neil said, reaching into his nightstand and taking out a gold foil-wrapped condom. Eden took it from him and tossed aside. He frowned slightly and asked, "What are you doing?"

"We don't need it yet," she told him, getting on her knees. "One good deed deserves another."

Neil leaned back and closed his eyes, letting out another moan as she took him into her mouth. Eden prepared herself to orally please him just as much as he had pleased her. Their lovemaking continued until they were both exhausted and satisfied.

"I swear, you are so amazing," he told her as he collapsed beside her.

"You can stop now. You already got the ass." She laughed.

"You really need to learn how to take a sincere compliment." Neil brushed a strand of hair that had fallen in her face and tucked it behind her ear. "I tell you you're sexy, beautiful, and amazing because you are all of those things and more, Eden."

Eden sat up, now feeling self-conscious. She knew he was being sincere, but it still made her feel funny. For most of her life, those were the words used to describe her sister, not her. Not that she wasn't all of those things, because she was, but she rarely heard them. The words that most people used when it came to her were smart, educated, nurturing. And she was fine with that because she was those things, too.

"I know." Eden shrugged. "I need to wash up."

"We can take a shower together," Neil told her. "I want to wash your beautiful, sexy, and amazing body. Come on."

After they showered, Neil pulled her close to him and wrapped her into his arms as they spooned. He talked to her about the meeting he'd had with the director. Eden was so happy for him and proud that he'd finally landed the job he'd wanted. But she was also still determined to get her sister a shot at the lead role, even if she didn't land it.

"Baby, just see if they'll consider her," Eden said, turning to face him.

"I will," Neil told her. "I'll bring her name up. We are having our first preproduction meeting next week. But I swear, if I do this, Eden, her ass can't be associated or involved in any more bullshit."

"She won't. I promise. I've been watching her like a hawk, and I'm telling you, she's good now. And I will make sure she stays good," Eden reassured him with a kiss. "Thank you."

She couldn't wait to let Riley know that there was a chance, although slight, for her to actually be considered for the part. She would have to call Riley's agent and tell him so he could be the one to tell her sister. There was no way she could tell her it was Neil who was making this happen for her. That would lead to too many questions that she wouldn't be able to answer.

"But we have something else to talk about, too," he said.

"What's that?"

"This is the biggest thing to happen to me, Eden. And when I walk that red carpet at the premier and those cameras are on me, I want you right there beside me on my arm."

Eden's eyes widened, and her breath got caught in her throat. "What are you saying, Neil?"

"I'm saying that we're going to have to tell Riley. I love you, and I'm not hiding you anymore. You're my lady, and I'm not hiding you from anyone anymore," he said, his eyes locking with hers. "We have to tell her. It's time."

Chapter 20

Bishop Walter Burke

"That sounds like a plan. I'll have my administrative assistant set up the meeting this week, and once you guys have come up with your final decisions for who you'd like to read, send them over and I'll take a look. I don't think this situation will affect the project at all, and we can move forward with the production schedule as planned. I will speak with you before the end of the week." Walter hung up the phone and began sifting through the folders on his desk.

"I know that call wasn't about what I think it was."

Olivia's voice startled him. He looked up and saw that she was standing in the middle of the study. He'd been so focused on the phone call that he hadn't realized she'd come in.

"Hey, sweetheart, what are you doing sneaking up in here?" he sat back in his chair and asked.

"Answer my question, Walter," Olivia said, taking a step closer to the desk where he was sitting. The room was massive, albeit smaller than his office at the church, which was where he conducted church business and had meetings. This was his study, designed specifically for sermon and Bible study preparation. There was a large mahogany desk, a comfortable leather chair and matching sofa, warm lamps, and a rug that covered most of the hardwood floor. Bookshelves held several Bibles, periodicals, reference books on leadership, preaching, theology, and commentaries. On the soft green walls, there were framed photos of his family and his favorite scriptures, not just for decor but for psychological reasons, reminding him of his "why." And then there was his coveted chipping and putting green located next to his desk, which he used quite frequently. Walter didn't need a man cave. To him, this was much better.

"What exactly are you asking?" He gave her an innocent smile, hoping her tone would lighten.

"Don't try to be coy," she warned him. "You can't be serious. I know you can't possibly be working when our son is lying in the hospital, fighting for his life. You can't be."

He looked at her emphatically shaking her head at him, and he knew it was going to take more than a smile to lighten her mood. "O'la, don't be like that. I know Malachi's in the hospital—"

"I can't tell," she interrupted him.

"But I also know I have a church to lead," he said, completing his statement.

"That phone call had nothing to do with church, and you know it." She glared at him. "You have an entire staff of ministry leaders and administrators to rely on to help take care of your ministry."

She was right, but he had no intention of telling her that, especially when doing so would probably make her even more upset than she already was.

"I also have other responsibilities and obligations I've committed to that have to be handled. They may not be directly related to Greater Works, but they are still important," he said. "There are a lot of moving pieces to getting this project done, Olivia, and a lot of key people involved. You know how hard I've been working on making this happen."

"I don't care if Jesus Christ Himself is involved. Nothing is more important than our son right now. Whatever meetings, conference calls, or anything else you're thinking about having ain't happening," Olivia snapped. "I called Bridgette and made sure she cleared your calendar until further notice. Preaching on Sundays in one thing, but outside work is another. Our family is in crisis right now."

Olivia turned and walked out of the study, and Walter jumped up and headed after her. He caught her just as she made it into the foyer and was about to walk up the stairs.

"You're being ridiculous, Olivia. I understand your being concerned, but you need to understand my position too. I have a family to support, including Malachi, and that includes making sure his medical bills are taken care of, and he has the best medical care available," he told her. He noticed her arms, which were folded across her chest, relax a little.

He added, "We don't know the extent of his injuries, but I do know he will wake up. And when he does, we will be prepared no matter what. He's possibly going to need around-the-clock care, medical equipment, therapy, and that's fine. He will have everything he needs, because I'm doing my part even while he's in that coma. I'm preparing, because the same way the church goes on, so does business. I'm making sure he has a home to come to when he's released. And I'm making sure you won't have to worry about anything other than him, the same way you've been doing. You know I've always taken care of this family, and that ain't gonna change, O'la. Everybody has to do their part. Your part is to go and be by his side. Speaking of which, I thought you were at the hospital."

"I was, but Micah is on his way to the hospital. Besides, Malachi had a visitor, so I left." Olivia told him.

Walter frowned and sat up in his chair. "Who's there? It better not be Jerry, because if it is—"

"Calm down, Walter. It's not Jerry. It's his friend Trey."

"Oh." Walter relaxed. He hadn't heard that name in a while. Trey and Malachi had been friends for years, and although he wasn't too thrilled to hear that his son's partying friend was there, he was glad it wasn't Jerry.

"Speaking of Jerry, he's been trying to reach you. You're going to have to talk to him at some point," Olivia said.

"There's nothing for us to talk about unless he's ready to stop lying to me about Malachi and why the hell he signed off on his prison release and said nothing to us about it," Walter said. "I don't have time to deal with liars."

"Who's a liar?" Micah asked as he walked into the study.

"Micah, what are you doing here? I thought you were headed to the hospital?" Olivia frowned.

"I am. I was waiting on Adrienne. She's stopping here on her way to the cookout down the street," Micah said.

"What cookout?" Walter asked.

"The one the neighbor invited us to," Olivia answered. "We can't go, so I asked her to attend on our behalf. But had I known having her do so would have caused you to not go be with your brother—"

"It didn't, Mom, and I'm heading out. I just wanted to see her before I left, that's all," Micah tried to explain.

"Don't you see her enough?" Olivia asked. "And can't you see her later? I wasn't going to be gone that long, Micah."

"Olivia, calm down. Malachi is fine. You said yourself that Trey was there with him," Walter told her.

"Trey? Trey Foster?" Micah seemed as surprised as Walter had been.

"Yeah," Olivia said.

"I'm surprised," Micah said.

"Why's that? He and Malachi have always been close." Olivia turned to face Micah.

"Because he's big time now, that's all. I guess I figured he wouldn't have time," Micah told them.

"They're friends. I don't care how big time he is," Olivia said. "Trey's not like that."

"What do you mean, 'big time'? Is he selling drugs? See, this is why I told you we needed to make a visitation list for Malachi, Olivia. He's only been out of jail a few days, and already he's been in a fire, and he's being visited by drug dealers." Walter shook his head.

"He isn't selling drugs, Walter. He does something with music," Olivia told him.

"Yeah, Dad. Trey's a big-time music producer now. He was even nominated for a Grammy. Besides, drugs were never his thing. That was—" The doorbell rang, interrupting Micah's sentence. He walked over and opened the door, greeting Adrienne with a kiss as she entered. "Hey, sweetie."

"Hey, you. Hey, Bishop, First Lady." Adrienne gave each of them a hug.

"Okay, she's here. Now can you leave?" Olivia asked Micah. "Or I can just go back up there and be with him. It's no big deal if you all need to spend some time together."

"O'la!" Walter wondered if she realized how rude she sounded, which was very much out of her character. But he also knew if he'd pointed it out, she wouldn't care. The only thing that mattered to her was Malachi.

"Did I do something wrong?" Adrienne asked with a worried look.

"No, baby, you didn't." Micah put his arm around his fiancée's neck. "Mama just needs some rest, and I need to get to the hospital."

"Oh, okay." Adrienne nodded. "Well, I just wanted to stop and speak before going down the street. I wish you were going with me so I wouldn't have to go by myself."

"He can," Olivia said.

"He can't. Olivia, you need to go upstairs and lie down." Walter walked over to his wife and looked into her tired yet beautiful face. She was still the most amazing woman he'd ever seen, and he was very much in love. He hated seeing her so stressed and exhausted. He touched her arm, but she pulled away.

"No, I'm fine. You're doing your part, and I'll do mine. I'll go and be with him since everyone else has more important things to deal with right now. Walter, you go work on your new movie and, Micah, you can go and be with Adrienne. I'm going to be with my son." Olivia stormed out of the room.

"Mom," Micah yelled.

"I'm sorry." Adrienne's voice was barely above a whisper, and she looked as if she was about to cry.

"No need to apologize," Walter said as he gave her a reassuring nod.

"It's my fault." Micah sighed. "I shoulda just left when I texted her. I didn't think she was leaving right then."

"You go ahead and go with Adrienne. I'll go, and it will be fine," Walter told him.

"You have to work on your sermon, don't you?" Micah asked.

"It's fine. I'll work on it later," Walter said. "You two go ahead and enjoy yourselves."

"I feel horrible," Adrienne said.

"It's fine. You did nothing wrong, and neither did Micah," Walter said with a simper in his eye. "I know my wife very well, and she did all of that simply because she wanted to go and be with your brother all along."

Chapter 21

Scorpio

"Girl, you know we were scared as hell, right?" Marcelo said.

"Hell, I was scared too," Scorpio told him, enjoying the feel of the brush he was putting through her hair. Although she still felt like crap, she was determined not to look like it. She'd finally been moved from ICU, and one of the nurses relented and allowed her to see herself in a small hand mirror. She was appalled. There was a slight bruise on the side of her face and dark circles under her eyes, and her hair looked like an unkempt, raggedy mess. Reaching Marcelo, one of her best friends who also happened to be her makeup artist and hair stylist, was her priority. Unfortunately, she didn't have her cell phone with her at the hospital. But Dina, her agent, came to check in on her and make sure her security detail was taken care of. She made the call to Marcelo, and once she was able to reach him, it didn't even take him an hour to get to the hospital to hook her up.

"We kept trying to come up here and see you. But they said you couldn't have any visitors, per your family's request. I'm gonna cuss King's ass out when I see him," Marcelo said with an attitude. "His ass knows that we are your family. Hell, we've been more family than he's been to you over the past year."

Scorpio was grateful for Marcelo's loyalty, but she knew she had to explain that he was angry at the wrong person. "It wasn't King who did that."

"Huh? Who was it then?"

"Yolanda," Scorpio told him.

"Yolanda who? Your Yolanda? As in your mother, Yolanda?" Marcelo cocked his head to the side and moved so he could face her. She couldn't help admiring the crisp, bright green button-down shirt he wore with a pair of jeans and Gucci loafers. He was heavyset, but that didn't stop him from being one of the best-dressed men she knew, and he was quite handsome. His locs were pulled up into a messy bun on top of his head. And at first glance, one wouldn't even know he was gay. But once he opened his mouth and his spunky attitude came out, there was no questioning it.

Scorpio nodded. "Yep, that Yolanda."

"Shit, let me hurry up and get the hell outta here. I don't need them kinda problems in my life," he said as he started gathering up the hair and makeup products that he had laid out on the bed tray.

"Marcelo, stop it. You're tripping." Scorpio laughed.

"No, you're tripping. I love you, Scorp. God knows it, and so do you. But I do not have the energy or mental space to deal with your mother. She is . . . well, you know how she is." Marcelo told her. He then yelled out of the room, "Cheddar, your ass ain't say nothing either. See how you do?"

Cheddar, who'd been posted up outside of Scorpio's room since she'd been moved from ICU the day before, poked his head in the door. "I didn't want to ruin the surprise."

"Calm down, Marcelo. She's out and won't be back for a while." Scorpio laughed.

"What the hell ever." Marcelo rolled his eyes as he picked up the brush and returned it to her head. His touch was a little more forceful than he realized and she flinched. "Oh, Scorp, I'm so sorry."

"It's okay." Scorpio grimaced. It seemed as if the pain was now shooting down her neck and through the entire left side of her body, which was the side where she sustained most of her injuries. "Did you bring the flat iron?"

"It's not okay. And I'm not putting heat anywhere near you, heffa. Ain't you tired of fire? I'm 'bout to slick this stuff back, and you'll be fine."

"Ugh, well, what are we going to do about covering these bruises?" she asked him.

"We're going to let them heal, that's what we're gonna do," Marcelo replied. "You look fine. Why are you tripping?"

"I don't look fine, and you know it. And I'm tripping because I need for people to see that I'm okay. Dina is gonna get me a new phone, but until then I need for you to take a pic of me and post it on your page and tag me so that people can see that I'm okay."

"What's the big rush?" Marcelo asked.

"Look, Dina told me they're postponing the swimsuit shoot, since I'm gonna be in here for a couple of days, then make a decision about the upcoming schedule. But I already know what the deal is. I'm sure I'm going to be replaced, and I don't want that to happen."

Marcelo gave her an empathetic look and sighed. "Girl, don't even worry about any of that. You need to focus on getting well."

"Oh, I'm doing that. But just tell me what you've heard. Who are they considering? Probably that bitch Farah, huh?" Scorpio asked, referring to another model who'd been on the rise, mainly because she was sleeping her way through the industry with both males and females. "Who is she screwing to get my spot?"

"It's not her. But I'm telling you, you don't need to be thinking about that right now. Besides, it's one shoot, not the end of your career."

"Don't act like you don't know how this game goes. And since when are you so passive? Hell, you're normally the one telling me let's get this money and show my face to the world. What's changed?" Scorpio frowned.

Marcelo paused and stared at her. "Scorp, because I almost lost my best fucking friend in the world, that's what changed. Do you know how scared I was, and then to have them refuse to let me see you or give us any updates about your condition? I didn't give a shit about any shoots, or covers, or anything else. I cared about you. That's all that mattered. Do you know how blessed you are to even be here?"

As the tears fell from Marcelo's eyes, Scorpio wiped her own now streaming down her face. She was blessed. The doctors had told her that repeatedly. And she was grateful to be alive, but she wasn't about to risk losing everything she'd worked so hard to have. She'd sacrificed to much. As much as her mother got on her nerves, one thing she taught her was how to be resilient and a fighter. And she was ready to do whatever she needed to do to hurry and get out of the hospital so she could get back to work.

"I know, Marcelo, and I'm sorry about the hell you've been through the past couple of days. Trust me, it hasn't been a picnic for me either." Scorpio reached for his hand, and he squeezed it. "But you and I both know this happening to me is giving folks the opportunity to come for my spot, and I'm not giving it to them. So fine, slick my hair back, but I'm telling you, you betta beat my face like it's never been beaten before," she said, using the term "beat" that industry professionals used when referring to makeup.

"Look, I ain't worried about nobody coming for your spot. There is only one Scorpio, and they know that," Marcelo said matter-of-factly. "You don't have nothing to prove. You need to be resting."

"I am resting, Marcelo. I've been stuck in this bed for days. I can't do nothing but rest. But I want to feel pretty. I need to feel pretty. It will make me feel so much better. You know you feel good when you look good." Scorpio winced again as she sat up a little farther in the bed. He went to help her, but she pushed him away. "I'm okay. I'm just a little sore, that's all. Come on, let's do this."

"Fine." Marcelo glared at her. "A simple, light beat."

"As if you could ever do anything simple and light," Scorpio teased. "And turn on some music."

Marcelo loosened up a bit as he grabbed his phone and turned on some music. Once he finished taming Scorpio's hair, he went to work on her face. Although his touch was light and she knew he was being extremely careful, it didn't stop the sharp pains from surging every few minutes. He paused each time Scorpio flinched, but she refused to let him stop.

"Are you sure you're okay?" he kept asking.

"I would probably be a little better if I had a damn drink." She laughed with her eyes closed as he put mascara on her lashes to thicken them. When he didn't respond right away, she popped her eyelids open and squinted at him. "Gimme!"

"Give you what?" he asked innocently.

"Whatever alcoholic beverage you got in that damn bag!" Scorpio told him.

"I will not. You're on IV narcotics. You betta push that damn button and grab a dose of whatever it is their giving you," Marcelo told her.

"It makes me sleepy. Come on, one little sip," she begged.

Marcelo reached into the bag and took out a silver flask and handed it to her. "Fine, one sip. That's it, heffa."

Scorpio took it from him and unscrewed the top, taking a sniff. Her nose wrinkled. "What is it? Jack?"

"Don't be picky. You don't want it, give it back." He reached for the flask, but she turned it up and took a big swig. The liquid burned just as hot going down her throat as the burns on her body, but it felt good.

"What the hell is going on here?"

Scorpio damn near dropped the flask she was still holding to her lips.

"Shit," Marcelo murmured, his eyes wide as they went from Yolanda, who'd just waltzed into the room, to Scorpio.

"Who the hell are you, and what are you doing in here?" her mother walked over and demanded.

Scorpio handed him the flask. In record speed, he twisted the cap back on and stuck it back into the bag, then began gathering up his things.

"This is Marcelo. You've met him before. He came to fix me up a little and visit. I invited him," Scorpio told her.

"Turn that damn music down," Yolanda snapped. "You're in here blasting that mess and drinking like it's a nightclub and not a hospital room. What if someone else had walked in and not me? You keep worrying about the press and blogs and what they have to say. You're in here giving them plenty to talk about."

Marcelo scrambled for his phone and turned the music off. "My apologies."

Scorpio shook her head and exhaled loudly. "No one else would walk in here. Cheddar is posted right outside the door. You're overreacting."

"I'm acting concerned. Someone needs to be thinking about your well-being. You should be in here resting and healing from trauma, and instead, he's in here playing dress-up. Ridiculous," Yolanda snapped.

Marcelo packed up the last of his things, and Scorpio saw the vein popping out of the side of his neck: something that happened whenever he was angry. She knew he was trying not to snap. Her bestie was trying to be respectful, but it was killing him.

"It's not ridiculous, and you owe him an apology. Marcelo, wait. We didn't take the picture," Scorpio said.

"Picture? What picture?" Yolanda frowned. "No one is taking a picture of you, especially in this condition and looking like that."

Again Scorpio winced, this time not from the pain in her body, but from the pain of her mother's words and the hurt she saw on Marcelo's face. His only response as he eased past her mother and out the door was, "Bye, Scorp."

"Did you have to do that?" Scorpio snapped at her mother.

"Do what?" Yolanda had the audacity to act as if she had no clue what Scorpio was referring to.

"Be rude and condescending," Scorpio told her. Not only had her disrespect caused Marcelo to leave, but she didn't even get the chance to see what she now looked like. Based on her mother's reaction though, his attempt at making her look presentable hadn't worked.

"I wasn't being rude or condescending. I was being sensible and looking out for your best interest."

"I was the one who told Marcelo to come to the hospital. My friends have been worried sick about me and couldn't even come and check on me." Scorpio wished she'd taken another swig of the liquor before her mother had walked in, because she needed it. Hell, she needed a whole fifth to deal with her.

"Sarena, I think you're confused about where the line between friends and family is drawn. You give people too much access to you, and then you complain about

the press being all in your business," Yolanda told her.
"And we need to think about getting rid of some of these
flowers. They're cluttering up the room."

Scorpio looked at the multiple vases of flowers spread
throughout the room. They'd been sent with well wishes
from everyone from King to her accountant. Her favorite
had to be the ones given to her from Knight, her stepson,
which he'd given to her with a hand-drawn card and
letter. She had missed him, and losing him was one of
the down sides to her breakup with her husband. She and
Knight had a special relationship.

"I like the flowers. They're fine," Scorpio told her.
"Leave them alone."

"Sarena, I know you've been through a lot the past
couple of days, but I wish you would stop acting like I'm
here to harm you. I'm not. As a matter of fact, I've been
out all day getting some things handled for you."

"What kind of things have you handled?" Scorpio
became concerned.

"Like finding you somewhere to live once you're released from here," her mother said. "Your house isn't
liveable, and you can't go back there. You probably
haven't even thought about that, have you? Well, I have.
I found a new home just as adequate as the one you were
living in. By the time you're released in a few days, I'll
have it ready."

"You didn't have to do all of that. King was working on it.
He was meeting with someone this morning as a matter
of fact," Scorpio told her, recalling the conversation she
and King had earlier. He was going over to talk to Darby,
the real estate agent, about renting the house across the
street from theirs.

"King? You really aren't depending on him to handle
your affairs, are you? You can't be that naive. He can't
even handle his own matters. He has his hands full with

that boy of his who's suddenly appeared. You don't have time to deal with a ready-made family, and you don't have to." Yolanda leaned over and adjusted Scorpio's pillows. "Sit back."

It did feel a little better, but Scorpio wouldn't dare admit it. "He's my husband. And I love Knight."

"Estranged husband," Yolanda corrected her.

"I don't need you to take care of anything. King can handle it." Scorpio sighed.

"Handle what?" King asked as he walked into the room. She was glad to see him and have someone to help take some of the pressure off from dealing with her mother by herself. "Hello, Yolanda."

"King." Yolanda's voice was flat.

"Hey. Handle finding us some temporary housing," Scorpio told him.

King walked over, leaned down, and kissed her cheek. "Damn, you look beautiful. Wow."

"Thank you. Marcelo came to visit." Scorpio smiled. "I was telling her you already handled it. Did you talk to Darby?"

"I did. But the house is under contract. Someone snatched it up this morning," he told her.

"Aw, damn." Scorpio sighed. "That would've been perfect."

"I know," he said. "But we'll find something else. Knight starts school next week, so I gotta hurry and get him settled in a crib. I really wasn't prepared even before all of this happened. But we'll be okay. All of us."

Scorpio saw the smirk on her mother's face, as if she was thinking, *I told you he couldn't handle anything.* She hated that she was sitting and enjoying that she might've been right. She thought for a second. She and King weren't on the best of terms, and she had no clue where their relationship stood at this point. But he'd been supportive and by her side while she was in the hospital, and even though she knew she wasn't in love with him, she did love him and considered him a friend. She also loved Knight as if he were her own son. Her mother couldn't understand any of this because she didn't want to understand it. But it wasn't her life, it was Scorpio's, and she knew if she didn't do anything, Yolanda would take over. She was not going to let that happen.

"No worries though. It's already taken care of," Scorpio told him.

"What do you mean?" King asked.

"My mom found us a place already. She's already working on getting it ready for us to move in. So Knight can pick out whatever he needs for his room, and you can help her with anything else." Scorpio grinned. She looked over at her mother and saw the look of sheer horror and confusion on her face. Scorpio was elated.

"Sarena, what are you talking about?" Yolanda's eyes widened, and she slid to the edge of the chair she was sitting on.

"You said you already found a new house and it was comparable to the one we already have. And we appreciate it. Right, King?" Scorpio glanced over at him and winked.

King raised his eyebrow. "We really do." He slowly grinned. "That was quite generous of you, Yolanda. But it's good to know that during times like this, family can pull together. Thank you."

Scorpio grabbed King's hand and said, "Hey, let's take a selfie and post it on your page and thank everyone for their prayers and support."

"That's a great idea," King said.

"I only wish Knight were here to be in it," Scorpio said as she posed for the cell phone camera that King was holding up. "Where is he?"

"He's at a cookout at the neighbor's house. The one who sent the basket of goodies," King told her.

"That's nice. Look at him making friends already." She turned and said to Yolanda, "Hey, you should come and be in the pics too. After all, we are a ready-made family."

Yolanda stood, placed her purse under her arm, and stormed out of the room.

Chapter 22

Lisa

"Everything looks amazing."

"Thank you, and thanks so much for coming." Lisa welcomed Micah and Adrienne into the backyard where the other guests had started to assemble. Riley Rodriguez, her sister Eden, and Peri Duboise and his friend April were already sipping sangria and nibbling on hors d'oeuvres. Marcus was serving as both grill master and deejay while her sons and their new friend Knight played around in the pool. It was a perfect day for a cookout, not too hot, and there was even a slight breeze.

"Can I do help with anything?" Adrienne offered.

"No, I have everything under control. You two can come on back and enjoy yourselves," Lisa said as she led the way to the deck. "We have more guests."

The attendees greeted the couple, and Micah introduced his fiancée.

"How is your brother?" Lisa asked. "We've been praying for him."

Micah looked over at her and said, "He's still holding on."

"That's good. And we'll keep praying." She touched his arm and nodded.

"We appreciate that," Adrienne told her.

"Make yourselves comfortable, and I'll be right back," Lisa said, then headed back inside to the kitchen.

"Who's that?" Shari, Lisa's younger sister, asked as she peeked out the window. "He's cute."

"Uh, he has a woman with him," Kendra, Shari's best friend, told her. "And based on how she's holding on to his arm, they're very much together."

Lisa laughed at the two women who'd arrived the night before. She was so glad that they'd arrived to hang out for a few days and help her with the cookout. She missed spending time with them and was glad that Marcus had asked Sam to leave their house so that they could visit in peace.

"She's right," Lisa said. "That's Micah Burke, Bishop Walter Burke's son, and the woman he's with is his fiancée."

"Damn it. I should've known he was taken. He's fine and saved. There was no way he woulda been single anyway." Shari sighed and went back to garnishing the bowl of potato salad.

"Girl, you're crazy," Kendra told her. "We're in Southern California. There are plenty of fine men around here."

"How many single men did you invite to this little shindig of yours anyway?" Shari turned and asked.

Lisa pretended to be focused on washing her hands, hoping to avoid the question. "Kendra, did you take the baked beans out of the oven?"

"They're not quite done yet," Kendra told her. "They need about another ten minutes."

"Don't act like you didn't hear me." Shari walked over and stood beside Lisa.

"Can you pass me a paper towel please?" Lisa politely asked, still lathering soap on her hands.

"Uh-oh, we know what that means." Kendra sighed. "Zero."

"Oh, my God, you're not about to perform surgery. Stop being so damn extra and answer my question," Shari whined.

"Hey, don't be mad because I'm protecting myself and my guests from foodborne illnesses. It's called safe food handling," Lisa replied as she took the paper towel Shari was holding out and dried her hands. "They won't be getting no food poison from over here. And to answer your question, I did invite an eligible bachelor. Well, at least I think he's eligible."

"Who is it? Is he cute?" Shari asked.

"He's handsome. Well, I think he is." Lisa shrugged. "He's another one of my neighbors."

"You only invited one guy who's single?" Shari asked.

"I told you I only invited the people in the neighborhood," Lisa explained.

"Oh, my goodness. Okay, Kendra, we'll definitely be hitting up some clubs this week, because my sister ain't looking out for us at all." Shari shook her head.

"Well, King Douglas did say he was coming back, so I already got my eye on him," Kendra announced.

"First of all, he's married," Lisa reminded her. "Second, he's too old for you."

"No, he's separated and has been for a while now," Kendra said. "And age ain't nothing but a number."

"Separated is still married," Lisa told her.

"I like older, mature men." Shari winked.

"Me too. They're experienced." Kendra gave her a high five.

"I'm gonna need both of y'all to calm down and stop acting thirsty." Lisa laughed. "It's so not a good look for either one of you."

"Don't hate because we're single and ready to mingle. Just because you've been tied down since you were a toddler doesn't mean you have to treat us like that." Shari pretended to be offended.

"Trust me, I ain't hating," Lisa told her.

"Besides, what does Scorpio have that I don't?"

At that moment, Marcus walked in carrying a large tray of grilled meat and said, "Uh, let's see: a modeling contract, a million dollar house up the street, a perfect body, and the face of an angel."

"Really, Marcus?" Lisa's head turned so fast to look at her husband that she almost got whiplash.

"She asked." He shrugged and placed the meat on the kitchen island. "This is ready. Where are the aluminum pans?"

"Oh, my God, no. Use the serving trays, Marcus. What is wrong with you? I know you see those Sterno trays we set up on the long tables," Lisa exhaled.

"Oh, I forgot we were fancy now. I remember a time when we would use cheap trays and aluminum foil. As a matter of fact, that's what we used night before last when I grilled." He looked at her from the corners of his eyes.

"And where is the new apron I bought you?" she hissed.

"What's wrong with this one? It's the one I always use." He ran his hands down the grimy black-and-white checked apron he was wearing.

"It's filthy, which is why I bought you a new one. Look at those stains." She pointed at the smudges of soot and barbeque sauce on the front.

"You're tripping," he said.

"Tell her again, brother-in-law," Shari said. "She's acting brand new around here."

"I'm gonna need all of y'all to shut up, and let's get this food ready. And if you're in here, who's outside entertaining our guests?" Lisa asked.

"So what was I supposed to do? Leave the meat outside?" Marcus asked.

"Here." Lisa handed him the serving trays to put the meat on and then headed back out the door, pausing long enough to say, "Don't forget about those beans in the oven."

"Are you sure you don't need help with anything?" Eden offered when Lisa stepped back onto the deck.

"I'm positive. My sister and her best friend are bringing the sides out, and then everyone can eat," Lisa told her as she arranged the plates and utensils in preparation for the food.

"Hey, Lisa, I hope you don't mind, but I invited a guest," Riley said.

"Who?" Eden and Peri asked at the same time. Riley ignored both of them and kept her eyes focused on Lisa, waiting for an answer.

"Sure, we have plenty of food," Lisa told her and motioned toward Marcus, Shari, and Kendra, who were bringing more food items out. "This is my sister Shari and my friend Kendra."

"Nice to meet you," Shari said, placing the pan of beans on the table.

"Oh, my goodness, you're even more beautiful in person," Kendra said, putting down the pan of macaroni and cheese.

"Everyone says that when they meet me," Peri gushed and batted his eyelashes.

"Shut up." Riley playfully punched his shoulder. "Nice to meet you too and thank you."

"Baby, can you turn down the music for a sec? And tell the boys to come over?" Lisa said to Marcus.

"Boys, come eat!" Marcus yelled out and waved toward the swimming pool.

"Uh, I thought you would've walked over and gotten them. I coulda yelled." Lisa shook her head.

"My bad, baby." Marcus shrugged, then yelled, "Make sure y'all dry off before coming over here."

"Okay, Dad!" their oldest son yelled back, causing everyone to laugh.

After the boys joined them on the deck, Lisa asked, "Micah, would you do us the honor and bless the food?"

"Most definitely," Micah said and got up from his seat. As soon as he rose, Adrienne grabbed his arm and walked so close to him that she nearly knocked him down.

"Clingy or nah?" Riley leaned over and whispered to Eden, loud enough for Lisa to overhear.

"Be quiet, and again, who the hell did you invite over here?" Eden whispered back.

"I thought you told me to be quiet." Riley smirked.

"Y'all are loud," Peri's friend April hissed.

"Let us pray," Micah said after the music was lowered. They all held hands and bowed their heads. After he was finished, the guests formed a line behind him.

"Lisa, honey, you have truly outdone yourself with this spread," Peri commented as Lisa began uncovering items on the table.

She had been cooking nonstop for the past two days, and her menu was extensive. There was a variety of everything: mac and cheese, corn on the cob, beans, salads, cole slaw, ribs, fish, burgers, hot dogs, steaks, chicken and shrimp skewers, chips, dip, and several desserts.

"This is downright indulgent," Adrienne said.

"And I'm going to enjoy every minute of it." Riley laughed as she piled food on her plate.

"Me too." Micah turned around and smiled back at her.

Noticing the slight frown on Adrienne's face, Lisa grinned nervously and said, "Please, eat up. There's plenty."

Marcus turned the music back up, and the sounds of *Maze Featuring Frankie Beverly* blasted from the surround-sound speakers. He walked over to where Lisa was standing at the end of the table and put his arm around her. "You did good, baby. Even with your fancy-ass trays. Everyone is enjoying it."

Lisa leaned against him and said, "We did good, even with that dirty apron you got on."

Everything was just as she hoped it would be. Her guests were laughing and talking, enjoying one another, and most of all, enjoying the food she'd made. Her sons had made a new friend. It finally felt like home. Lisa made herself and Marcus plates, and they sat down and joined everyone else. The conversation quickly turned to the fire.

"I heard the police have started an investigation. They think it may have been arson," Peri told them.

"You think someone burned King Douglas's house down on purpose? Why?" Eden asked.

"It was his and Scorpio's house, remember? Although she doesn't live there. But they both got them crazy fans," Peri replied.

"But people couldn't have known they live out here. Hell, until this happened, I doubted if anyone even knew this neighborhood was back here. It had to be an inside job," Marcus said.

"Nah, King wouldn't have burned his own house down. Besides, he wasn't even in town that night. It had to be someone else, and that's even if the fire was set intentionally," Lisa said.

"I heard they're looking for some woman. So it had to be one of his fans," Riley said.

"So, he ain't got male fans?" Peri teased.

"Fine, a man in a wig who looked like a woman." Riley shrugged. "Or Scorpio could just be lying. All of the neighbors were outside that night as soon as that fire happened, and I didn't see anyone else."

"So where is the single dude?" Shari leaned over and asked Lisa, who was sitting beside her.

"I guess he decided not to show," Lisa told her.

"What single dude?" Marcus asked a little too loudly. Now everyone was looking at Lisa, waiting for her answer.

"Uh, Jonah. His house is at the end of the cul de sac," Lisa said.

"The weird white guy?" Riley asked.

"The dog whisperer." Peri nodded.

"Wait, you ain't tell me he was white, Lisa. And you know I don't do dogs." Shari said, putting down the rib she was holding.

"Or white boys," Kendra added. "No offense, Peri."

"None taken." Peri winked at her.

"Hold up. Y'all acting like I was trying to hook you up with him or something. I invited him to eat, the same way I invited everyone else," Lisa told her. "This ain't *Love Connection.*"

"Trust me, you wouldn't want to be connected to him anyway, boo," Peri offered. "He hardly ever leaves his house."

"He seemed nice when I went over there," Lisa told them.

"Yeah, I've talked to him before, and he does seem cool." Micah nodded.

"Maybe he'll come later." Marcus shrugged.

"Well, he'd better hurry, because this macaroni and cheese is about to be gone." Riley laughed. "I need to get me some more of that."

"Me too." Micah stood up.

"I'll get it for you," Adrienne told him and grabbed his plate. Seeing how everyone was staring, she quickly added, "I want some more myself and that potato salad."

"Lisa, we have gotta chat, honey. I'm serious when I tell you I can use you and your culinary skills. I'm always looking for a great caterer," Peri said.

"I would love to chat with you about that," Lisa said, flattered by his offer.

"Yes, and she has a staff that can help," Shari told him and pointed at herself and Kendra.

"I thought y'all were here to party and meet guys, not work," Marcus commented.

"We can do both," Kendra told him. "And she can pay me in peach cobbler."

"Oh, snap. I forgot the cobbler," Lisa said, standing up. "I'll be right back."

"I'll help," Marcus offered and followed her back inside. Once they were in the kitchen, he asked, "Baby, what are you doing?"

"Getting the cobbler." She looked at him strangely, wondering what he was referring to. "Can you grab that whipped cream out of the fridge?"

"That's not what I'm talking about."

"Well, what then?" she asked.

"You telling Peri you were interested in catering, that's what."

"I am interested. You know how much I love to cook, Marcus, and bake."

"You can cook and bake for your family. You don't need to be working for nobody else," Marcus said. "We got money. You don't need a job."

"This isn't about money, Marcus." Lisa sprinkled cinnamon on the cobbler that she'd just removed from the holding oven. "It's about doing what I love."

"You love your family. What about us? We planned on traveling with the boys this summer when they got out of school. And we still haven't finished getting settled in our house."

"We can still do that. Calm down, Marcus. It's not like I said I'd start working for Peri tomorrow. I said I would talk to him." She sighed.

"But I know you, Lisa. You'll talk to him, and the next thing you know you'll be cooking for baby showers and baking wedding cakes. And then when are you gonna have time for the new baby?" Marcus asked.

"New baby? What new baby?" Lisa almost laughed until she saw her husband was serious.

"I told you I wanted us to have another baby," he replied, looking both hurt and confused.

Lisa didn't know how to respond. The last thing she wanted to do was argue with her husband, especially with a yard full of guests on their deck. She picked up the cobbler and said, "Marcus, we can talk about this later, okay?"

"About what? The baby or the catering?"

"Both," she said, relieved when his eyes softened and he smiled at her. "Now grab the whipped cream so we can get back out and have fun with everyone else."

"I'm right behind you, boo." He leaned over and kissed her. "There better be some mac and cheese left out there, too, because I want some more."

"Then you'd better hurry up." She smiled.

"If it ain't, then you'd better get ready to whip me up another pan later tonight, naked." He winked.

"Lord, please let it all be gone." Lisa looked up and pretended to pray as they walked back out the door.

"Well, well, well, looks like I got here just in time," a voice called out from the side of the house.

Lisa stopped so fast that she almost dropped the cobbler. Her mouth dropped open, and she stared, hoping she was imagining things.

"What's wrong?" Marcus asked, then turned his head in the direction she was looking.

"Baby, you made it," Riley yelled and swiftly walked past them, then ran and gave their unexpected guest a hug and a kiss.

Sam lifted her off her feet and said, "I told you I'd be here, beautiful. I wouldn't have missed seeing you for the world."

"Oh, shit," Marcus mumbled.

"Everyone, this is my date, Sam," Riley announced, pulling Sam by the hand.

Kendra stood and rushed toward the house. Shari followed. Everyone else stared at Riley and Sam as they walked hand in hand. Lisa didn't move. She couldn't move. She stood in place, her entire body shaking with anger. Marcus had assured her that Sam was gone and they wouldn't have to deal with him. Now here he was in their backyard.

"What's up, people? What's good, Marcus?" Sam grinned at them. Then, releasing Riley's hand, he walked over and said, "Let me help you with that, sis-in-law."

"What are you doing here, Sam?" Marcus demanded, taking the cobbler from her hands.

"I told you I invited him," Riley answered and then said, "I didn't think it would be a problem. Especially since he might be moving into Harrington Point soon."

"What?" Lisa snapped.

"That's right. I put a bid on the house up the street." Sam grinned. "We're about to be neighbors."

Chapter 23

Malachi Burke

"Hi, Mr. Burke. I'm Xandria, and I'm gonna be your nurse tonight," Xandria Carter said softly as she entered the hospital room. She scrolled through his chart on an iPad and familiarized herself with his case. Then, placing it down, she walked over to the sink and washed her hands. As she pulled on a pair of latex gloves, she walked over to his bed and told him, "You are the talk of the ICU, that's for sure. I thought I was gonna have to give a blood sample and a polygraph before they let me in here to check on you. That security they got posted up at the door ain't no joke, but I hear they are nothing compared to your mother."

Malachi Burke was her first patient after being off for nearly two weeks. She heard about him as soon as he was admitted into the intensive care unit where she had worked for the past two years. For days since he had been there, her coworkers had been texting her nonstop about the son of Bishop Walter Burke and the chaos he was causing: hospital security, personal security, media calling for information and trying to sneak in to take pictures. None of that mattered to Xandria. Her only concern was the care of her patient, who was now lying in a coma and had been for the past week since being in a fire. He was intubated and on a ventilator, but according to his chart, the doctors had slowly been weaning him off the sedatives. He should have regained consciousness a few days ago, yet he hadn't.

"So it looks like somebody's sleepy and doesn't want to wake up? We gotta fix that now, Mr. Burke," Xandria told him. She spoke to him as she would any other patient, knowing that even comatose patients still had the capability of hearing things around them. "Okay, let's see how you're doing today."

He lay motionless, several IVs running into his arm and hands, connected to a heart monitor and an automated blood pressure cuff. She took his temperature, and then placed in her ears the stethoscope hanging from her neck, rubbing it to warm it a bit before slightly opening his hospital gown and placing it on his chest. Satisfied with the rhythm of his strong heartbeat, she then reached into her pocket and took out a small flashlight. Gently, she opened his eyelids slightly and shined the light into his eyes. She noticed a slight dilation of his pupils and said, "Well, that's a good sign. Let's try something else."

Xandria placed his hand into hers and couldn't help but notice how long his fingers were. He had nice hands, and she wondered if he played the piano. She stared into his face as she pinched the nail bed of his thumb as hard as she could. Then she saw it: a slight wince.

"Oh, so you don't like that, huh? Good, good."

"Well, well, well, look who finally decided to come back to work." Xandria looked up to see her coworker Gina walking into the room. "Welcome back, Carter!"

"Don't even try it. I was only gone for a few days. Y'all probably didn't even notice I wasn't here."

"You were definitely missed. This place does not run right without you, and with all the attention Mr. Burke here has brought, it's been ridiculous around here," Gina said, pointing to him. "I swear, Mr. Burke, if you weren't so handsome, I would talk about you."

"Don't listen to her, Mr. Burke. Even if you weren't handsome, she would talk about you." Xandria shook her head. She and Gina had worked together in the ICU of the hospital for the past three years and had become the best of friends.

"No change, huh?" Gina asked.

"Nope, but I think he may be playing a little possum. He's reactive, and I get the feeling that he's listening."

"Mr. Burke, you need to stop. Got your parents and your brother all stressed out and causing all this commotion on the floor. Because of you, all the bosses and hospital bigwigs stay up here, and we can't chill like we want to. Don't nobody come to work to *work* every day." Gina laughed, and so did Xandria, and suddenly, there was a loud beeping in the room. Xandria rushed to the head of the bed to the heart monitor connected to his chest.

"See? I told you he was listening," she said.

"At least we know he has a sense of humor. This is the most we've gotten out of him since he's been here. Maybe he likes you," Gina suggested. "As fine as he is, that wouldn't be a bad thing."

"You're crazy." Xandria shook her head. She picked up the iPad and began noting this in the chart.

"Meet you later in the cafe?" Gina asked.

"Sure thing," Xandria told her. She went back to focusing on the notes in her patient's chart. When she was finished, she looked back at him and said, "Okay, Malachi. Can I call you Malachi? Good. So I convinced your parents that you were in very capable hands for the night, and I told them to leave. So I don't want no problems, okay?" she said. "But I think what we need to do is clean you up a bit. You could use a bit of a shave. And how about we turn on a little bit of music for you? Maybe that will make you feel better."

Xandria picked up the remote and turned to the music stations on the TV. The first one was a punk rock one, and she quickly hit the button. The next song that she heard was a mellow soft rock. She shook her head and said, "Nah, you don't seem like the soft rock type. You're a preacher's kid, so you probably enjoy gospel." She found the gospel station and turned it up and continued watching him. His eyes remained closed and his face emotionless. She paused and then said, "Hmmm, let's try this."

Another click of the remote and a hip-hop beat came from the television. Then she saw it: a subtle move in his face. She turned up the volume a little and waited, but there was nothing. She turned back to the gospel and stared at him. He didn't move. She clicked back to the hip-hop station, and sure enough, his eyebrow moved.

"Oh, you're a rap fan, huh? Okay, I see you, Mr. Malachi. Personally, I prefer R&B, but this ain't about me. It's about you." She laughed as she grabbed the plastic hygiene container from the bathroom area of the room and turned on the water. When it was warm, she wet a washcloth, which she used to clean his face. Then, with the care and precision of a surgeon, she shaved his face, rapping along to the music as she did so. When she finished, she stood back and admired him again. "Damn, you are a cutie."

Suddenly, his eyes opened. They stared at one another for a moment, and then he finally whispered, "So are you."

Xandria gaped, and then she smiled. "Well, well, well. Welcome back, Mr. Burke. I knew you were playing possum. I'll get the doctor, and I guess I need to call your folks and let them know you're awake."

Malachi's hand slowly reached and touched her arm. Shaking his head, he said, "Not yet. Please, not yet."

Epilogue

Jonah Harrington

Jonah was in the middle of preparing lunch when he heard the doorbell ring. He turned the stove on low and covered the pot of homemade chicken soup, grabbing a dish towel to wipe his hands as he headed to answer it. His favorite canine companion, Dash, was right on his heels.

"Can I help you?" Jonah asked the man who was standing on his doorstep.

"How ya doing? I'm Detective Adam Frazier," the man greeted him.

Jonah didn't smile back. He just stared. Dash sensed Jonah's composure and began growling. The detective glanced down and backed up. Jonah looked past him to see the squad car parked in the driveway.

"Dash, stop," Jonah said gently, and the dog quietly sat down beside him. Jonah reached and gave him a gentle pat on the head.

"I'm investigating the fire that happened last week. I understand you were one of the first people to call it in, and your house appears to be the closest one. Did you happen to see anything or anyone?" the detective asked.

"Nope, I didn't," Jonah told him. "Why are you investigating the fire? I thought it was started by something in the garage."

"Well, no, it appears that it may have been a deliberate act."

"Really?" Jonah blinked.

"Yes, sir. Mrs. Douglas has reported that there was an unknown female who assaulted her right before the fire occurred who may have had something to do with this. Did you notice any female in the neighborhood that night?"

"No, I didn't," Jonah said.

"Well, I can't imagine anyone getting out here without a car. Did you see any strange vehicles that night?" Detective Frazier asked.

"Nope, not at all." Jonah shrugged.

"I'm told you were the first one to arrive at the house and you helped Mrs. Douglas and Mr. Burke escape. Did either one of them say anything to you?"

"Well, he was the one who pulled her out the house. I just helped him lay her down, and then I called 911. Neither one of them said anything," Jonah told him.

Detective Frazier reached into his pocket and handed Jonah a business card. "If you remember anything, please give me a call."

"Sure thing." Jonah took the card and watched as the detective got into his vehicle and drove away.

He hated the police and had since Lydia's death. For weeks after she died, he was interrogated over and over again. They seemed determined to prove that he had something to do with it. His life was miserable until the final autopsy report came in and cleared him of any wrongdoing, and even afterward he still felt like he was a wanted man. His life had come crashing down, and all he could do was vanish. He left everything and everyone and found solace in what he had one day hoped would be the surprise of a lifetime for Lydia: the house he now lived in.

Jonah and Dash went back inside. He walked into the kitchen, thinking about the fire and the questions Detective Frazier asked. He also thought about the things he didn't tell the detective. He didn't tell him about the black Honda Civic, which was now parked in his garage covered with a tarp. He didn't tell him about the torn shirt Dash found near the backyard, and he didn't tell him about the woman who had been hiding out in his upstairs bedroom for the last two days. He made a bowl of soup, put some crackers on a small plate, grabbed a bottle of water, and made his way up the steps with a tray carrying it all.

"Lunch is served," he told her when he walked inside the bedroom.

She was standing by the window, peeking out, dressed in one of his T-shirts. "Oh, my God!" she hissed. "Was that the police?"

"Yeah, it was," he said. "Come on, get back in bed so you can eat."

"What did they want?"

"They're still investigating the fire." He placed the tray on the nightstand beside her.

"Shit. What did you tell them?" she asked, limping back over to the bed. Her ankle was bandaged, and her face was slightly bruised.

"I didn't tell them anything. Mainly because I don't know anything," Jonah said.

"I can't believe this! I never meant for any of this to happen, I swear! Shit just got crazy and . . ." She broke down and began crying uncontrollably.

"Hey, it's okay. Come on, eat something," Jonah told her. This was something Jonah had gotten used to over the past few days. As a matter of fact, when she wasn't asleep, she was crying. Those were pretty much the only two things she did: sleep and cry.

She was a pretty girl, young, petite. Had she not been wearing the blond weave in her hair, she would be the spitting image of one of his all-time favorite celebrity crushes: Tatyana Ali. He had tried time and time again to find out information about her, but the only thing he was able to get from her was that her name seemed to be Squirt and that the fire was a mistake.

As he watched her slowly eat the soup he prepared, Jonah hoped that his helping her wouldn't turn out to be a mistake of his own.

To Be Continued